"Why did you do it?"

Khefar paused before locking the door. "Do what?"

"Plead my case in the Hall of Judgment. You promised you'd keep my soul from Shadow, but we were among the gods of Egypt. Even being fed to Ammit would be better than being taken by Shadow."

"Neither sounds appealing to me."

"With Ammit there's no danger of becoming the very thing I hunt," Kira reminded him. "You didn't have to ask for my soul."

Why did he do it? Those five words circled endlessly through her mind, still unanswered. Yes, he had a sworn mission to save lives, to redeem himself for all the lives he'd taken. Yes, she'd been one of his charges. She clearly remembered that as she lay dying in the remnants of the club, a Messenger had told him that there were other lives that he could save, that failure to save her didn't mean damnation for him. Yet he'd slashed his wrist to pour his immortal blood onto her very mortal wound in an effort to save her life.

Praise for *Shadow Blade:*
Shadowchasers Book One

ALSO BY SERESSIA GLASS

Shadow Blade

SERESSIA GLASS

SHADOW CHASE

SHADOWCHASERS BOOK TWO

POCKET BOOKS
New York   London   Toronto   Sydney

Pocket Books
A Division of Simon & Schuster, Inc.
1230 Avenue of the Americas
New York, NY 10020

This book is a work of fiction. Names, characters, places, and incidents either are products of the author's imagination or are used fictitiously. Any resemblance to actual events or locales or persons, living or dead, is entirely coincidental.

First Juno Books/Pocket Books paperback edition August 2010

JUNO BOOKS and colophon are trademarks of Wildside Press LLC used under license by Simon & Schuster, Inc., the publisher of this work.

POCKET and colophon are registered trademarks of Simon & Schuster, Inc.

For information about special discounts for bulk purchases, please contact Simon & Schuster Special Sales at 1-866-506-1949 or business@simonandschuster.com.

The Simon & Schuster Speakers Bureau can bring authors to your live event. For more information or to book an event contact the Simon & Schuster Speakers Bureau at 1-866-248-3049 or visit our website at www.simonspeakers.com.

Designed by Esther Paradelo
Cover design by John Vairo Jr.

Manufactured in the United States of America

10 9 8 7 6 5 4 3 2 1

ISBN 978-1-4391-5877-7
ISBN 978-1-4391-7705-1 (ebook)

To Paula, for cross-checking my mythology.

To John Vairo Jr. and the Pocket art department,
for my kick-ass covers.

And especially to Larry—
thanks for helping me find Balance.

SHADOW CHASE

Chapter 1

Coming back from the dead was exhausting work.

Not that Kira Solomon had done much more since her resurrection than survive a celebratory feast with a demigod, an immortal warrior, a bureaucrat, an ageless woman, and two friends she'd accidentally tried to kill.

Then again, that was more than enough. As glad as she was to be on the right side of the grass, she'd had just about all the celebrating she could handle.

She leaned against the whitewashed column supporting the porch overhang, waiting for Khefar to show up with his car. The bungalow was situated in a beautiful old neighborhood in Ansley Park in Midtown Atlanta, tree-lined and gentrified, not far from the High Museum and Piedmont Park. Where else would Balm live other than some century-old neighborhood on the National Register of Historic Places?

Kira wondered if the other residents of Ansley Park knew their sometime neighbor was a woman of unfathomable age who headed an international clandestine organization. An organization dedicated to fighting the evil of the Fallen: their human hosts, Shadow Avatars, and all those who consorted with or were descended from the original Fallen—demons, halflings, hybrids, and other beings of Shadow.

Somehow Kira didn't think that was something that could be shared over tea and cookies with the neighborhood welcoming committee.

Right now, she could do with a soothing cup of tea herself. Anything to fight the chill that still clung to her bones despite her ever-present gloves and the black faux leather jacket she wore over charcoal wool trousers and a gray turtleneck sweater. All Kira wanted to do was go home, settle down on the couch or in her altar room, and relax with a mug of chamomile.

It was hard to be thrilled to be alive when so many weren't—like the innocents who'd been on the receiving end of her bad Shadow-induced flipout. Feeling the weight of those deaths while playing happy with her friends and coworkers had been a burden almost impossible to bear. She was looking forward to having some time to herself, in her own space, surrounded by her own belongings.

The front door to the bungalow opened. Kira stiffened as Wynne stepped out. She should have been happy that her friends still wanted her around, but she couldn't get past the guilt of what she'd done to them, especially Zoo. Even though Wynne's husband seemed to be fully recovered, Kira knew he bore a jagged dark scar in his olive skin, thanks to her.

Wynne leaned over the porch rail, her pink hair a shocking contrast against the orange and bronze fall leaves of the neighborhood trees. Dressed in a pair of desert-print army combat uniform trousers from her former military life and a black sweater that looked as if it had been on the losing end of a catfight, Wynne Marlowe was every bit the contrast she presented: a disciplined soldier with an unpredictable nature, a petite woman with a sweetheart face and an expertise in tae kwon do, a big-hearted woman who took as much pride in the spells her husband wove as the weapons she forged.

"You know, now that this is over, the four of us should go somewhere guaranteed to be uneventful," Wynne announced. "Maybe Antarctica. It can be like a couples' vacation."

"A couples' vaca— Did Zoo add a little extra herb to your tea?"

"I'm being serious, Kira." Wynne turned to face her.

Kira backed up a step, maintaining the space between them. "You're being crazy. I'm not part of a couple."

"Now who's dipping into the herbs? I'm not blind. I was there when Khefar saved you and brought you back from—wherever y'all went. Something tells me he wouldn't do that for just anybody."

Kira shoved her gloved hands deep into her trouser pockets. Her dying memories swirled along the edges of her mind, much like the leaves scattering around the bungalow. Khefar had saved her. He certainly hadn't had to, not the way he had. She'd tried and failed to come up with a good reason why he'd endangered himself to save her. She did know, however, that it wasn't because they were a "couple."

"Wynne, there's no couple stuff going on between Khefar and me."

"Why not? Don't you want it to?"

Wynne might look like a pink punk pixie, but she was as tenacious as a terrier. Where the hell was

Khefar and his car? "It's not a question of want. The reality is that he lives—and has lived for thousands of years—to complete his redemption so he can die and be reunited with his family in the afterlife. I've got the most dangerous job on the planet with the possible exception of those people who take lava samples from active volcanoes. One day, sooner or later, I won't be able to pull off a miracle. I'll fail even more spectacularly than I have in the last couple of weeks, and that will be it. There won't be any coming back. Khefar and I, we're both short timers. Our clocks are winding down."

The terrier made a puppy-dog expression. "But—"

"Wynne." Kira closed her eyes for a brief moment, dreading what would come next. This wasn't going to be easy, and she would rather have waited. But what she had to say needed to be said, and sooner was better than later.

"You're a good friend, a true friend, and I appreciate you and Zoo having my back in combat and in normal life more than I can ever say."

Wynne narrowed her eyes. "Why does it feel like there's a humongous 'but' coming? Like you're breaking up with me?" Her pale face paled further as surprise widened her eyes. "Wait. *Are* you breaking up with us?"

"Not the friendship," Kira said quickly. "But I can't have you guys helping me with Chases anymore."

"Why?"

"Because *I'm* the Shadowchaser. I've got the training and magic to take on the Fallen, and I barely survived the encounter. You guys aren't even part of Gilead's support staff. You're not protected!"

Wynne folded her arms across her chest, looking like a petulant teen. A petulant teen who just happened to be an excellent marksman and weapons master. "We're protected. We've got skills, weapons, and my man's a witch. There's no reason why we can't still have your back."

For a moment Kira couldn't even form words. "Have you forgotten what happened a couple of days ago? I almost killed you and Zoo!"

Wynne's hand cut through the air between them. "That was a one-time thing and not your fault! You were doped up on Shadow and out of your mind. We don't blame you for what happened in the cemetery!"

"I know." Kira kept herself as still as possible. She didn't want to accidentally touch Wynne, even with thick jackets and her gloves between them. Magically downloading every bit of her friend's thoughts, emotions, and memories, and possibly draining her life-force just wasn't high on the list of things she wanted to do, ever. "I know you don't blame me, and I'm grateful. So very grateful. But . . . it was hard seeing Zoo like that, seeing you seeing your husband like that. It was hard finding out I had done that to him without even hesitating."

"Kira." Tears shimmered in Wynne's lashes. "You were defending yourself. You thought we were trying to hurt you. You even warned us to stay back!"

"It doesn't matter." Kira didn't know how she could make her friend understand, but she had to try. "I need you to try to understand where I'm coming from on this. It's too dangerous now. I don't think it's going to get any less dangerous. The Fallen know they can hurt me and other Chasers, make me do things that go against everything I stand for."

"But—"

"They pushed me into Shadow, Wynne!" She pulled her gloved hands out of her pockets, wrapped them around the porch railing. Somehow she forced her voice back to normal. "They changed me, and they won't stop until they drag me kicking and screaming to the other side. I'm not taking anyone else with me."

"We won't let them!" Wynne scrubbed at her eyes, leaving a smear of black eyeliner across her cheek and knuckles. "We can help like we always do!"

"No, Wynne. You've done your time on the front lines. You and Zoo deserve a little peace and quiet."

"Since when have we done peace and quiet?"

Kira dragged out a smile. "Okay, your version of peace and quiet. Either way, you guys need to tend to your business, to the family you want to have. Helping me makes you both targets, and I can't do what I need to do when I'm worrying about you."

Wynne set her jaw. "That's what this is really about, isn't it? You think we're a liability."

"I didn't say that!"

"You didn't have to." Wynne stepped back toward the front door. "I guess now that you have an immortal warrior and a demigod on your side, you don't need two humans getting in the way."

Kira winced. That was true and not true at the same time. Because Wynne and Zoo were human and fragile and her friends, she wanted them safely out of harm's way. If they stayed away from her they'd be safe—safe from the things Kira Chased, and from

Kira herself. How could it be wrong of her to feel that way?

"Well." Wynne sniffed, then brushed her arm across her face again. "I guess I'd better tell my husband that us lowly humans aren't wanted around here."

"Wynne, please try to understand."

"Oh, I understand, all right. It's a tactical thing. You don't bring BB guns when the enemy is packing howitzers. We slow you down. Better for everyone if we're off the field."

Wynne went inside without another word. Kira lowered her head, trying to deal with the anguish. Her friendship with the Marlowes had just suffered a mortal blow. Probably neither would forgive her, but at least they'd be alive to hate her.

"You did the right thing."

She looked up. Khefar stood on the walkway, keys in his hand. With his dark braids, ebony skin, black jeans, and leather jacket, he stood out in sharp relief against the bright autumn day.

"Yeah." She pushed upright, throwing her own black and blue braids back over her shoulders. "I know it was the right thing to do. It still hurts like a bitch."

He nodded. "It will for a while, but at least they'll be safe."

She made her way down the stairs, joining him on the walkway. "Will they? Be safe?"

"As safe as anyone can be in this battle. Going after the enemy's loved ones is an age-old tactic." Which Khefar knew all too well; that was how he'd lost his family four millennia ago.

She followed him to the car. Going back into the

house to say goodbye would have been suicidal. "We sent the Fallen back to Shadow. Most of the hybrids helping him are out of commission one way or another."

Khefar nodded. "And yet it doesn't feel finished, does it?"

"No." The thought depressed and excited her at the same time. She mulled it over as they made their way out of Ansley Park and back to East Atlanta. They'd defeated Enig, the Fallen who'd infected her with Shadow as part of his plan for world domination. They were alive. Every sense she had, Normal and not, told her there'd be no rest anytime soon.

Separating the Fallen from his Avatar and sending him back to Shadow was a victory. She knew that. The costs, though, the costs were just too much.

"Are you all right?" Khefar's voice was even, unemotional.

She glanced over at Khefar. The Nubian was the epitome of calm collectedness as he eased the Charger to the curb in front of her converted warehouse home. Of course, being a semi-immortal who'd survived four thousand years would probably make anyone confident. Obviously coming back from the dead after coming face-to-face with ancient gods in the Hall of Judgment was all in a day's work for him.

She sighed. "I guess I'm still tired. Resurrection takes a lot out of a person."

"It does at that," he replied with the air of someone who knew what he was talking about. Since he'd died more than a few times, she figured him to be an expert by now.

She automatically scanned her neighborhood, searching for signs of anything untoward before getting out of the car. Sunshine gleamed off the spires of downtown Atlanta proper, less than a mile away. Buildings and variegated trees stood out in sharp relief against the perfect robin's-egg-blue sky. It was a normal mid-afternoon, with normal people going about their normal business, completely and blissfully unaware of how close to not-normal their lives had come. The fact that they didn't know, wouldn't ever know, meant that she'd done her job right. For the most part.

She realized with a start that she had no idea what day of the week it was, or even whether it was October or November. The crispness of the air could indicate either month, though the lack of Christmas banners hanging from the streetlights suggested it was still October. Not a weekend day given the light traffic. Not that it mattered. Shadowchasers punched hybrid Shadowlings, not clocks.

For a moment, she thought about hopping on her bike and zipping up I-75 to catch the fall foliage in the North Georgia mountains, perhaps including a stopover in the faux-Alpine village of Helen, only to remember that she hadn't taken the time to get her motorcycle fixed after the altercation with the seeker demon. She wanted her bike back. Hell, she wanted her life back.

Two weeks. In just over ten days her life had irrevocably changed. Her mentor, Bernie Comstock, had been killed by a seeker demon because of a sentient dagger—the dagger Khefar now wore strapped to his hip. Khefar just happened to be a four-thousand-year-old Nubian warrior and the only person she'd been able to touch without devastating and often deadly effects since reaching puberty. Together she and the Nubian had managed to destroy the Fallen who'd controlled the seeker. They'd all but died in the process, faced judgment in the Hall of Gods, and been called out by their respective patron goddesses—Isis for Khefar, Ma'at for Kira. That was all after Kira had been drugged by Shadow and, while out of her mind, killed more than half a dozen innocent people and almost taken out her best friends as well.

Kira was a Shadowchaser and, now, the Hand of Ma'at. She was also tainted by Shadow. Somehow the first two hadn't cancelled out the third. Above all, though, she was indebted to this Nubian who'd risked his afterlife to save her, especially since he hadn't had to.

"Have you gone to the Hall of Judgment every time you've died?" she asked Khefar as he got out of the car.

He paused to engage the alarm. "No, not since the first time."

She could hear the reluctance in his voice loud and clear as he joined her at the front door. The man had four thousand years' worth of information and parsed it out like a miser.

"I guess that makes sense," she said, wanting to know more. Needing to know more. He had to have some idea. "I mean, it would be torture in a way, having your soul weighed with your charge from Isis unfinished. What do you think it means that you went there this time?"

"Even after four millennia I cannot profess to understand the minds of the gods." He used the palm scanner to deactivate her security system, then unlocked the front door, which surprised her until she remembered she'd reset everything for him assuming her confrontation with the Fallen would be her last. Had returning from the dead affected her memory?

"Maybe you went there because I did, because it was my first time . . . well, dying," she said, following him into the house. "Because you tried to save me."

He'd sliced his wrists open to treat her wounds, hoping his near-immortal blood would counteract the effects of the Shadow-infused dagger. He wasn't supposed to do that. He had promised to use the Dagger of Kheferatum to unmake her, to guarantee that Shadow wouldn't be able to trap her soul and make her an Avatar for one of the Fallen.

He grunted instead of answering. She hadn't really expected more, but it still rankled. Fine. She'd get information even if she had to pummel it out of him.

She tossed her jacket onto the back of the couch, then moved to the center of her crowded living room, planted her fists on her hips. "Why did you do it?"

He paused before locking the door. "Do what?"

"Plead my case in the Hall of Judgment. You promised me that you'd keep my soul from Shadow, but we were among the gods of Egypt. Even being fed to Ammit would be better than being taken by Shadow."

"Neither sounds appealing to me."

"With Ammit there's no danger of becoming the very thing I hunt," she reminded him. "I would have been content with whatever fate my Lady Ma'at deemed fit to give me. You didn't have to ask for my soul."

Why did he do it? Those five words circled

endlessly through her mind, still unanswered. Yes, he had a sworn mission to save lives, to redeem himself for all the lives he'd taken. Yes, she'd been one of his charges. But she clearly remembered—as she lay dying in the ruins of the destroyed nightclub after the defeat of the Fallen—a Messenger had told him there were other lives he could save, that failure to save her didn't mean damnation for him. Yet he'd slashed his wrist to pour his immortal blood onto her very mortal wound in an effort to save her life.

On top of that, he'd pled her case in the Hall of Gods before Isis and Osiris and Ma'at, with the other Egyptian gods bearing witness. He'd saved her life and, in doing so, ensured that he'd have to stick around as her fail-safe.

"Khefar."

"Enough already." He moved past her, stripping off his jacket, tossing his keys on the kitchen counter. "I am content with the choice I made. Why aren't you?"

She bit her tongue. Truth was, she just wasn't used to anyone making sacrifices for her, not without wanting something in return. Even her handlers had wanted her performance as a Shadowchaser. They'd gotten what they wanted and they'd both lost their lives in the process. Kira had yet to determine what the Nubian wanted, but she'd find out soon enough. Khefar might have saved her life, but she still didn't trust him with it.

That didn't mean she couldn't be polite. He *had* saved her, after all. "Thank you, for everything."

He nodded. "What's next?"

She didn't have a clue. Ma'at and Isis had told them

they still had work to do, but hadn't told them what that work was. Balm had given her time off from her Shadowchasing duties and, after the spectacular destruction of the Fallen at Demoz's club, she doubted if any Shadowling in Atlanta would try to cause trouble for a good long while.

If neither the goddesses nor Balm had plans for her right now, there was one thing, she realized, that needed to be done, perhaps the most important thing. "I need to go to London."

"Comstock?"

She nodded, trying to ignore the wrenching of her heart. When you could count on one hand the people you cared for and trusted, losing one of them was difficult. When that person was your mentor and surrogate father, the loss was devastating. "I promised that I'd take his ashes back to London and speak to his solicitor. It's been almost two weeks since he . . . died."

"When do we leave?"

Khefar was like that, always so matter-of-fact. Assuming he'd accompany her to London without a protest from her. What else could she do? The last time she'd gone off by herself she'd killed half a dozen innocents. She was firmly a team player now.

"As soon as possible, I suppose. Balm offered to fly us there on her way back to Santa Costa."

Khefar lifted one of her books from a stack near the couch, a history of the Toltecs. She locked her muscles against the involuntary urge to grab the book from him. It was still difficult having someone in her space, touching her stuff. Harder still to resist yanking up his shirt and running her hands all over his hard body.

The image almost made her whimper. She really, really wanted to know what it would be like to stretch out beside him on her bed, to know the warmth of his skin beneath her hands. She wanted to know the touch of his hands moving over her skin, cupping her breasts, making her feel alive and human and wanted.

"You don't sound like you wish to accept the offer." He flipped through the pages slowly, like a bibliophile considering a beloved book. He had such long fingers.

"Balm has a top-of-the-line Gulfstream that's configured for four crew and fifteen passengers," she said, looking away. "She can get us there soon enough, but once we land she'll probably try to find some reason to stay in London while I . . . while I take care of Bernie's wishes. It's going to be hard enough to do what needs to be done as it is. My experiences with Bernie and my experiences as a Shadowchaser are still separate in my mind. He is . . . was my professor, my mentor. Not my handler. I never knew him in that role while he was alive. If Balm's there, Bernie's connection to the Gilead Commission is all I'll think about."

He perched on the couch's arm, balancing the open book on his knees. "Then decline her invitation. You can take time to settle things here and she can return to Santa Costa to inform the Commission of your replacement."

"My replacement?"

He looked surprised. "Of course. The head of the Gilead Commission is no fool. She probably already has a shortlist of candidates along with a list of Chasers she can move at a moment's notice in an emergency."

"Spoken like a military man."

"The Balm of Gilead always thinks strategically," Khefar told her. "Don't think that she doesn't. It's part of why she and Sanchez get along so well."

Kira had noticed that, during their celebratory feast at Balm's safe house. The leader of Gilead and the Atlanta section chief had been too buddy-buddy for Kira's comfort. It made her think the two had strategized more than once where Kira was concerned. Sanchez—who seemed to be a toe-the-line, follow-the-rules, file-it-in-triplicate bureaucrat with no fondness for a hotheaded Chaser who preferred effective practicality to perfunctory protocol—had been itching to replace Kira for some time. Knowing the section chief, Kira was sure Sanchez would be happier if Atlanta was a Chaser-free zone altogether.

Balm always had plans within plans. Kira had learned that the hard way, growing up on Santa Costa in the Commission's castle-like stronghold. From the moment Balm had taught her how to eat without reliving every step of her food's production, preparation, and progress to the plate she ate it from, she'd been trained to be a weapon used at the Commission's discretion.

It hadn't been an unbearable life, just a hard one. Kira had accepted the hardships as punishment for nearly killing her adoptive sister. She'd endured the training because giving up or giving in had never been an option even when she couldn't eat food she hadn't picked herself. She'd had to survive, had to succeed, because becoming a Shadowchaser was the only way she knew how to atone.

Khefar's voice softly intruded on her thoughts. "What's got you thinking so hard?"

"The past and the future." Kira moved over to the couch, which meant moving closer to the Nubian. She tried not to think about all that touchable flesh within arm's reach. "I didn't think becoming the Hand of Ma'at meant I'd be giving up my Shadowchaser duties. I don't even know what being the Hand of Ma'at means. When your god calls you to service, you don't say, 'Gee, let me think about it.'"

"I certainly wouldn't." He touched the Isis knot etched into the skin at the base of his throat. "Being called means that you become her instrument. You answer when she calls and do her will as she sees fit."

Kira touched the mark at her own throat, the feather of Ma'at. The goddess had bestowed the Feather of Justice on Kira after claiming her in the Hall of Judgment, just as Isis had renewed her claim on Khefar. As far as Kira was concerned, she'd always belonged to Ma'at; the tattoo just made it official.

Still, she didn't know what it meant, what she'd have to do. What Khefar had told her was fine and dandy, but it wasn't anything concrete. She needed to *know*. The search for answers had ruled her entire life; this was no different. Unfortunately the goddess hadn't given her an instruction manual.

"I guess we'll find out soon enough what's expected of us. There's enough to process here as it is."

"Yes, which is why you shouldn't worry about it now. Let's take Comstock's ashes to London as he wished so that you can say goodbye to him properly. We can handle the rest later."

There was that word again. *We.* It was a challenge to think in terms of another person, having to account for another in everything she did or needed to do. Another change, and one that made her distinctly uncomfortable.

"So how long have you known Balm?" she asked, just to think about something else. The entire topic of the mysterious Balm of Gilead was a pretty big something else. Kira doubted that Balm was a subject she could ever completely learn. But every shred of information she could obtain might be of value, especially when the lack of knowledge could bite her in the ass.

He looked up from the book. If the stack by the coffee table was any indication, he'd gone through at least one a day since taking up residence on her couch. She couldn't decide if she wanted to run her fingers over the pages as he had or never touch them again. Both options bothered her.

"You make it seem as if the head of Gilead and I are friends."

"I heard that exchange between you two at Balm's house. You have to admit, it seemed like you were well acquainted. She evidently has tried to recruit you—more than once, from the sounds of it."

"She has." He didn't seem happy she'd remembered the conversation. The closed book hit the couch between them.

"When was the first time she tried to make you a Shadowchaser?" When he hesitated, she rushed on. "I know you're about four thousand years old, and Balm hasn't aged a day in the fourteen years I've known her. Can't you give me something here?"

"If Balm hasn't 'given you something,' as you say, I

cannot see how it would be appropriate for me to reveal to you what she has not."

"Oh come on! We died together. We faced judgment together. You're sleeping on my couch and I've only known you for a week. We left 'appropriate' in the dust a long time ago!"

A muscle in his jaw twitched. "It's been almost two weeks. While the start of our association was unusual—beginning with you shooting me—I have been nothing but appropriate with you."

Great. She'd just insulted him. She'd never get information now. That he acted like he didn't even remember that they'd kissed more than once was just icing on a screwed-up cake. "The start of our association was me holding a gun on you. I didn't shoot you until you helped me with the seeker demon. And for the record, I never said you were anything other than appropriate. I just wanted—"

"How long are we staying in London?"

His change of subject was like running into a wall, more damaging to pride than body. She shoved herself up off the couch and to her feet, needing to put room between them. "Why? Got something else on your schedule?"

He stilled as if he'd just caught himself before doing or saying something they'd both regret. "At the moment, no. You are still my duty."

Ouch. Obviously the Nubian had more than the dagger in his arsenal. She folded her arms across her chest, holding back hurt and anger. "Speaking of duty, I hadn't thought about putting a time limit on my duty to Bernie, so I don't really know how long I need to be in London. I've got to talk to Bernie's solicitor and do whatever needs to be done legally since he left me his apartment and everything in it. Who knows how long that will take? On top of that, I haven't been to London since I graduated, so I'd like to visit the university while I'm there, especially the Petrie Museum."

"Then might I suggest taking Balm's offer? She's going to London anyway, so the trip will be far less expensive than booking last-minute trans-Atlantic flights on a commercial airline."

"You're worried about expenses?" She realized then she didn't know if Khefar had money or not. Either she'd paid or the Nubian's traveling companion, the demigod Anansi, had pulled whatever was needed into being. "I figured someone as old as you would have learned a thing or two about saving pennies."

"Over the course of my life I've seen financial systems rise and fall." He slipped to his feet and continued, his voice and posture stiff. "So yes, I've learned a few things about money. However, I'm more concerned with the logistics of taking a commercial flight. Neither of us are leaving our blades behind, and we both have other items we don't want to leave to the vagaries of airport security or international shipping."

She immediately looked at his hip, the Dagger of Kheferatum resting in its sheath. An ancient blade with the power to destroy and create, its presence in her life the last couple of weeks had caused more grief than she'd seen since losing Nico in Venice six years ago. So much grief, and yet she still craved the blade. Proof of just how messed up she'd become.

The taint of Shadow the Fallen had inflicted on

her pulsed through Kira. Sending the Fallen back to Shadow—and nearly dying in the process—hadn't been enough to offset the stain. It reminded her that she still had work to do, still needed to balance her scales and bring her soul firmly back to Light. Becoming the Hand of Ma'at hadn't given her a free pass.

Kira's hand dropped to the handle of her Lightblade, and the hunger backed off. "All right. I'll call Balm, tell her we'll fly out with her. I guess I'd better put in a call to the solicitor too, let him know I'm coming."

"Good idea." He grabbed his car keys. "I'm going to go to the pharmacy, pick up a few toiletries," he announced. "Do you need anything while I'm out?"

"Nothing you're willing to give me."

Kira wondered if a basilisk could match the stare he gave her. "You have no idea what I'm willing to give you," he said.

"Well if it's not information, it doesn't really matter anyway," she retorted, her ears warming. How the hell was she supposed to work with someone who kept her flustered, guilty, *and* in the dark?

"I'm just going to that shop down the street," he said, heading for the door. She hadn't engaged the metaphysical protections when they came in, so he could escape easily. "I shouldn't be more than half an hour."

"Thanks for the warning," she muttered, then flopped back on the couch as he left. There were a ton of things to do before she could leave the country, but her mind refused to focus on any of them. All she could think of was the sacrifice Khefar had made on her behalf, a sacrifice that hadn't had to happen. Above all was the rapidly fading joy she'd felt in Ma'at's presence, and how very dull and uninteresting the world seemed in comparison.

Her thoughts drifted back to Khefar. Was it so wrong to want answers? She supposed that after wandering the world for four thousand years, one learned to accept things as they happened. Or grew to assume one was always right. It sure would explain his arrogance and his lack of communication.

Khefar. Kira just didn't know what to make of him. She knew him, but she really didn't know him. All that she knew about him she'd learned from touching his dagger. Unlike with other people, when she touched Khefar, she didn't get bombarded with his thoughts, memories, emotions. She didn't drain his energy. No, when she touched Khefar, she got smooth skin, hard muscle, warm body. All she felt was the man.

An overbearing, arrogant man who would happily take all her choices from her for the sake of his damned honor.

"So not going to happen," Kira whispered to herself. "I'm going to get answers, with or without your help."

Chapter 2

Anansi was waiting by the car as Khefar left Kira's house. That he hadn't ridden over with them meant he wanted to talk to Khefar alone. Which more than likely meant the conversation wouldn't be good.

Khefar unlocked the car. "Did you enjoy your tête-à-tête with the Balm of Gilead, Nansee?"

"Immensely." The old man, nattily turned out in his usual suit and tie topped by a black wool coat, opened the passenger door, then slid into the seat. Of course, the demigod could have disarmed the car's alarm with a touch, but he enjoyed playing human when it suited him. "It's been a century or so since I've spoken with that particular incarnation."

"She's still formidable no matter what her manifestation," Khefar said, climbing into the driver's seat. "Kira asked me how long I've known Balm."

"Bound to happen sooner or later. What did you tell her?"

"Nothing." He started the car. "Said it wasn't my place."

The demigod snorted. "Things went downhill after that, I'll wager."

"You win. I cut her off with talk of London, but she's still not happy."

"Kira Solomon is not one to be satisfied with non-answers and half-truths," Nansee said, hands lifted as he played cat's cradle with a length of string that might have been in a pocket or might have just as easily, for the demigod, appeared out of thin air. "If you learn nothing else about the Shadowchaser you've tied your life to, learn that."

The car bucked, then stalled. Khefar wrenched the gearshift back to neutral. "I have not tied my life to hers."

Nansee barked with laughter. "My boy, that's a good one. You usually don't joke, riddle, or smile. The Chaser's had a positive effect on you already."

Khefar bit the inside of his cheek. "I am not joking." He eased the car forward again. "I have not tied my life to Kira's."

He could feel the old man's stare. "I don't think you realize what you were getting into when you agreed to be the Chaser's fail-safe," Nansee said. "Don't let a couple of kisses cloud your judgment."

"I'm not letting kisses—wait a minute." Khefar glared at the spider. "Were you peeking?"

The demigod attempted to look offended. "My dear boy. I'm a demigod, not a Peeping Tom."

"Right." Irritated, he shot through the intersection with more speed than needed, then forced himself to slow down. "Kira Solomon's is one of the lives I need to save before I move on. You told me that yourself. So no, I don't think my judgment is clouded."

"Of course not," Nansee said, the lack of conviction in his voice clear. "Tell me this then. Why did you do it? Why go through such extreme measures to save the life of one person, even if that person is a Shadowchaser?"

"Not you too." Khefar resisted the urge to pound the steering wheel. "Can neither of you leave me alone on this? Isn't it enough that I did it, and it's done?"

"Hmm." The old man sat back. "So the Chaser has also wondered. I should think, son of Nubia, that you also need to wonder why you saved Kira Solomon, and find the answer soon."

Why had he saved her? That was the question he'd asked himself repeatedly since returning from the Hall of Judgment. He was still wondering why, still not finding answers. He hadn't thought about it, he'd just reacted. He'd saved her because that was what he was supposed to do, and because it was Kira. The reason was that simple and that complicated. All he knew was that when he made a vow, he kept it. He'd promised to be Kira's fail-safe, to use the Dagger of Kheferatum to unmake her soul to prevent it being harvested by Shadow. He'd also promised to save her life if he could.

Kira. What a study in contradiction. A seasoned warrior at twenty-six, a young soul bearing old burdens. A woman who distanced herself even from people in the same room, but also a little girl desperately wanting somewhere to belong, someone to belong to. A killing machine packed into a supple gymnast's body, and a woman needing to touch others without lethal consequences.

She could touch him, though. Kira could take off her gloves and run those slender, strong hands over his chest, drape her sleek cinnamon-skinned body across his. He could ease the hunger in her dark-brown eyes that Shadow had lightened to hazel, a hunger that had nothing to do with taking his dagger and everything to do with basic human need.

It would be the right thing to do. He wouldn't be taking advantage of her, not when he'd be giving her, giving them both, something they both wanted. It wouldn't be unfair to share intimacies with the Shadowchaser, even knowing that his time was short. It wouldn't be cruel to nurture the attraction between them, even knowing he would leave this earthly plane as soon as he'd saved his final soul and his centuries-old obligation finally ended. Would it?

Or would he be doing Kira more harm than good? Would such a relationship ultimately leave her worse off than she had been before?

"Such thoughts crowd your mind," Anansi observed, breaking into Khefar's thoughts. "What has caused this particularly dour expression this time?"

Khefar pulled into the parking lot of the pharmacy, but made no move to kill the engine or get out. "You heard her after she found out she'd killed those innocents, Anansi. You saw what that knowledge did to her. It put her in a vulnerable place, a dark place, exactly as Shadow wanted. I couldn't let her stay there."

Khefar remembered that place, the very bottom of a well of despair. After returning home in triumph after being rewarded by the pharaoh himself only to find his village decimated and his wife and children murdered, nothing had remained save grief and rage, and he'd combined that with the royal favor he'd curried to lead an army bent on retribution. It hadn't been enough. Nothing had ever been enough.

"I killed sixty-four thousand out of rage and grief.

She killed a dozen by mistake after being poisoned with Shadow. Yet each death sends you deeper and deeper into darkness. I know what that does to the mind and to the soul. She needed hope in order to face the Fallen who killed her mentor and attacked her."

"There is a difference between protecting someone's soul from Shadow and slicing open your own vein to keep her alive," the old man pointed out.

Khefar's fist thumped against the steering wheel. "Was I supposed to let her die?" he finally asked. "Was I supposed to let her go before the gods unprepared? It is human nature to offer comfort as one can. Can I do less?"

"Ah. So you're finally feeling human again?" Nansee smiled. "Thank the gods. Or rather, thank me."

"Very funny." Khefar shook his head at the demigod, then finally killed the engine. "I will continue to help Kira in any way that I can because it is my duty and my charge. Isis and Ma'at sent us back because we have work to do, and apparently they want us to do that work together."

The car suddenly felt too confining. He got out and headed into the store, needing to clear his head. Unfortunately his thoughts followed him inside.

Why the hell would Kira and Nansee question the reasons why he'd saved her life? There were no reasons—it had needed to be done and he did it. Why would they make him feel guilty for that, as if he'd made a mistake? He remembered Kira's expression as she'd confessed that she carried the taint of Shadow after her first encounter with the Fallen. It had taken an unbelievable amount of courage to ask him to be her judge, jury, and executioner, and yet she had done so. Not out of fear for herself, but for fear of the harm she could do to others should she become a pawn of Shadow.

Khefar couldn't blame her. He wasn't a Shadow-chaser, but he'd seen enough skirmishes in the eternal battle over the last four thousand years. Seen the impact of Shadow on innocent lives. He'd seen good men and women tarnished by Shadow, people who'd been corrupted into becoming Avatars, vessels for the Fallen to inhabit.

The only way the Fallen, the über-powerful off-spring of Chaos and Shadow, could enter the human world was to inhabit a human host. The only ways for the Fallen to take possession of a person were either to accept a willingly offered invitation—in exchange, of course, for power—or to inhabit a "shell": a human systematically and utterly corrupted to become a suitable dwelling for evil.

Once so completely debased, the human host, Khefar knew, was essentially lost. It had been a bitter lesson to learn, and one he'd never forget. One of his charges, a bright young man brimming with promise, had been corrupted by the lure of power. Khefar had tried to use the Dagger of Kheferatum to excise the Shadow from the boy. What had remained was an abomination, something far less than human. Sorrow had torn at Khefar as he'd called the dagger's true power and unmade his charge.

That loss had cut deeply. Yes, there were other souls to save, but he'd lost that young man twice—once to Shadow, and then forever to the Void. He'd promised himself then, and silently renewed that promise now, that he'd never lose another charge to Shadow. It was a promise he intended to keep.

He remembered Kira lying in his arms after defeating the Fallen, the Shadow-drenched dagger lodged in her shoulder. How she'd smiled up at him through the agony, hopeful that she'd done enough to balance her scales but trusting that he'd use his dagger to unmake her soul. He hadn't wanted her skill, her bright promise, to be snuffed out. He hadn't wanted her to die—not because it would affect his tally and delay his entry into the afterlife, but because he didn't want to lose her.

Gods help me.

He quickly finished gathering supplies, then cashed out and left the store. Nansee leaned against the car, a tangle of red licorice dangling from his fingers. "Food you can play with," the demigod announced in pure delight. "I love this stuff."

"I'm sure it's a step up from how you used to play with your food," Khefar answered, loading his purchases into the Charger's trunk. He wondered if Kira would let him store his car in her garage. She'd probably demand information again, he'd refuse again, and she'd become angry again.

"Anansi." He moved around to the driver's side. "I have a question for you."

"Uh-oh." The old man made short work of his candy. "Back to serious already. Did the salesclerk call you 'sir' or something?"

Khefar just looked at him. The old man threw up his hands. "All right, what is this question you wish me to answer?"

"Earlier you urged me to discover the reasons why

I chose to save Kira as I did." Khefar leaned against the car. Afternoon had begun its inevitable reddish-purple slide into evening; the temperature would drop soon. For the trip to London he'd have to trade the leather jacket for the trench coat, which suited him fine. Just made it easier to hide his dagger. And guns.

"So I did." The demigod leaned on the roof on the other side. His reflection shimmered in the shiny black surface, flitting among his various forms. "Is that the question, or are you still conjugating verbs in your head?"

"You seemed to be urging me to discover the reason quickly," Khefar continued, ignoring the old man's barb. "And you asked me that after returning from a meeting with the Balm of Gilead. I know the two of you. I know you both have your threads in the fabric of the present and past in order to determine the patterns of the future."

The old man lost his jesting expression. "You've been around long enough to know this is so," he acknowledged. "And that we're not the only ones who make such weavings. Your question is?"

"What's going to happen to Kira?"

Nansee's expression became distinctly uncomfortable. "I'm not sure what you mean."

"Don't play games with me, old man." He jabbed his finger into the roof for emphasis. "I did what I did because I didn't want to lose Kira. She burns bright with promise and goals unfulfilled. She needs to continue, for herself and for the Light. Is Kira's life threatened?"

"She's a Shadowchaser. Her very calling is one of danger."

"Anansi." Khefar waited until the demigod looked directly at him. It wasn't an easy thing to hold a deity's gaze, but he was concerned enough, angry enough, to do it. "We were elevated by Isis and Ma'at, then sent back. You and the Eternal Woman have been in conference in a way that you haven't been in more than a century. The last time you confabbed with the Balm of Gilead, a country collapsed. So tell me: is there a danger of losing Kira?"

Nansee sighed, an old man's weary sigh. "There is always danger, son of Nubia. I can only surmise, and Balm agrees, that your new status exposes you both to new dangers. We worry for our charges, especially when the potential futures we are used to seeing have become covered with storm clouds."

For the West African demigod to worry, things had to be dire indeed. Khefar thought of the vow he'd made to Kira to unmake her soul, the vow reaffirmed in the Hall of Judgment and sanctioned by Isis herself. He didn't make vows lightly, but he'd assumed it was one he'd have to be concerned with later instead of sooner. From Anansi's expression, time was no longer a luxury he had .

"How long?"

Nansee shook his head. "I don't know. Balm told me that she hasn't been able to see Kira's path since before Comstock was killed. And she didn't see Comstock's end at all. It is as if Kira's fate and her path are being deliberately obscured. Balm claims she has no idea what shrouds it."

Khefar digested that bit of news. From his past contact, he knew Gilead in general and Balm in particular kept tight rein on their Chasers. He had learned that both kept their eyes focused on Kira even more intently than other Chasers. Even if the Chasers sometimes went off the radar, the handlers were easy enough to track—and since the rise of satellites and global communication, this was simpler to accomplish and more precise than ever. If Gilead knew where you were, they had other means of knowing what might be going on with you. For the Commission to not see trouble brewing for a Chaser or their handler was unprecedented.

A sudden thought struck Khefar. He turned to Anansi. "Balm thinks Comstock's and Kira's futures were obscured because of my dagger, doesn't she?"

The old man's expression soured further. "She didn't use those exact words."

"She probably used something pithier."

"She did question the timing of you losing your dagger and its coming into Comstock's possession."

Sudden anger burned Khefar's throat. "As if I deliberately got myself killed and the dagger stolen in Germany in hopes that it would find its way to Comstock in London and then here to Kira?"

"I agree that it would be a most audacious and incomprehensible plan." Nansee dipped his head. "Nothing like your usual strategic approach. We both know, however, that your dagger has a mind of its own. Especially when it comes to whom it chooses to serve."

Khefar thrust a hand into his jacket, fingers wrapping around his dagger's sheath. "The Dagger of Kheferatum wouldn't take an innocent life in the quest for a new master." At least, he didn't think so. Then again, it had been several centuries since he'd had a crisis of faith on the level of the one recently suffered in Germany when the dagger had been stolen.

"Perhaps." Doubt filled Nansee's voice. "Still, I would feel better if I knew you had a true grip on the blade."

Khefar knew Nansee's interest was mostly self-centered, given that the Dagger of Kheferatum could unmake a god. "Don't worry, spider. The dagger still recognizes my hand."

The demigod looked mollified, if not convinced. Khefar knew the spider god wanted more proof, and he couldn't blame the old man. The Dagger of Kheferatum was a dangerous force, imbued with the power of the god Atum to destroy or create. What the dagger created remained in existence. When the dagger destroyed, it removed its target from the fabric of existence—humans, Fallen, gods. Not even atoms remained.

"The dagger remains mine until Atum himself comes to claim it from me," Khefar said. "No one will take it from me."

"Not even the Shadowchaser?" Nansee asked.

Khefar stared at the demigod, his constant companion for millennia. This was the longest the old man had ever gone without a joke or a smile. Now this question. Did Nansee worry that Kira would try to take Khefar's dagger? She'd already touched it a couple of times, and the dagger itself had tempted her more than once. Khefar knew she still coveted his blade and that the taint of Shadow was probably at the root of it. He knew Kira struggled against the desire to possess it. If Shadow gained more of a foothold . . .

"No one will take the Dagger of Kheferatum from me. Not even the Shadowchaser."

"As it is spoken, so shall it be," Nansee said. "May all the gods and goddesses stand with you."

Khefar jerked open his car door. Nansee could treat his words like a vow all he wanted. Khefar had simply stated a fact, no oaths necessary. He'd lost the dagger once; it wouldn't happen again. If Kira made a try for his dagger, he'd take that as a sign that she'd become Unbalanced, and he'd have to fulfill his promise to her.

He turned back to Nansee. "Does Balm know about the pact I have with Kira?"

The old man shook his head. "I think, if she knew, she would do everything in her power to remove you from Kira's life."

"And we both know the Balm of Gilead has a lot of resources at her disposal," Khefar muttered, sliding behind the wheel.

Nansee walked around the car to Khefar's side. "Unfortunately she doesn't see the event with the Fallen as the end of your duty to Kira, and neither do I. I suspect she'll be less friendly than usual."

Khefar sighed, started the car. "It's going to be a fun trip across the Atlantic."

Nansee shut the door as Khefar rolled down the window. "I do not envy you that, Medjay. I suggest you spend the trip sleeping as much as you possibly can to stay out of Balm's way. I'll meet you and our Shadow-chaser in London."

Chapter 3

After ending her painful call with Bernie's London solicitor, Kira indulged in a long, steaming shower before slipping into her standard black cargo pants, black work boots, and a chocolate brown long-sleeved knit shirt. Feeling somewhat human again, she made her way down the spiral staircase to the lower level of her home. The image of Nerfertiti emblazoned on the back wall greeted her as she stepped into her office. Kira was tempted to open the passageway to her private chambers. She wanted to perform a Weighing of the Heart ritual to see just how out of Balance her soul actually was. With her other responsibilities looming, the ritual was an indulgence and a worry she couldn't afford. However Unbalanced her soul, she had a job to do, a duty to Ma'at, to Bernie.

She moved around her desk, then settled into her ergonomic chair. She'd have called Balm if she'd remembered to ask Balm for her Atlanta phone number after the lunch feast. Assuming Balm even had a phone in the Atlanta digs she hadn't bothered to tell Kira about. More secrets, more reasons to be pissed.

Usually she communicated with her surrogate mother in dreamwalks, structured scenes in the place between dreaming and waking. With Balm being so close, Kira figured she should be able to reach out to the head of Gilead without having to go into a dream state.

She closed her eyes and took a deep breath, her hands splayed flat on the desk as she willed her body to relax, her mind to quiet. It was difficult to do given her frustration with the Nubian roiling so close to the surface of her conscious mind. Just because he had a few thousand years on her didn't mean he was the boss.

She filled her mind with the sound of the ocean crashing against the rocks on Santa Costa, the feel of the sunshine as it bleached sand and stone, the scent of the briny breeze rustling through the bushes, the place that had been home and prison and proving ground.

Balm. Balm, can you hear me?

The answer was immediate. *Of course, Daughter, is something wrong?*

No. Just wanted to take you up on that flight offer. Hope it's not too late.

Balm's amusement rippled across their connection. *Not at all. The pilot informs me that we are cleared to leave shortly after sunset. We're at DeKalb-Peachtree airport. Shall I come and get you?*

The Balm of Gilead in her sanctum sanctorum? *That's not necessary.*

All right, Kira. Are you sure there's nothing wrong? Your friends seemed quite upset after your departure.

Kira suppressed a groan. Gods, what had she been thinking to have that conversation with Wynne at Balm's house? She should have waited until they'd gone home, maybe called them before heading to the airport. But no, it had needed to be done and delaying or phoning later would have been the coward's way.

Daughter?

Just a disagreement between friends. She could only wish it were something so simple, instead of a fundamental shift in how she and the few people she trusted interacted with each other. *I'll try to talk to them again when I get back from London.*

Excellent idea. Then I'll see you at the airport.

See you soon, and thanks.

You're very welcome, Daughter.

Balm pulled away. Kira slowly swam up through layers of her subconscious, then blew out a relieved sigh. Balm hadn't asked about Khefar or Anansi, and Kira saw no reason to bring them up. She had a feeling the conversation wouldn't go as well.

She opened her eyes. Bernie's pocket watch gleamed up at her from the smooth desk surface. The watch, like most of his favorite things, was an antique, a heavy, quadruple-hinged timepiece made in the mid-nineteenth century with an eighteen-karat-gold case and porcelain face. It was one of the few non-Egyptian pieces that Bernie considered his pride and joy.

Loss cut through her again. Balm had been her guardian since Kira was twelve, but Bernard Comstock had truly been like a father to her. He had been her professor and her mentor. Only after his death did she learn that he was her Gilead handler, and had been almost since she'd first arrived in London.

The betrayal hurt a little less now, with new pains supplanting it. But the loss . . . the loss would stay with her for a long while.

She stripped off her left glove and reached for the watch, only to hesitate before touching it. Reading objects was never an easy thing, even though she'd been using her extrasense to catalog artifacts for years. But objects belonging to those who'd died violently, cherished mementos used daily, those were tough to shield herself against. Khefar's dagger had tossed her across the room after she'd read it.

Bernie had come to her when she'd touched a mere travel voucher. Rather, it had been a construct of Bernie, her magic, and her subconscious, interacting with Kira almost as the man himself would. Touching his blood had forced her to relive his death at the claws of a seeker demon. What would touching his pocket watch, an object he had loved and carried daily without fail, do to her?

Only one way to find out. She called her extrasense as a protective measure, slowly using her innate magic to push through the Veil of reality. Blue-green light flickered along her arm and hand, the turquoise tinge a visual reminder of her brush with Shadow.

Her fingers curled around the gilded case. For a moment, nothing. Then, like spilled watercolors, her Normal vision streaked and ran, the colors blending, changing to amber. Disorientation gurgled through her as everything she knew as reality flowed and ebbed. Then matter became solid again, solid but *changed*.

Instead of sitting in her desk chair, she sat in a Range Rover. Instead of the walls of her office, she saw the sands of the Giza Plateau spread out before her, the city of Cairo just beyond to the northeast. And beside her, behind the wheel, sat her mentor, the recently deceased Bernard Comstock.

"Bernie." She swallowed. "You look good."

He smiled, years peeling away from his bronze features, making him even more dashing in his safari khakis. She felt decidedly out of place in her dark Chaser's gear. "Not too shabby for a dead man, eh? I must say, being rather like a ghost agrees with me."

"Does that mean that you're happy, then? You're okay?"

"Happiness is relative, Kira." He stared out at the plateau. "Digging season begins in a few months. I hope I'll be able to see some excavations then. Should be an adventure."

Bernie's kind, dark eyes regarded her solemnly. "You've had some adventures of your own, I understand."

She barked out a laugh. "That's putting it mildly."

He nodded, the wide brim of his hat keeping the sun from his face. "I'm glad you made it through both your ordeals, and that you trusted the Nubian at the end."

A reminder that if she had trusted Khefar sooner, she might not have killed innocent people. "I'm sorry."

"You could have asked me. I'm here to help you."

"I know that, now." She hesitated. "I—I just wasn't sure what I'd see, touching your personal things."

"You won't have to witness my death again. I told you before, I'm a remnant of Bernie and your memories of him, powered by your magic. Because I'm neither here nor there I can see things that you cannot, and I'll share what I can with you."

"Meaning there will be things you won't share with me."

"More like 'can't share.'" He adjusted his hat.

"There are rules and I must work within them. You know without me saying that I am no less determined to see you live a long and happy life now than I was when I was alive."

Kira dipped her head. It felt good to have someone concerned about her welfare for her sake instead of their own, but she wished that someone were flesh and blood, not a ghostly figment of her magical imagination.

"Did you know you were going to die?" she asked, the words bursting from her. "Is that why you took all these elaborate steps to make sure I could communicate with you? You knew you were going to die and didn't tell me?"

Bernie's hand lifted off the steering wheel, but even in death he checked his instinct to touch her. "I was an antiques dealer long past sixty," he said softly. "Death had been a constant companion for quite some time. But no, I didn't know for certain that I would die when I brought the dagger to you. Even if I had known, I wouldn't have told you. I would simply have enjoyed the time I had left with those most important to me. Would you not have done the same?"

He was right. There was no way that she'd burden Wynne and Zoo with her imminent death. Even now, she wanted to distance her friends from her Shadow-chaser life and the stain of Shadow she carried. They'd helped her for the last few years and almost lost their lives because of her. It was time for them to move on. Even their former lives in the military were less dangerous than helping her fight Shadow.

"No, I wouldn't tell anyone. But that doesn't change

the fact that I want you here. I need you here, Bernie, especially now."

"I know, Kira." His hand hovered over hers. "Use my watch to contact me whenever you have a need. It will ensure that enough of me manifests for you. I would advise you to keep it near you for the next little while."

Kira sighed, feeling the weight of responsibility settle heavily on her shoulders. "Sending the Fallen back to Shadow wasn't the end, was it?"

Bernie shook his head. "You already know the answer to that. There are things you will still have to do for Balm, things you have to do for Ma'at. And a couple of things I need you to do for me. So much responsibility on your young shoulders, but I believe you're more than capable of shouldering it."

Glad somebody thinks I'm capable. "I'm flying out to London tonight, on Balm's plane. I've called your solicitor to let him know I am coming. Is there anyone else you'd like me to contact?"

He tapped a finger against his chin. "There are still a few colleagues at the Petrie who should know. Mr. Braithwhyte—my solicitor—will have already informed the clerks at the antiques shop. I would very much appreciate a nice memorial tea there, and you need to meet the people working there anyway."

Need to? Not really. But for Bernie, she'd go through the motions. "I'll see to it. What would you like me to do with your ashes?"

"The ashes are no longer me, but I wouldn't mind if you'd bring them here, to the plateau. We'd always said we'd join an excavation here one day. I sincerely regret that we won't be able to do that."

She wiped at her eyes. "Maybe I'll go to the Valley of the Kings, and while I spread your ashes, we can pretend we're discovering a new tomb."

He beamed. "Excellent idea."

She hesitated, not wanting to spoil this reunion of sorts with bitterness. "What about your colleagues at Gilead London? Do you want me to invite any of them to your memorial?"

"No." His expression tightened. "I didn't go into the office very much, Kira. As far as I'm concerned, no one there could be considered a friend. Balm will soon make a discovery to that effect."

"Are you saying that Balm's in danger?"

"I do not think so. At least, not at this moment. The Chaser and handler in London, something seemed a bit off with them . . . it's entirely possible that the Nubian's dagger was intended for them, and accidentally fell to me. I do fear, however, that taking my ashes back to London is but the start of your adventures there."

Adrenaline steamed through Kira's veins. A Chase. Not one of the Fallen, perhaps not even hybrids, but an investigation she could submerge herself in, and push aside her own problems.

"Don't worry, Bernie. I'll look into taking care of the arrangements and look into the London Chaser. If there's something to find, I'll find it."

"I'm sure you will." He grinned. "Now get out of my Rover. We've both got things to do."

The vision slowly faded into the reality of her office. Her hands shook as she closed the pocket watch, then pulled her gloves back on. She'd keep it, and

Bernie, close. She had a feeling she'd need to rely on him heavily in the days ahead.

Khefar made his way back to Kira's, his mind spinning. Not that he'd expected that everything would be fine and dandy since he and Kira had been called by Isis and Ma'at, but he'd hoped Kira would have at least one day of peace. One day in which she could just be herself. A day in which they'd have opportunity to move beyond a handful of kisses and combat training into something more stimulating, more dangerous.

He shook his head. It probably wasn't a good idea to think about Kira like that. He'd saved her because he was honor-bound to do so, because that was the only way to reunite with his family. The Light needed more soldiers, not fewer, and it would have been a tragedy for Kira to leave this world so soon.

More or less settled in his thoughts, Khefar parked, gathered his belongings from the trunk, then made his way back inside Kira's. She'd been busy while he had been gone. The riot of books, papers, and artifacts seemed a little more streamlined. A duffel bag already waited by the door. He dropped the one he'd retrieved from his trunk beside it, then took his purchases over to his second bag tucked beside the couch. One good thing about the trip to London would be getting back into a real bed, though the couch was hardly the worst place he'd had to bunk down.

"Already packing, I see."

"Yeah." She crossed to the dining table she used as a worktable. "Balm's flight plan was cleared, so we're flying out tonight."

Her irritation hadn't abated in his absence, he noted. Not that he blamed her. He stared at her, at this woman he'd known for less than a month. A woman who infuriated him, excited him, terrified him, and at moments even humbled him. The things that had happened to her would have broken most people, yet she persevered, urged on by the need to defend, and in some ways, to atone. In that, they were kindred spirits.

"You disapprove of my packing methods?"

"What?" He noticed then that she'd stopped in front of her repurposed dining table. An open suitcase lay atop it. "No, why would you say that?"

"You're frowning." Her gloved hands flexed as she shoved what looked like bed linens into the case. "Granted that's a normal look for you, but I promise I'm not over-packing. I always take my own sheets and towels when I travel."

Why would he be angry at her method of packing? Clearly he needed to work on his diplomacy. He shoved his purchases into the second duffel. "That makes sense. Given your ability, I guess staying in a hotel frequented by hundreds of different travelers would wreak havoc on your extrasense."

"It's easier to just tell the hotel staff that I have a disability combined with severe allergies. That and the 'Do Not Disturb' sign usually get them to leave me alone during my stay."

"What about when you're chasing and you have to bunk down in a hurry?"

She closed the suitcase. "Gilead usually has a transit house, or I make sure to stay at a Light-staffed hotel. If I'm deep in a Chase I usually don't sleep until it's over. I stay in my gear and keep on the move until the Chase is done. Then I come home and crash for a couple of days."

It hadn't occurred to him how she'd had to adapt in order to function with her gift. "It's a wonder you leave your house at all."

"I've learned to block most of the impressions I could get hit with. Usually, public stuff just comes across as a dull background roar—like thousands of television channels playing a thousand different shows. It's only the private things, the violent things, that break through my barriers."

"Like my dagger."

She nodded once. "Like your dagger. And Bernie's death."

He considered that. "You don't get impressions from me, but the dagger did talk to you. Do you think you would get impressions from a personal object of mine?"

She stopped mid-motion, her body language indicating caution. "I don't know. Are you saying that you want me to get a read on something of yours?"

Khefar shoved his left hand into the pocket of his jacket. All he had left of his former life was a part of a necklace his wife had worn, around which he'd wrapped a few strips of fabric from his children's clothing, tucked into a small leather pouch dangling from a suede thong. A pitiful, fragile reminder of what he'd lost, what he'd been working for so long to regain.

His wife, his two sons, his daughter. He held fast to the hope that they were well and waiting for him in the afterlife, enjoying their time in the Field of Reeds.

He believed they didn't blame him for not having been there, for having protected the pharaoh's firstborn instead of his family, but he could not be sure.

"You have their names," Kira said softly, her eyes dark with understanding. She pulled off one of her gloves. "You already know that speaking their names gives them life here and now. But I understand wanting more, wanting another connection to what you had. If you wish, I can try to get a hit from whatever you have there in your pocket." She held out her hand.

Khefar's finger's clenched around his ancient memento. The need to know pulsed through him—the need to recapture the faces of his loved ones, reclaim snippets of their lives. To know that they hadn't suffered before they died.

"No." He cleared his throat, forced determination into his tone. "No, but I thank you for the offer. There's no telling what you may discover or what effect the discovery would have on you. The dagger threw you across the room, you said. If that could happen with my blade, I don't want to imagine what this would do to you."

A ghost of a smile curved her lips. "You think it could be worse than anything else that's happened to me?"

"Precisely why I don't want to try. You've just come out of three days of unconsciousness after journeying through the underworld. Your system could still be overwhelmed and your extrasense could still be spotty."

"My extrasense is fine." She pulled her glove back on. "There's no reason to be afraid of what I might discover. I saw plenty already . . . thanks to the dagger."

"I'm not afraid of what you'd see." Not completely. He didn't fear what Kira would think of him based on her vision, but what she would tell him.

"Whatever." She jerked the suitcase off the table and lugged it over to the door.

He followed her. Evasiveness didn't work with the Shadowchaser; he'd already learned that. Time for truth.

He touched her shoulder, knowing the contact would get her attention. She flinched, then straightened to look at him. Emotion swirled in her eyes: anger, hurt, and abrasive grief. He knew then that as much as he wanted a connection to his family, he would never again ask Kira to read him. What he'd gain would be offset by what she'd lose, and he couldn't accept that.

She lifted her chin, determined, defiant. "Say what you need to say. I still have things to do."

"Kira. I'm worried about you, about the taint of Shadow on your soul, the tragedies that have marked you. The burdens you already carry would overwhelm a lesser person. I don't want to add to them if I can help it. I have carried this for four thousand years. I don't know if any pleasant memories are still attached to it or not. Because of that, I don't want you to take a risk on my behalf."

She stared at him as if trying to mine the truth in his face. Finally some of the heat left her gaze. "I need to finish up here."

He let her go. "Is there anything I can do to help?"

She gestured to the garage. "I cleaned up my bike

parts so you can pull your car inside. I've already arranged for a taxi to take us to the airport. It should be here in about an hour."

"Thanks for making room for the car." He paused. "And I wish to apologize for earlier. It's been a life-changing time for both of us. I know you think I am deliberately keeping things from you, but I'm not. As long as I've been aware of the Gilead Commission, there has always been a woman named Balm at its head. You, having grown up in the Commission's stronghold, probably know much more about the organization that I could ever hope to discover."

She didn't look convinced, but thankfully she decided to leave it be. "The spider's not coming with us?"

"He has alternative methods of travel," Khefar explained. "He said he'll meet us in London."

She snorted. "So he doesn't want to be trapped on a plane with Balm either. Too bad he couldn't let us tag along."

Khefar shuddered. "I'm not sure we'd survive sliding along his webs."

"Good point. Opening a slice into reality in one place and then stepping through to another place would probably drive a human insane." She smiled. "Then again, Balm has that effect on people too."

"It's like choosing between a rock and the proverbial hard place."

"Yeah." Her smile slipped. "That's how it usually goes. And it's us poor ants at the bottom who get buried in the landslide."

"Then I say we are neither ants nor at the bottom of the pile." He held a fist out to her. "Deal?"

She bumped his knuckles with her own fist. "Deal. You mind if we stop by the DMZ before we head to the airport?"

"No. Let me take a shower and change and I'll be ready to go. I'm curious myself to see how the club fared."

Chapter 4

As the taxi pulled to a stop Kira noted that the club seemed undisturbed from the outside. The complex still reeked of a concrete and steel postmodern homage to urban decay. It was too early for crowds to line the sidewalk seeking entry. Instead, workers clogged the entrance, signage on their trucks touting various repair and building specialties. The phrase *hive of activity* came to Kira's mind.

Kira asked the driver to wait, then looked at Khefar as they made their way to the front door. "Granted I was too busy dying, but I didn't think we did that much damage to the club."

"I was a little distracted with trying to keep you alive, but part of the reason you died was because you went through a window and fell two floors to the pit."

Kira rolled her shoulders. The last time she'd been in the Goth-industrial club, three days ago, had been to deliver a fake Dagger of Kheferatum to Enig, one of the Fallen, or rather his human Avatar. Enig, who'd killed her first handler six years ago, who'd wanted to create a new world order, who'd wanted her to join him and injected her with Shadow to ensure her cooperation.

She forced the thoughts—and most important, the emotions—away. Demoz, the DMZ's owner, had to be around somewhere. Even though last week she'd basically been a one-woman smorgasbord for the psychic vampire, she had no doubt Demoz would be ready to feed again.

A bouncer lounged in the doorway. From his build to his features to the artful arrangement of his shiny obsidian hair, he looked like he could have made a lucrative career as a sumo wrestler, if not for the spice of "other" about him. Though his stance was casual, his eyes assessed every worker entering and leaving the club.

He straightened as they approached. "Chaser Solomon. Mr. D. said you can go on in."

Kira pursed her lips. The bouncer's tone sounded downright respectful. Something to do with taking out one of the Fallen and then coming back from the dead to tell about it, no doubt.

She turned to Khefar. "Looks like we're expected." Kira didn't know whether to be happy about that or not.

"Mr. D. passed down the word yesterday," the guard said helpfully. He was a step up from the DMZ's usual door enforcers; he actually used his brain. "You don't have to worry about checking your weapons either. Someone will take you to the boss."

Kira frowned. Khefar shrugged, his frown matching hers. Apparently he didn't know what to make of this effusive greeting either. At least they'd be able to remain armed. She didn't think Demoz would try to trick her, but she'd used his club to bring down a Fallen. She had no doubt the other side would do something similar, especially given Demoz's infamous neutrality.

A skittering of awareness along her extrasense

warned Kira that some version of the DMZ's security measures was active. "Don't know how far we'll get," she said, "but let's not try to force our way past the coat check."

Khefar nodded, and they made their way into the main entrance. New decor greeted them beyond the double doors. The gunmetal-gray walls were now lined with what looked like sheet metal held in place by thick bolts. A pair of white leather couches sat beneath two stripes of pale blue neon along one wall. A contrasting set in black leather sat opposite beneath two strips of dim yellow neon. One side: Light; the other: Shadow.

"Looks like the vampire's done some redecorating since we were here," Khefar observed. "Definitely makes a statement."

"Yeah, Demoz is a true opportunist," she answered, wondering where Morey the eel and his tank were. She couldn't remember the changeling's huge fish tank taking any damage during the fight three days ago, but anything could have happened after she'd died.

"He's probably been planning changes for a while, waiting for the right moment—or an insurance claim. After all, why repair when you can renovate?"

"You know Demoz well," a lilting voice said, then laughed.

Kira turned to see a young woman in winter-white wool trousers and a pale blue sweater approaching them. It took Kira a moment to place her as the Light-filled woman who worked as Demoz's personal assistant.

The woman stopped in front of them, a beatific smile lighting her smoky eyes, a gleaming contrast to her copper skin and coal-black cap of curls. "It is a pleasure to see you alive and well, Kira Solomon."

"Thank you . . . you know, I never got your name."

"You may call me Yessara."

"Yessara. I think you've met Khefar."

The woman extended a hand to the Nubian, who shook it warmly. "It is good to see you restored as well. And you both bear new marks. You have an Isis knot and Kira wears Ma'at's feather."

"Yes." Khefar dipped his head. "We were called by our goddesses during our away time."

"Away time. That's one way to put it." Yessara gave another one of her easy smiles. "Congratulations to the both of you. It is truly joyous to be so blessed."

Joyous, nervous, scared off her ass—Kira felt all of those things, but she kept it to herself. She simply didn't know how far up the Light chain Yessara went, and she couldn't afford to push away any potential allies.

"I just wanted to thank you again for everything you've done for me, but especially for finding and returning my Lightblade to me."

Yessara waved a graceful hand. "You've already thanked me, Chaser Solomon. Nothing more is required. Now, if you'd like to see Demoz, I'll be happy to take you to him. Just follow me."

The Light-imbued woman led them down the hallway from which she'd come, instead of through the double doors leading to the bars and triple-tiered club area divided between Light and Shadow. They stopped before an elevator. Yessara waved her hand in front of a panel and the doors slid open in response.

Kira followed the young woman inside, Khefar

silently at her back. The doors closed and the elevator started its descent.

Kira kept a protective layer of extrasense in place out of habit. While she had every reason to trust Yessara and few to the contrary, heading down deeper into Demoz's compound was stepping into uncharted territory. She needed to be prepared for anything because anything could be prepared for her.

Needing a distraction, she turned to Yessara. "May I ask you a question?"

The other woman faced her, hands clasped loosely in front of her. "You may."

"Why are you here, working for Demoz?"

"Where else should I be?"

"Um, I don't know—somewhere more nurturing, like working in a spa or something?"

Yessara laughed. "I've been told I have a relaxing effect on people. Reason enough to be where I am, doing what I do. Besides, it's a good job with great pay and benefits."

It was a good answer, but hardly satisfactory. Why would someone at an obviously high Light level like Yessara be content with being the gofer of a psychic vampire? Perhaps it wasn't about being content, but about duty, being where one needed to be. If Yessara wasn't a part of Demoz's staff, wasn't close to the neutral vampire, Kira's Lightblade would have been lost to her for good.

"Looks like we've arrived," the assistant said. A soft *ping* answered her, then the doors slid open. Yessara stepped out into a surprisingly bright yet utilitarian corridor, full of people and product moving about.

Obviously this was the staging area of the club, the way Demoz managed to cater to several hundred humans, hybrids, and others who entered his club each evening.

Yessara guided them down a corridor to a room marked "Office" by a plain black and silver nameplate. One quick knock, then she opened the door, gestured them inside. Demoz waited within, looking so unlike himself that it took Kira a moment to process what she saw.

For one thing, the vampire, whose skin could accurately be described as the color of tar, had his jacket off, his white dress shirt stretching the laws of physics as it worked to contain his considerable bulk. For another, he looked as if he was actually working, poring over a sheaf of papers stacked beside a laptop, a smartphone clutched in one beefy hand. A bank of monitors dominated one wall of the office, showing various areas of the DMZ complex.

"Wow, Demoz," Kira said, "you really do work and stuff?"

The vampire looked up, an oversized grin splitting his midnight face. "Kira, you did make it through!" he exclaimed, lifting his bulk out of the huge oxblood chair. "That wonderful Sanchez woman told me that you would, but I wanted to see with my own eyes."

Wonderful Sanchez woman? "You're buddy-buddy with the Gilead section chief now?"

"You know it's important to cultivate relationships with the movers and shakers of the city. Besides, Estrella Sanchez is a very intriguing woman."

Demoz was interested in Sanchez? "You're intrigued by Sanchez? I think I just threw up a little."

"She's fascinating, and can be useful," Demoz said, clearly enjoying Kira's discomfiture. "But if you must know, I'm not interested in Chief Sanchez in the way you seem to think."

Well, that's a relief. "Are you interested in anyone in the way I seem to think?" Gods, dying had apparently removed her social filters. She couldn't stop her curiosity or need for information, but she usually found more subtle ways to get the answers she wanted. Like putting someone in a half nelson.

Or observation. Demoz cut his eyes at Yessara, who busied herself with straightening the stack of papers at Demoz's elbow. The psychic vampire averted his eyes to peck at his keyboard, but Kira knew what she'd seen.

A psychic vampire and a . . . whatever Yessara was, which was probably something close to a "peace angel," a being with the ability to filter out unpleasant thoughts and emotions, usually as a person slept. They weren't really angels, of course, but enough Renaissance painters had captured them as rosy-cheeked cherubs that the moniker had stuck. Someone who filtered out negative energy would be attracted to a being who considered that energy food, and vice versa. If that symbiotic relationship developed into something more, she couldn't fault them for it.

Demoz cleared his throat. "Are you going to finally introduce me to the enigmatic man beside you, or will I have to do it myself?"

It was as good a segue as any. "Demoz, this is Khefar. Khefar, Demoz."

The two men shook hands, testing each other as

males of any species seem to have a habit of doing. "Very unusual mental pattern there, Khefar. Then again, our Kira seems to prefer the unusual. Normal bores her to tears."

"Then it's a good thing I'm not normal," the Nubian said. "I'd hate for her to become bored with me so early in our association."

"Really?" Demoz said, thrusting a wealth of meaning and question into the word as he resettled into his chair, Yessara standing beside him. He turned his assessing gaze—which was almost a physical touch coming from the psychic vampire—to Kira. "So, what brings you by my establishment today, Shadowchaser?"

"Just wanted to see for myself how your repairs were going," she told him, lowering herself to balance on the edge of the navy microsuede guest chair. Khefar took a spot just behind her and to the left, where he had plenty of room to draw a weapon if need be. With Yessara beside Demoz and Khefar backing her, what should have been a casual conversation had taken on the feel of a crime boss meeting, at least to Kira. "I also want to get an idea of the general mood around here and the rest of the city since we sent Enig back to Shadow."

Demoz steepled his fingers. A large Herkimer diamond sat in a thick silver band on his middle finger, taking up a sizable chunk of real estate on his left hand. Given that she'd destroyed his massive clear quartz specimen a few days ago, the vampire probably had to use the gem as a backup power amplifier.

She felt the brush of his power as he reached out, sending thin feeders throughout the club. It enabled him to sample from a large group of people instead of having to drain one victim at a time as younger vampires had to do. If you killed your food every time you ate, you'd soon run out of food. Luckily for every class of vampire that used humans for nourishment, the human population bred much faster than they did.

Demoz opened his eyes with a satisfied sigh, the black-on-black of his irises gleaming like dark stars. Kira had to be glad that he hadn't smacked his lips. "It's been a curious mixture of respect and awe," he finally said. "Fear is there too, of course. What you did here, and how you did it, has spread throughout the halfling and hybrid communities here in town. I'm sure it's probably all over the Internet as well."

"Great." So much for going back to low-key.

"I see you've gone through even more changes since the last horrible time I saw you," Demoz said, his hand hovering at his own thick-jowled throat.

Yessara leaned forward. "Both Kira and her general have been elevated by their respective goddesses," she told Demoz. "A most happy occasion."

Kira could all but see the wheels spinning in Demoz's head as he decided whom he'd sell the information to. She didn't mind in this instance—unless she wore scarves or turtlenecks for the rest of her life, people were bound to see the mark she bore at her throat—but now she'd have to be even more aware of what she shared with Demoz.

"It's definitely an honor," she said, wondering why Yessara had referred to Khefar as a general. She was, of course, correct. Khefar had held the rank from his pharaoh and, she suspected, many times since. But how would Yessara know that? It made her wonder again how high up in the Light hierarchy Yessara was, how old the girl was, and what her real reason for being in the DMZ was. "Being the Hand of Ma'at isn't something I take lightly."

"I doubt any of the denizens of Atlanta will take it lightly either," Demoz added. "What I don't know is if you've just made your job harder or easier. Several local halfling and Shadowling leaders threw in their lot with Enig. They had to, out of self-preservation. Defying one of the Fallen buys you a painful one-way ticket back to Shadow. When you took Enig down, Gilead took down several leaders, and you've left a halfling power vacuum in your wake."

"Damn. Should have known something like that would happen. Is there anyone local left with the skill and power to unify the halflings?"

"There are some who think they do. I don't think anyone's going to try to make any moves anytime soon, especially once word gets out that you're still around. Not until the memories of you dispatching a Fallen and a seeker demon have faded."

She nodded, trying to decide what to tell the information broker. She decided on truth. "I'm going to be out of town for a couple of days, taking the handler's ashes back to London. Sanchez will have plenty of Gilead teams on the streets while I'm gone. If there's anything you think I should know, she can get in touch with me."

"Of course. I'll be happy to speak with Section Chief Sanchez, especially since she's been kind enough to arrange for a new slab of quartz crystal to be shipped here from Mexico as a replacement for the specimen I lost."

Sanchez doing something nice for a hybrid? It was a new day after all. "I assume you'll cleanse it before installation."

Demoz managed to look affronted. "Kira. I'm grateful, not gullible. I'll make sure there are no eavesdropping enchantments or other spells on the crystal before it even enters the club. Gilead is paying for quite a few repairs, and I see no reason why they shouldn't. Because of that, I consider our accounts even, nothing owed on either side."

Kira doubted that Sanchez would think so, but she'd leave that for the chief and the vampire to settle. They were both grown-ups.

"Okay then." She rose. "Have there been any sort of repercussions for you?"

"For me? No. The DMZ was acting in its usual capacity as neutral ground for two opposing factions to come together. Though you didn't seem so opposed that night." He regarded her solemnly. "I'm glad to see my observations were in error. After all, the goddess of Truth and Order would hardly elevate someone touched by the chaos of Shadow, would She?"

"I haven't heard of anything like that happening before," Kira answered honestly. "Take care of my city while I'm gone, Demoz."

"Of course. And make sure your 'general' takes care of you while you're gone."

Despite every intention not to, Kira gasped. Demoz broke into a grin, a grin that soon became a guffaw. "Oh, now that is priceless!"

"Demoz . . ." She didn't reach for her Lightblade, but it was a close thing.

The vampire held up his hands. "Don't worry, though, I'll keep that information all to myself. Who would believe me anyway?"

His booming laughter followed them out into the hall. Khefar looked at Kira. "Mind telling me what was so amusing back there?"

"Actually I do," she told him, stomping her way back to the elevator. "You're not the only one capable of keeping secrets. Even obvious ones."

Chapter 5

Balm's Gulfstream sat in a private area of the DeKalb-Peachtree Airport. The top-of-the-line jet would get them and their belongings across the Atlantic in under eight hours, less with a tailwind. It still meant she'd be trapped all night in a metal cylinder several thousand feet above the ocean with no hope of escaping Balm or Khefar. If she was lucky she'd be able to sleep for most of the flight. She had the feeling, however, that she'd used up a good portion of her luck returning from the dead.

Kira and Khefar got out of their taxi as the driver hurried around to the trunk to unload their bags. A couple of members of the flight crew took their luggage as Khefar paid the driver. The head of Gilead watched the activity, a thin slip of a man standing beside her at the foot of the stairs.

As Kira watched, Balm spoke softly to the young-ish man, who then went up the stairs and into the plane ahead of her. "Who is that?" Khefar wondered.

"The better question is probably 'what' instead of 'who,'" Kira said as their taxi left. "Balm usually has an assistant with her at all times. When she's not on Santa Costa, her assistant usually doubles as a pretty lethal bodyguard. No telling what he turns into when she's threatened."

Balm didn't smile as they approached. "You didn't tell me that the Immortal Warrior travels with you, daughter of mine," Balm said, all but glowing in the sunset with her cream-colored wool coat draped about her.

"Must have slipped my mind," Kira answered, mental shields firmly locked down. Her hand dropped to her well-worn canvas messenger bag, feeling the corner of Comstock's carefully packaged urn. "If there's going to be drama about this, we can travel some other way."

Balm lifted her chin. "The invitation has already been extended and accepted. No need for drama here. The crew will see to your belongings. I trust you packed light?" She turned on her heel and climbed the stairs into the plane.

Kira turned to Khefar. The Nubian wore his usual inscrutable expression. "Don't worry. I'm not going to ask because you're not going to answer anyway."

She entered the plane, moving past the crew area and galley to the passenger section. Decorated in earth tones with large reclining seats, a couch against the starboard side, and a four-seater dining area, the interior of the private jet was luxurious, but Kira had expected nothing less. The Gilead Commission operated under the umbrella of a private multinational conglomerate called Light International that conducted business for the Light all over the world, with Balm as its chief executive officer. Centuries of investments and donations fueled and funded the organization's philanthropic activities as well as its paramilitary skirmishes against Shadow.

Kira knew from growing up on Santa Costa, Gilead's private island in the Aegean, that Balm took her role as CEO very seriously. No matter what time Kira walked the halls of the Gilead stronghold, Balm was awake, overseeing Chaser selection, managing acolyte training, reviewing field actions with the other Commissioners, placing her assets where they did the most good. That was in addition to all the decisions of running the business and altruistic endeavors of the company. The nonstop activity was like a hurricane with Balm at its center. There were times when Kira thought the woman was hardwired into some giant Gilead database.

Khefar came in behind her. "I thank you, Balm, for your hospitality."

"You're welcome, Khefar, son of Jeru, son of Natek." Balm inclined her head, then settled onto the couch. "Never let it be said that Gilead withholds hospitality from those in need of it."

Khefar sketched a slight bow. "May your hospitality continue for centuries to come. If you'll indulge me, I haven't fully recovered from our return from the dead. I'll avail myself of the chairs here."

He settled his dark gray trench coat closed about his body, then folded himself into one of the generous leather chairs. Kira had no doubt he'd be asleep before the pilot could taxi to the runway.

"Daughter," Balm called from the back of the plane, "why don't you come sit near me? We still have much to catch up on."

Kira refrained from sighing and headed toward the rear of the plane. When Balm went into mothering mode, Kira usually ended up the worse for wear. It meant Balm wanted her to learn something, and Balm's lessons were always hard learned.

"What are you thinking about?" Balm asked as Kira settled into the club chair opposite the couch.

"I'm thinking that the more I learn the less I know," Kira said, turning up the collar on her battered all-weather coat and carefully maneuvering in her chair so that none of her skin touched the seat. No telling what sort of reading she'd get from the leather. The flight crew finished their last-minute preparations. Balm's assistant looked up from his smartphone, smiled briefly, then returned to his messages. "Then again, you and the Nubian aren't exactly the most talkative people I've had to deal with."

"I'm willing to talk now."

"So you are. Which, I have to say, worries me."

Balm glanced out the window as the plane began to taxi. "Sometimes I am so focused on the big picture that I forget there are other things that are also important. Much has happened in the last few weeks, Kira. Information is vital for all of us, especially when dealing with the Fallen."

Kira hesitated, slouching in her seat as the plane smoothly rose into the air, gained altitude, then leveled off. The plane's air had a hint of seabreeze to it, as if Balm had somehow found a way to capture Santa Costa's balmy winds.

A sudden pang of homesickness surged through her. Despite her love-hate relationship with Gilead, the island stronghold was the one place she'd lived longest, and Balm the one person who'd been a constant in her life. She wished she could talk to Balm—really talk to Balm as if the head of Gilead truly was her mother, and not the woman who'd become her guardian after her adopted parents dumped her on Gilead's doorstep. She wished she could talk to Balm about the innocent people she'd killed while strung out on Shadow; the excruciating weight of the guilt; about the remnant of Shadow that had twined itself deep into her core, so deep that not even sacrificing her life and killing the Fallen had expunged it. She wanted to talk about how nothing in her world made sense anymore and she was only pretending to have her shit together.

This was Balm, however. She was the head of Gilead first and last. Any other Shadowchaser with Kira's problems wouldn't go confessing all to Balm like some supernatural Mother Superior unless they wanted to be brought in for refinement. A Chaser infected by Shadow, whose soul was weighted away from the Light, would be marked for elimination. Kira had asked Khefar to be her fail-safe in case she slid too far because she couldn't trust herself not to fight her Gilead comrades. So no, she couldn't tell Balm just how tenuous her hold really was. She had to fake it for now.

"I told you what I know about the Fallen when we were at your house," Kira finally said. "I know I still need to write up an official report for you, but I was hoping to wait a little bit on that before turning it in."

Balm sighed. "You're on leave right now, Kira. I don't expect you to turn in work related to your duties as a Shadowchaser until you return to active duty."

That reminded Kira of something Khefar had

mentioned earlier. "So you're not going to choose a replacement Chaser for Atlanta?"

Balm kicked off her shoes to lounge on the couch. Something about the pose reminded Kira of frescoes she'd seen in Pompeii. "What nonsense is this? I've already told you that you'll always be a Shadowchaser as far as I'm concerned. No one will make you evacuate that deplorable warehouse you call a home."

"My warehouse suits me just fine. If you're not aiming to replace me, why send Chasers to interview with Sanchez? You did know about that, didn't you?"

How a woman lying on a couch could look down her nose, Kira wasn't sure. Balm managed it with ease. "Very little goes on in this organization without my knowledge or approval." Her eyes flared blue, then returned to normal with a blink. "For instance, a young Pakistani man is currently going on break in Gilead Sydney. I do believe he's having a nice bit of fruit salad."

"You've proved your point." Kira shifted in her chair, manipulating the controls to convert it into a reclining seat. She'd long believed Balm was some sort of oracle; now she wondered if the head of Gilead was actually the Oracle. It would certainly explain why Gilead was based on Santa Costa. "I still don't understand why you sent them, especially without telling me."

"Perhaps I wanted you to care more about your role as a Shadowchaser," came Balm's surprising answer. "And perhaps I wanted Sanchez to appreciate you more."

"By comparing me to your other Chasers? I'd think that would convince Sanchez even more to be rid of me."

"Or it will convince her that despite your complete disregard for rules and authority, you really are the best that Gilead has to offer in standing against Shadow. Your successful Chase of the Fallen—as much as I disapprove of your methods—showed that."

Kira shrugged off the compliment. "I'm merely the product of my training. After nearly a decade of being forged into what you wanted me to be, I can't be anything other than an efficient Shadow-killing machine."

If Balm disliked her comment, she showed no sign. If anything, her expression was entirely too knowing for Kira's taste. She closed her eyes, not ready for compassion or understanding or, worse yet, pity.

"Tell me honestly, Daughter: are you going to be okay?"

Kira opened one eye. Balm lay in the berth across from her, serene and eternal as always even twenty-five thousand feet above the Atlantic. Kira had known Balm since she was twelve, and now, some fourteen years later, she and the head of Gilead, with her smooth bronze skin and long brown hair, looked more like college roommates than mother and daughter.

"I don't know, but I'm going to have to be, aren't I?" she answered, wishing she'd done as Khefar had—chosen one of the recliners in the forward part of the Gulfstream near the crew section. The Nubian had settled into his chair and immediately fallen asleep as if he hadn't a care in the world. He looked so peaceful she wanted to throw something at him. Like her Lightblade.

Balm gave a discreet cough. "I think you should consider coming to Santa Costa after you've finished in London. You've been through a lot—you deserve a rest."

"Rest? I feel like I've spent more time unconscious in the last two weeks than I have awake and upright." She shifted in her berth. "If I went back to the island with you, we'd have a row before the plane stopped taxiing."

"We're not having a row now," Balm pointed out.

"That's because I'm going to pretend to sleep as soon as I figure out a way to end this conversation. Even if we didn't fight, I'd have nothing to do but terrorize your acolytes. Are you sure you want to turn me loose on Santa Costa?"

"I think you could have an edifying effect on my students. No doubt Gilead is already abuzz with what you did in Atlanta."

Kira suppressed a shudder. She didn't want to be known for what she'd done in Atlanta—killed half a dozen innocents, nearly killed her friends, lost her handler, nearly lost her soul to Shadow. "All the more reason not to go. Dealing with the London office will be bad enough."

"I'm going to be in London for a several days. I can make sure that no one bothers you while you're handling Comstock's last wishes, but I would like to know what you're planning to do afterward."

"Planning? I just came back from the dead this morning. I think I'm doing good to put one foot in front of the other right now."

"Kira." Balm put a world full of reproach into saying her name. Then she cleared her throat. "You should know, everyone who works for Gilead has a settlement given to their heirs in the event of their death. Since Mr. Comstock designated you as his heir, you'll get his settlement. It's part of why I'm accompanying you to London."

Kira was sure that Balm didn't travel around the world to personally offer condolences when a handler or Chaser died, especially since most of the Chasers were orphans, but she decided she'd keep that opinion to herself. "Thank you, but you know I don't care about that."

"I know you don't, but he did. Comstock was very adamant that you be looked after."

Kira had to look away as grief ambushed her again. Bernie had been looking after her for years, from the moment she'd met him at University College in London to instilling a part of himself in his personal items. She was carrying his pocket watch with her, just as he'd suggested, tucked in an inside coat pocket.

She resisted reaching for the watch. Despite having "talked" with Comstock earlier in the day, she wanted to talk to him again. It bothered her, though. When she defused magical artifacts for various museums and private collections, each successive handling drained the intensity of the magical residue until there was nothing left. If she kept talking to Comstock, would his essence too eventually fade to nothing? She didn't want to be without him, without his advice, his easy jokes, the warmth and affection he freely gave her.

The scent of herbal tea brought her out of her reverie. Balm now sat at the table at the rear of the plane with a silver tea set and a platter of sandwiches before her. "When was the last time you ate, Daughter?"

"At your house, that humongous meal you and the spider god laid out for us." Kira swung her feet to the floor. The ambient light had been lowered sometime after takeoff, shrouding the bulk of the interior in near-darkness. She could just make out Balm's assistant in one of the reclined seats near Khefar at the front of the plane.

Balm looked at her over the top of a sheaf of papers, a pen and two pencils tucked in her dark waves. "You didn't eat a lot then, I noticed. I've got a nice chamomile tisane and some light sandwiches. Come sit with me."

It was a usual ritual for them, a way to apologize without either side capitulating. Puberty had been a hormone-raging madness for Kira, who, still stung from losing her adoptive family, had chafed under Balm's militant ideas of discipline and behavior. Many of their discussions and training sessions had ended with tantrums and broken objects. With teatime they were able to set aside their frustrations and Kira's growing pains and establish common ground. It had become so much a part of their dealings with each other that Kira didn't think herself capable of discussing anything personally or emotionally important with Balm without a cup of tea in her hands. Only Nico's death in Venice and its aftermath hadn't been soothed by tea.

Kira joined Balm at the table. Her stomach immediately growled. She stripped off her gloves, then tented her hands above her serving. Her hands flared blue as she mentally opened the pathway between Normal and not, reaching through the Veil to call her extrasense. One short, concentrated blast, and she could eat and drink without being bombarded with the steward's life story.

Balm added a dollop of honey to her tea. "Tell me, what do you think of the Nubian?"

Kira looked up from her sandwich, glancing over her shoulder at the sleeping man. He had headphones on, she noticed. What sort of music did a four-thousand-year-old man like to listen to? She didn't know, and it made her realize that while she knew some of his past, she had precious little knowledge of who Khefar was now. "What I'd really like to know is, what do *you* think of the Nubian?"

"He's a strong fighter, smarter than he lets on, loyal to a fault. He takes the protection of his charges very seriously. And his pain runs so deep there's no way to measure it."

Kira had figured that much. She wasn't an empath, but she knew pain and guilt had embedded themselves into Khefar's very fiber, permanently covering the man he'd been before. "Did you know him before he died the first time?"

Balm raised an eyebrow. "Kira, to ask your elders such a question. How old do you think I am?"

"Do you really want me to answer that?" Kira lowered her voice again. "Can I trust him?"

"Do you trust anyone, daughter of mine?"

Kira didn't. Not completely, not anymore. If she ever had. She trusted Bernie's ghost. Maybe. What kind of person did that make her? "It's safer not to."

"Safer, perhaps. Not necessarily better." Balm nodded in Khefar's direction. "He will work to earn your trust, work to hold to the vows he has made. He will save a life for every life he took, and more. He will protect you as long as his vows compel him to, or die trying."

Kira frowned, wondering if Balm knew Kira had asked Khefar to be her fail-safe. She obviously knew Kira was or had been one of the sixty-four-thousand-plus lives he had to save to cancel his debt and move on to his afterlife. "How did you know that I was one of the lives he needed to save?"

Balm smiled. "I can't reveal all my secrets in one night, my child."

"How about this: can you tell me why you seem to have a problem with him? It can't be just because he refuses to become a Shadowchaser."

Balm's expression shuttered. "He hasn't told you?"

"No, he hasn't." Irritation blossomed in Kira's gut. "Looks like you don't want to tell me either. Did you have a relationship with him?"

"Mind your cheek, Daughter." Balm adjusted her wrap about her shoulders. "To answer your question, no, I have not had carnal relations with the Immortal Warrior. Our interactions have strictly dealt with Light and Shadow."

Whatever that means, Kira thought. "Still, you must respect him if you've tried to recruit him before."

"As I've said, he has impressive skills and an equally impressive battle résumé. Who would not want someone with his abilities on their side? Unfortunately for Gilead, Khefar answers to a higher power. And now so do you."

Kira touched the feather imprinted at the base of her throat, the mark of her patron goddess, Ma'at. Proof that she had gone to the Hall of Judgment and survived, proof that Ma'at had called her into direct service. Proof that she was needed and necessary, though she had no idea what for.

"Kira."

She looked back at Balm. The other woman's dark eyes shone bright in the dim light as she leaned forward, her right hand stretched across the golden marble tabletop. "Never think, for one minute, that I am anything less than proud of you and what you've accomplished. I know that this is a difficult time for you but I promise, I am here for you for whatever support you need. Not just as the head of Gilead, not just as Balm. Do you understand?"

Kira blinked rapidly, then carefully slid her hand across the smooth surface, stopping a hairbreadth from Balm's fingertips. It was as close as she could get, as she dared to get, in the real world without her gloves. Neither of them knew what would happen if Kira were to touch Balm, and that was reason enough not to. Despite how frustrating Balm had made her life, Kira didn't want harm to come to her.

She raised her gaze, staring back at the woman who had saved her, who loved her. A tough love to be sure, but love all the same. Because of this woman, Kira could suffer loss, suffer grief, suffer threats to her existence, and still survive. That was a precious gift, and no one would take it away from her.

She still didn't know much of Balm's history, but she knew the head of Gilead had never mentioned children. Had Balm had a family in her former life? Had she been a mother? Had she somehow lost them or been taken away from them? Or had the Light chosen her early, elevated her before she could have a chance at a normal life? Was that part of the reason why Balm had claimed Kira as her daughter, so that she could have some measure of a family?

"Thank you, Mother, for everything you've done for me. And I make the same promise to you, to be here for you for whatever support you need. Not just as a Shadowchaser or the Hand of Ma'at."

Balm smiled, a simple happy smile Kira was glad to see. With so many losses in such a short time, Kira intended to hold on to what she had left no matter what.

Chapter 6

This wasn't exactly how she'd expected to return to London.

Summer would have been best. Much better than this cold, rainy November day, a bit of a shock after the bright warm days and cool nights of Atlanta in autumn. Still, she'd rather be out in the rain in London than in a plane with a prickly Balm and recalcitrant Nubian. She'd definitely rather be out in the rain instead of in this stuffy office in North London, sitting in front of the ornately carved desk of one Mr. Stanley Braithwhyte of Cooper, Johnstone, and Braithwhyte.

Kira kept her gloved hands carefully knotted in her lap, barely listening as Bernie's solicitor divulged the contents of the will. It was all she could do to keep her emotions at bay, to stave off the memories and continue functioning.

"Ms. Solomon."

Kira looked up, suddenly aware that the forty-something-year-old lawyer with the neat haircut, quiet tie, and unassuming features had called her name a time or two before. "I'm sorry."

She scrubbed a hand over her face. She'd insisted on coming straight to the solicitor's office instead of checking into the hotel, wanting nothing more than to get this deed done. Braithwhyte probably didn't approve of her travel-creased clothes, bleary eyes, or refusal to shake hands. Or her knapsack with Comstock's urn cluttering up the edge of the antique gnarled wood desk that looked as if it had belonged to Richard the Lionheart's solicitor.

The solicitor folded his disturbingly smooth hands atop his copy of the will. "Ms. Solomon, perhaps we should continue at another time. This is obviously an extremely difficult time for you."

Kira's composure nearly cracked. She did not want to have to go through this again. "No! No, it's just been a trying couple of weeks. Please continue."

Calm gray eyes regarded her, clearly assessing, probably wondering why an antiques dealer would leave his estate to a former student living abroad. She met his gaze, refusing to shift nervously in her chair, refusing to feel uncomfortable. "Is there something you wish to say to me, Mr. Braithwhyte?"

"Ms. Solomon, I know that your relationship with Mr. Comstock wasn't . . . traditional."

She straightened, focusing on the lawyer. If he'd wanted to get her attention, it had worked. "What are you implying, Mr. Braithwhyte?"

He held up his hands. "Nothing untoward, I assure you. I just want you to know that I have been Mr. Comstock's solicitor for years. The trust and level of disclosure he placed in me was absolute. I'm sure, were these circumstances different, you'd have already sensed something out of the ordinary here?"

His peculiar phrasing made her curious. She lowered her shields, allowing her extrasense to discreetly well up through her pores. Braithwhyte's eyes brightened from gray to silver, the pupils elongated to slits. A greenish aura swirled around his head and shoulders.

Gods. The lawyer was a hybrid, part human and part demon. She hadn't thought to scan the law office simply because it had never occurred to her that Comstock would do business with demons. How would she know, though? She and Bernie had never discussed the battle between Light and Shadow, never discussed the dangerous aspects of her job chasing down the Fallen and their Avatars. They hadn't even discussed the possibility that the things of nightmares actually lived and walked among humans. And because she didn't know how much Comstock knew, she could very well have walked into a trap set by a demon lawyer.

A demon lawyer. She had to swallow a sudden gurgle of laughter. *You need to get it together, girl. This isn't the time or place for jokes. Being this type of careless can get you killed.*

"Did Bernie know that you're not fully human?" she managed to ask, feeling the weight of her Lightblade against her right hip. She'd lose seconds freeing it from the folds of her coat, but stripping her gloves off would take longer. Braithwhyte hadn't given her a reason to use the blade or her power. At least not yet. It didn't mean he wouldn't try something.

"Yes, Mr. Comstock was well aware of my background."

If Bernie knew the lawyer was a demon, or half-demon, why would Bernie have retained him or his firm? Entering into any type of agreement with demons was a tricky thing that required equal amounts of patience, skill, and luck. Even then, if the demon wrote the contract, there would be built-in loopholes. Seemingly benign language could become a deadly trap if the contract were breached.

A chill slid down her back. Bernie somehow was able to communicate with her in the here and now, despite being two weeks dead. Had he entered into some sort of Shadow agreement, contracted through this firm so that he could advise her from his afterlife? *Please, Ma'at, tell me he didn't do this.*

"Do you execute soul contracts, Mr. Braithwhyte?" She didn't know the Chaser assigned to London, but she had to believe that whoever it was wouldn't allow demon lawyers to do soul business in London.

"I am not a purveyor of souls, Chaser Solomon," the solicitor said, leaving no doubt that he knew exactly who and what she was.

She sat forward, ready to act. "I didn't ask if you bought and sold souls, Mr. Braithwhyte. I asked if you execute soul contracts, agreements that are binding on a client even after their death."

"Ms. Solomon." The lawyer did a perfect imitation of an offended Brit. "This law firm has been here for decades, serving both the human and hybrid populace. Note, I said *hybrid*, not Shadowling. In all that time, we have never coerced a client or taken advantage of the desperate. Furthermore, I would remind you of free will. Mr. Comstock told me you were of the belief that what a being does is more important than what a being is. Was he wrong?"

Chastised by a demon. She really was losing it. "My apologies, Mr. Braithwhyte," she said, forcing herself to settle back in the chair. "I think you can understand why I'm a little off my game right now."

"Of course," the lawyer replied, back to his solicitous self. He leaned forward in his chair again. "If I may be so blunt, you don't have the head for this at the moment. Why don't you take some time to rest, perhaps reacquaint yourself with London? Most of the things that absolutely need to be done have been taken care of. Also, other than being the executor of Mr. Comstock's will, I've managed other legal aspects of his affairs. I would be honored to continue in that capacity for you, but understand should you wish to retain someone else."

By the Light, she hadn't thought that far ahead. She hadn't thought beyond walking into the firm's office. "Oh, um, yes. Considering what you know, it makes sense to continue on as you have."

He smiled. Kira was sure it was meant to be comforting, but it just felt oppressive. She was smothering beneath kindness. "I'm sure you've already booked a hotel, but Mr. Comstock's flat isn't far. I have a list of its contents that I can inventory with you if you like, but there are some objects that Mr. Comstock specifically requested that you view alone."

She straightened again. "Excuse me?"

"There are some artifacts in Mr. Comstock's flat that contain messages that can only be revealed using your particular talents," the solicitor explained. "I was specifically instructed to inform you of this."

She almost reached for the pocket watch. Thank goodness, she'd have something else of Bernie's to reach him through. She wasn't in danger of completely losing him all over again.

Braithwhyte continued. "No one from your organization has been allowed in the flat, as Mr. Comstock took great pains to insure that his home remained free of the trappings of his secondary occupation."

The lawyer pushed a plastic sleeve across the desk to her. She could see a key and a folded sheaf of papers through the clear material. "Mr. Comstock's key, and an inventory of his personal items. There are several nice restaurants near his flat with excellent takeaway. Take your time and get back to me when you're able. I've also included my contact information."

"Thank you, Mr. Braithwhyte." Kira pursed her lips, a minor fight to keep her emotions under control. She trembled, the urge to flee tightening her muscles. Facing down one of the Fallen would be preferable to dealing with this. "If you don't mind, I think I will take you up on that offer and come back later."

She stood, almost knocking the chair over. The solicitor rose. "Are you all right, Ms. Solomon? Perhaps I should call someone."

"No, I'll be all right. I just need to get some air, clear my head." She reached for the urn, its weight minuscule compared to the weight of guilt threatening to choke her. "I'll call you when I'm ready to return."

She fled the office, thankful for her coat, her gloves. She felt twelve again, huddled in a battered coat several sizes too large, garden gloves duct-taped to her wrists to protect herself and those around her. Feeling as if the world had ended and everything she'd known and cared for had been ripped from her. She'd defeated one of the Fallen, faced death, and spoken with the gods of Egypt. Yet dealing with a lawyer and the loss of her mentor was more than she could handle.

Finally, cool, damp air. She stopped on the sidewalk, head tilted back, gasping for air as the mist touched her face. The coolness did nothing to calm her; sudden anger surged through her instead. She lowered her head, clenching her fists to keep from screaming. She hated this, hated feeling weak and ineffectual. Hated feeling like she'd failed Comstock or, worse, that she'd killed him.

"Kira, are you all right?" Khefar loomed over her. Where had he come from?

"Were you waiting out here all this time?"

"It hasn't been that long." His hand settled on the middle of her back. The contact felt good, and she used it to anchor herself. "Nansee's just arrived, so we decided to wait with our things in the rental. What's wrong?"

"Nothing, I just—it was more intense than I expected." She straightened, clutching her messenger bag close to her body as Londoners streamed past them. "The lawyer gave me the keys to Bernie's flat. If I know him, he's got a room scrubbed for me. I think I'd rather go there than the hotel. It's not all that far."

"Of course." He'd pulled his braids back into a neat, thick ponytail. With the all-weather coat, worn jeans, and heavy black boots, he looked like he fit in here and now, instead of in Nubia four thousand years prior. "Is this something you wish to do on your own?"

She stared up at him, then looked past him to see Nansee sitting in the back of the hired car. The demigod beamed, then waved, and she automatically waved back, an involuntary smile rising up through her misery. Who could be sad when a god smiled at you?

These two had seen plenty of death over the course of Khefar's epic journey to save a life for every life he'd taken. The Nubian might not be forthcoming with knowledge, but he was generous with his support. Even the spider god helped in his own non-interfering, just-collecting-tales sort of way. She could move through her grief with their help.

"Actually, I'd like to run by the Petrie Museum before going to his flat. Maybe we could grab some food on the way back and I could share stories of Bernie with you and Nansee. I think that would be a good way to honor him."

He guided her to the car. "You know there's no way Nansee would pass up the opportunity to share stories. And if there's food involved, he'll probably even get there before us."

"You know I'm all-hearing as well as all-seeing," Nansee said as Khefar opened the door for Kira. "Take care who you insult, Medjay."

Khefar climbed in, then shut the door. "If you were really all-hearing, you'd know that's not the worst insult I've thrown at you."

Kira asked the driver to take them to the Petrie, then settled back, feeling better than she had since arriving in London. One breath at a time, one day at a time, and she would survive this.

She closed her eyes, conscious of the Nubian on one side of her and the demigod on the other, still good-naturedly needling each other. Looking at Khefar's profile, it was too easy to remember sparring with him, the ease with which he'd removed his shirt so they could grapple with each other. She could remember pinning him to the floor, seeing the sparks in his eyes as she'd slowly and thoroughly run her hands all over his chest and arms.

Skin hunger flared inside her, almost painful. She wanted to touch him again, to let her fingers trail up and down his skin. She wanted to press her body against his, to feel another human being without hurting him or psychically downloading his entire life history. Before him, it had been so long since she'd touched another person in tenderness. Before him, it had been her first handler, Nico, during a romantic weekend in Venice after they'd found a way to suppress her extrasense.

She'd been punished for that, punished for wanting to have a semblance of a normal life. Nico had died while she'd been literally powerless to prevent it. She'd buried him, and with him, her desire to ever know intimacy again. Until the Nubian.

There were plenty of reasons not to go there, though. Being intimate meant being vulnerable. More than that, she didn't know how long either of them had. Khefar had vowed to save a life for every life he'd taken as a Medjay bent on avenging his family's death. Sixty-four thousand, eight hundred and thirty-one lives. After four thousand years, he was almost done. He'd already saved her once. He had one more life to save before his total would be fulfilled and he'd be free to join his family in the afterlife. That had been his motivation for four millennia. She couldn't even begin to think that she stood a chance of keeping him at her side.

She balled her hands atop her knees. She didn't have forever anyway. The taint of Shadow still lived inside her. She could still feel it, curling inside her like the feel of seaweed brushing against her skin as it sometimes did when she went free-diving on Santa Costa. If his ancient oath didn't hold Khefar here, his vow to her would. One day he'd have to fulfill his promise to destroy her if Shadow overpowered her. He'd have to use the Dagger of Kheferatum to unmake her, until less than atoms remained. She didn't want him to hesitate, or to grieve over the act. Would he let his possible attachment to her override his promise, his ability to do what needed to be done?

Khefar wrapped his fingers around her gloved hand. She looked over at him, startled, but he continued talking to Nansee as if holding her hand was the most natural thing in the world. Maybe it was, for him.

Thinking he'd change his mind, she slowly uncurled her fingers. He gave her hand a squeeze, then threaded his fingers through hers. The contact, even through the synthetic material of her glove, warmed her. She relaxed by degrees, allowing herself to indulge in the promise of possibilities. Khefar would do what needed to be done. He would do what he could to save her, and if he couldn't save her, to stop her. She had to trust him. She had to take a chance. Because she didn't think she could take much more pressure without some sort of relief.

Minutes later, the car pulled onto Gower Street. Kira leaned forward. "Can you stop here, please?"

"Is anything wrong?" Khefar asked.

"No, I just think I'd like to walk for a while."

He nodded. "Nansee, do you want to take the car around for a bit, then come back to get us?"

"Sounds like an excellent idea," the demigod said. "It's been several years since I've been in London."

"Good, we'll give you a shout when we're ready to go." He turned back to Kira. "Are you left-handed or right-handed?"

"Either, if I have to," she answered.

"I know, but which do you prefer?"

"I'd rather draw my Lightblade with my right hand, if I had my druthers."

"Good." He left the car, then reached in to help her out. Once she gained the curb, he stepped to her left side, wrapping his right hand around her left. "I taught myself to be ambidextrous," he told her, "but I prefer to draw my dagger left-handed. Works well for us, it seems. Take your gloves off."

She stared at him, surprised he'd even suggest it. "Are you kidding? Millions of people come through here. The college has been around for two hundred years. I can't walk down this street without gloves on!"

"Okay then, just the one."

Keeping her gaze on him, she carefully stripped the glove from her left hand. It freaked her out to be standing barehanded on a busy sidewalk on a chilly, misty November afternoon, all sorts of people milling around them.

He wrapped his fingers around hers, then drew her close. "See? That's not so bad, now is it? We can pretend to just be two normal people, walking down the street hand in hand."

"That was your plan? Shock me with the

over-the-top request to take off both my gloves so I'd compromise on removing just the one?"

He smiled at her. "Worked, didn't it?"

"I guess it did." She fell into step beside him, trying to shake the weirdness of walking hand in hand. It had been six long years since she'd done something like this, something most people took for granted. Nico had been her handler, but more than that, her first and only lover. He'd died because of her, because she'd wanted a weekend of being Normal, of being intimate.

But Khefar can't die, a voice whispered inside her head. *If he does, he'll always come back. Don't you want to know what it's like to touch him, to really touch him?*

She did want to know, badly. The need for that sort of contact, a physical connection to another human being, ate away at her like a cancer.

Khefar squeezed her fingers. "Tell me about the Petrie Museum. You said Bernie worked there?"

"He was a professor. The Petrie is part of the Institute of Archaeology at University College, London. I came here shortly after losing Nico to get my BA in Egyptian Archaeology. I literally bumped into Bernie in front of a textile exhibit in the Petrie. Even after I graduated and he retired from university, he continued to be a mentor. Of course, I had no idea that shortly after meeting me he'd been tapped to be my new handler."

"That's pretty quick, isn't it?" Khefar asked. "For Comstock to become a handler so soon?"

She nodded, guiding him along Gower Place to Gordon Street. "Handlers have their own specialized training. Nothing as rigorous as what Shadowchasers go through, but it can be pretty intense. They have to be everything from tacticians and researchers to psychologists and medics. I guess Bernie's experiences and interests went a long way toward allowing him to bypass a lot of the usual training a handler gets."

"I can see that. From what I learned of him when tracking my dagger, he seemed to be a true Renaissance man."

"He was. He loved the past, loved antiques, but loved learning new things too. Technology of all types fascinated him, whether it was the latest smartphone or an ancient Mayan calculator. His enthusiasm was inspiring, even as I questioned my sanity for wanting to be an archaeologist."

"Why would you question it? You obviously have a personal reason for studying ancient Egypt."

"My touch ability, remember?" She squeezed his fingers for emphasis, but also because she could. "The first thing I had to do as a freshman was learn how to do stuff like making pottery, working with wood, and collecting and processing wild foods. I knew how to do the wild food part because I couldn't eat processed food after I hit puberty, but the rest of it?" She shook her head. "It was only four days, but we called it Hell Week. It really was like that for me, between trying to do copper smelting and flint-knapping without passing out, to explaining to my classmates that no, I didn't have leprosy or phobias that would impede my archaeological fieldwork."

"How did you explain everything to your class-mates? I can't imagine they left you alone about it."

"No, they didn't. I had explained the gloves, keeping most of my body covered, and my inability to shake hands or touch my fellow students by saying I had a rare neuropathy that made contact painful. Comstock had been one of the advisors on the trip and I confessed to him that I sometimes got impressions from things I touched and it was just easier to keep gloves on. He accepted it right out of the gate, said he even knew a psychic or two. Somehow he worked things out for me, and I didn't have issues after Hell Week ended."

"He looked out for you from the beginning."

"Yeah, he did. That's just the way he was." *And still is,* she thought to herself.

She fell silent, and luckily, he left her to it. Memories crowded her mind, memories of her time in London. Even having a reputation among her classmates of being "a bit off" had been tolerable, simply because walking through the Petrie's collection, going to class, cracking open books, staying up late studying, and subsisting on ethnic takeaway with an occasional Chase in between had gone a long way toward easing her grief over losing Nico.

Now she was back in London, back at university, back to grieving a loss. Once again, going into the Petrie to gaze at artifacts of lives gone by would act as a panacea for her soul.

She stopped outside the museum's entrance. So much had changed since she'd been through last, but it was good change. Progress stopped for nothing and no one. She looked up at him. "Come on. I'll give you the nickel tour of the collection, and we can compare notes. Whoever is more historically accurate has to buy dinner."

"You're on."

The tour of the Petrie Museum went better than Khefar had expected. Even though the museum had moved to a new location, Kira had a wealth of memories and anecdotes to share, about both Comstock and the collection. It was obvious she'd have been at home following in her mentor's footsteps either in field study or teaching. And that Khefar would be buying dinner.

On the ride to Comstock's flat, however, she once again fell silent and brooding, and he knew she dreaded the idea of being among her mentor's personal possessions. He couldn't blame her. Comstock's death was a deep wound that would take time to heal.

Khefar stood behind Kira as she stiffened her back, straightened her shoulders, then unlocked Comstock's flat. She pushed the door wide. "Welcome to Bernie's."

"What a charming place," Nansee exclaimed, his voice overly bright and cheerful. "Very retro."

Khefar had to agree, adding his coat to Kira's on the rack by the door. Comstock's flat was much like the man himself: nicely turned out and harkening back to another time. The main room seemed right out of a Victorian parlor, dark woods and heavy fabrics framing the windows, settees, and chairs. A gracefully carved three-section bookcase overstuffed with leather-bound books took up the largest wall next to a burgundy wingback chair and a brass reading lamp. The handler's adoration of Egypt was evident in the profusion of replicas and original artwork from various periods that overflowed every available surface, both horizontal and vertical.

Kira stopped in the center of the room, her bags in her gloved hands. She'd been unusually quiet on the ride over from the museum. Knowing how much she craved human contact, he'd wanted to pull her against him, to offer her some measure of comfort. He worried about her, worried about the streak of Shadow he'd seen in her eyes. He knew enough to know that finding Balance would help her, setting joy against despair, love against hate. So many things had happened to her in the short time that he'd known her. She'd powered through simply because she'd had a job to do. Yet she didn't have a Chase now, and he wondered how much more tightly she could be wound before she'd snap.

"Bernie had a serious love for Egypt, as you can see," she said, gesturing about the room.

"Not only Egypt," Khefar said, pointing to a collection of silver and pewter frames on a mahogany writing desk. One of the gilded frames held a picture of a much younger Comstock with his arms around a stunning African woman in traditional Cameroon-style dress.

"That's Bernie's wife," Kira said quietly. "They had roughly five years together, more than thirty years ago. He never remarried after he lost her, so he considered himself a bachelor professor."

Khefar looked at the profusion of photos on the table. Most of the pictures were of Kira by herself, or Kira with Comstock. A large gilt frame displayed a photo of them both on what could only be the Giza plateau. "Looks like he considered you the daughter he never had."

She gave a jerky nod. "He told me that more than once. Other than the fieldwork I had to do as part of my course study, we were able to go to Cairo one March. I'd wanted to be able to do a full year there, but Balm had already given me three years without a dedicated area to monitor, and she needed me to take over Atlanta full time. By that time Bernie already knew about my touch ability but looking back, I know now he had already been assigned as my handler and debriefed by Balm."

"He never said anything to you or gave you any indication that he knew about your Shadowchasing duties or being picked to be your new handler?"

She shook her head. "No. I'd told Bernie I had some type of ESP, but he found out about the full range of my extrasense when we were observing a new piece the Petrie had found in its collection, a Middle Kingdom amulet that was rumored to be cursed. It was—it had a Shadow trap attached to it that ate away at a person's vitality. I had to touch it to defuse it. Bernie saw me, touched me, then got thrown across the room for his trouble. Luckily my extrasense was concentrated on the amulet, so he only came away with singed eyebrows and injured pride."

"He knew about the curse and wanted to protect you from it. It's why the piece hadn't been displayed before," Nansee said, his hands behind his back as he examined Comstock's eclectic collection. Khefar could see the concern in the demigod's eyes, which was enough to worry him. Neither of them wanted a repeat of Atlanta, but the only sure way to prevent an incident would be to use his dagger against Kira.

He wasn't about to let that happen. Unmaking her would be a last resort, not a first line of defense. He'd vowed to save her, after all. As long as there were still threats against her, that vow held.

"Bernie was always looking out for me," Kira said quietly. "He was so good-natured and warm about it that it didn't feel intrusive, like it sometimes does with Balm. It's why I considered him more of a father figure than a mentor or my professor. I learned how to survive thanks to Balm, but learning how to live? That was Bernie's doing."

She passed a gloved hand above the collection on the table. "I crashed here a couple of times after I was assigned to Atlanta," Kira said quietly. "Mostly because Bernie already knew about my touch ability, but also because I wanted to make sure he was managing okay."

"You missed him."

"Of course I missed him. He was the closest thing I had to a dad after I was sent to Santa Costa. He didn't think I was a freak because I couldn't touch anyone. He didn't throw me away when he found out."

She pressed her lips together. "We made the one trip to Cairo, but never had the opportunity to take part in a dig together. That was one of those 'one day' dreams. You know, 'One day we'll make the greatest discovery since Tutankhamun's tomb,' that sort of thing. I suppose that won't happen now."

"It is cold comfort, but I think you'd honor his memory by still making the trip while holding him in your heart."

"True enough. I think spreading his ashes in Giza or Luxor would be a nice thing to do before heading back home to Shadowchasing. If I'm still supposed to Chase, that is."

"Oh, I think there are plenty of stories still out there for you, Kira Solomon," Nansee said. "Why don't you get settled and I'll go order from that Indian restaurant we passed on the corner. If the Nubian's buying, I want to make sure we get a wide variety of dishes."

"Everything's about food with you, isn't it, old man?" Khefar asked, shaking his head.

"Who doesn't like to eat?" Nansee patted his stomach. "Nothing is better with a good story than good food and good drink. Except perhaps, a good woman."

"Don't even think about it," Khefar and Kira said in unison.

The old man beamed as he stood. "The expressions on your faces delight me. All right, then, I suppose I'll content myself with a good woman telling a good story. Be back shortly."

"I'm going to set up my room," Kira announced after the demigod left, carrying her bags to a closed door just off the living room.

"If you're planning to stay here, then I'm staying with you."

She stopped for a moment, then nodded. "You and Nansee can fight over who gets Bernie's bedroom."

Khefar didn't think the demigod would stay over, but he kept that to himself. "We'll work something out. Do you need some help?"

She smiled. "I think I can manage to make a bed up all by my lonesome. Besides, I brought a traveling altar with me. I'm going to set that up too."

He let her go, wondering if she intended to perform the Weighing of the Heart ceremony again, or in her case, weighing her soul. She'd told him that the last time she'd done it, her soul had been heavier than Ma'at's feather. Ma'at had stayed final judgment then, and when they'd both died and gone before the gods in the Hall of Judgment, neither of them had been weighed then. Instead, they'd been claimed by their respective goddesses and sent back into the world.

That had to be a good thing. Ma'at wouldn't have claimed Kira and sent her back if Kira was in imminent danger of losing herself to Shadow. At least, he had to hope not.

Chapter 7

Anansi had procured a veritable smorgasbord of dishes, firing up Kira's appetite. "This looks amazing, Nansee. Thanks for getting it."

"Of course, dear girl, of course. But you know I want stories in payment. For instance, you and Mr. Comstock taking a camel ride."

Kira grimaced as she ripped into a piece of buttered naan. "Ah, yeah. My first and only camel ride. What I got from that experience, other than a bruised bum, is that camels are evil."

She recounted the attempted camel ride across the Giza Plateau with Comstock and some fellow students and soon had them laughing uproariously. She followed the tale with her attempts at keeping a fire sprite from destroying Comstock's antiques shop while he helped a customer out front. It felt good to share with the Nubian and the demigod, to not hold back as she'd habitually done with others, even Wynne and Zoo. It was like having a wake, a way to honor the man who'd meant so much to her, and a much better way to pass an afternoon than sitting in a demon lawyer's office going over a will.

"Well, children." Nansee climbed to his feet. "There's a perfectly good hotel reservation still on the books. I see no reason to let it go to waste. As quaint as this flat is, it's not meant for three people."

Kira stood as Khefar gathered their takeaway containers and carried them to the kitchenette. "Thank you, Nansee. I appreciate what you did for me."

"For you? No, I just wanted good stories and good food," he told her, then spoiled the statement with a wink. "But I'm glad you were able to remember the good times you had with one who clearly means a lot to you. It's a sure way to have your loved ones live on in your heart."

She nodded, feeling much better than she had when the day began. "Well, then enjoy the hotel, storyteller. Don't run up the room service, or I'm gonna have to hurt you."

Nansee sighed dramatically. "It's so hard for a demigod to get respect these days. Khefar, a word?"

Kira concentrated on clearing away the remains of their meal as Khefar stepped into the hallway with the demigod. The Nubian had been nothing but considerate since she'd all but crashed into him outside the solicitor's office. His spending time with her as she walked through the Petrie had helped to make the visit bearable, even happy, instead of bittersweet. She was more than willing to forgive and forget their disagreement in Atlanta. Sometimes it just took too much energy to stay angry.

Tomorrow she'd finish with the lawyer, maybe revisit some of her old haunts, and try to decide what to do with Bernie's things beyond the few items he specifically wanted her to have. Things he'd put his essence into. Keeping the flat was a no-brainer. So was keeping all his notes, books, and artifacts. Eventually she'd have to decide between leaving all that in the flat or transporting it back to Atlanta. But for now, she'd fly to Cairo so she could take care of Bernie's ashes as he wished, then she'd get back to Atlanta and her job. Everything would be fine once she started Chasing again.

Khefar returned. "What are you thinking?"

"About all the things I still have to do," she answered. "I've got to go back to the solicitor's office tomorrow and finish up some paperwork. Plus, Braithwhyte told me there are a few things that Bernie especially mentioned for me to keep, but I don't know what, exactly, they are. I'll need to figure out what to take back to Atlanta with me and what to leave here. And then there's the rest of this stuff . . ."

He glanced about the room. "Surely everything's important to you? This is Comstock's home. Memories of him—good memories of him—are in everything he owns. Would you really part with his belongings?"

"No, I wouldn't. I couldn't. Not yet." She shoved her hands through her braids and changed the subject. "I want to take a shower."

Khefar nodded and turned his attention to an overflowing bookshelf.

She hid in the shower for a while, then changed into a navy warm-up suit emblazoned with the University College London logo across the chest. She found Khefar comfortably ensconced in Bernie's "reading chair," evidently enthralled by some tome he'd discovered. The book appeared to be written in Greek. It occurred to Kira that the warrior had probably read Greek since before English was a language.

Leaning against the doorframe, she asked, "Good read?"

"Homer always is." He closed the book and looked up. "This is a 1711 edition of the *Iliad*," he said with an appreciative smile. "There's a matching copy of the *Odyssey*. Probably just reading copies for Bernie. Anyone else would keep them behind glass."

"True. And this place"—Kira gestured—"is full of treasures. But what I'm most interested in is . . . Braithwhyte said that Bernie left direct messages for me in a few specific objects."

"You can do that? Leave messages in objects, I mean."

"Bernie can. Or could. He left messages in his personal effects that led me to the Fallen in Atlanta. How he did it, I don't know. Just another thing about my mentor that I was—and am still—clueless about."

She moved deeper into the room, emotional weariness making her sluggish. "I'll have to take those things home with me, or ship them over. I also need to check out Bernie's security system and magically augment it to make it truly secure. And I have to inventory everything—his extensive collection of mementoes and artifacts, the books, the furniture . . ."

"You don't have to do any of those things right this moment." He stepped closer to her. "Are you all right?"

No, she wasn't. Her nerves felt stretched tight, like harp strings ready to be plucked. Only she didn't think she could manage any heavenly melodies. "What's it gonna take to get people to stop asking me that?"

"People believing that you're okay."

"All right." She spread her arms. "I'm fine. What

did Nansee want to talk to you about that I wasn't allowed to hear?"

"He's worried about you too." His hands clamped down on her shoulders. "And you're not fine. You haven't been fine since Comstock died."

"You didn't know me before Comstock died." Something that felt like a smile pulled at her lips. "Maybe this is my version of fine."

"You know I don't believe that." His grip eased, but he didn't move his hands. "What can I do to help?"

She stared up at him, wondering if he really meant it, wondering if she dared let herself be vulnerable with him. He'd saved her life, brought her back from the dead. He was the only person on earth whom she'd been able to touch without harming. If she couldn't be vulnerable with him, there was no hope.

"I'd like to take advantage of you."

"Really?" Midnight eyes gazed down at her. "And how do you think you could take advantage of me?"

"By touching you, getting you to touch me back." She slowly brought her hands up to settle on his waist. If he wanted to move away from her, this would be the moment. He didn't.

"The only way that you would be taking advantage of me is if I weren't willing," his said, his voice a low rumble. "I'm very willing."

"For what? For how much?"

"As much as you want." His hands slid down her shoulders, down her arms, to her hands. His fingers tugged at her gloves, slowly pulling them off and freeing her hands. Then he linked their hands, fingers threaded together. "As much as you need."

She shivered at the contact, so ordinary for most people, so intimate and extraordinary to her. The simple touch resonated through her. She brought their joined hands up, pressed her lips against them. "I need to feel you, Khefar. Feel something other than this sharp, brittle chill in the pit of my stomach."

Rising to her toes, she kissed him. She felt him stop breathing, holding himself still, waiting for her to move. "I need your help," she whispered against his mouth. "Please kiss me."

He did, cupping her face between his palms, his lips moving over hers. Oh yes, this was what she'd needed, this decadent distraction. Her fingers twisted in his T-shirt, tugging it up so that she could run her hands over his abs.

He sucked in a breath, then really kissed her, a deep slide of mouth-to-mouth that made her toes curl. She wanted, needed, to feel more. She lifted her hands away from his skin long enough to tug at his shirt. "Take it off."

He stepped back, his heavy gaze never leaving hers. Slowly he gripped the hem of his shirt and just as slowly pulled it up, over, off. Her mouth went dry as she watched perfect, honed muscles flex beneath his dark chocolate skin. Something ignited inside her, something beyond simple skin hunger. The sweet sensation thrummed through her with a slow steady burn, and she realized it for what it was: desire.

She reached out a hand to touch him, slowly, conscious of the blue glow suffusing her fingers. She hesitated. Her hands were tools, weapons used to protect and attack. Never just hands, never touching for the simple pleasure of touching.

When she hesitated too long, he stepped closer, causing her fingers to brush against the deep, dark suppleness of his skin. Muscles flexed beneath his shoulders as she lightly ran her hands over them and down his chest. The tingle in her fingertips shot up her arms and spread through her chest, making her heart pound. He was amazing. This was amazing.

A four-thousand-year-old Nubian warrior with the chiseled physique of someone not quite thirty. Living, breathing, beautiful, able to touch and be touched. His body fascinated her, had since the day they'd met, and she gave herself over to the joy of discovering it.

Her fingers skirted around the edge of the fetish necklace he wore. It hung just past his collarbone and the base of the Isis knot tattoo, a dark leather cord strung with glass beads, some cowrie shells, and a leather pouch. That pouch, she guessed, was what he reached for in his pocket back in Atlanta. It contained mementoes of his family, things that helped him remember his long-dead wife and three children.

She pressed her palm flat against his chest, just above his heart, then looked up. His expression was as serious as usual but his eyes were equal parts wary, watchful, wanting.

"It's okay," she whispered, dropping her gaze to the sight of her hand stroking over his heart. "It's okay if we don't go further than this. Right now this is more than enough, so thank you for letting me have it."

"You're most welcome, Kira," he said, his voice a raspy rumble. His index finger slid along her cheek, then tilted her chin up until their eyes met. "But this isn't all that you want, is it?"

"No." She could barely get the word out through her dry mouth. It wasn't all she wanted. Not after six years, six long years of not touching another human being. Not after losing Bernie. Not after finally, finally finding someone she could touch without hurting.

Keeping his gaze on hers, Khefar reached up, his hands sliding behind his neck. The leather cord loosened. She stepped back, breaking contact with him. He caught the pouch in one fist, the cord ends dangling over his knuckles as he held it close to his chest. "Does this bother you?"

"Of course not," Kira replied. "That's your connection to your family, and you should keep it close. I keep Comstock's pocket watch with me now. Does that bother you?"

"No." He pushed the treasured memento into his jeans pocket. "Come here."

They came together again. Her mouth grazed Khefar's shoulder as he pulled her close, caging her in his arms. The warmth was incredible, the feel of his heartbeat against hers beyond wonderful. "I've wanted to feel your hands on me for the longest time."

"I've touched you before." His eyes clouded. "When I carried you out of that cemetery. When I pulled that blade out of your shoulder. When I tried to hold the wound closed to keep you from bleeding out."

Kira stroked his cheek. "Obviously we need some new memories of you touching me."

Stepping back from him, she pulled her thin sweater up over her head. For a moment she almost wished she had a thing for sexy lingerie, but other than the weekend with Nico, she'd never had a need or desire for anything other than serviceable front-hook bras. Judging from Khefar's expression, she didn't need to.

She reached out, wrapping her fingers around his. Slowly she brought his hands up, pressed his palms against the slope of her chest, leaned into him. "How about this?"

"This . . . is good," Khefar said gruffly, the rough pads of his fingers stroking over her skin, the fabric of her bra. "You're glowing."

Kira raised her head. Sure enough, a pale blue glow suffused her arms, her cleavage pressed against his chest. "Oh. I guess I'm excited."

His fingers traced the straps of her bra. "Makes me wonder what'll happen when you're really excited."

"Are you willing to find out?" She certainly hoped so.

"Gods, yes." His nimble fingers quickly unhooked her bra. "You'll let me know if this gets too intense for you?"

"Compared to what?"

"Right. You only do intense."

Her bra slid down her arms and hit the floor. Kira kept her eyes on his, anticipation coiling in her gut, hungry, so hungry for his touch. She felt the slightest touch, the backs of his hands lightly grazing her skin. Then Khefar turned his hands to cup her breasts. She had to close her eyes against the sensory overload. Her breasts ached, felt full, heavy, and ultra sensitive as her nipples brushed against the scattering of hair covering his chest. Her whole body felt prickly, with a wealth of sensations zipping along her synapses.

It amazed her that she could be like this with him,

half-naked with him, and still want more, so much more. As if he knew it, he pulled her close again, letting her feel the weight and bulk of his body against hers, feel his hands in her hair, his breath and his heartbeat, close, so close.

She pressed her lips against his jaw. "Come with me to my room."

They made their way to the spare bedroom, then quickly removed the rest of their clothes, placing their daggers on separate nightstands. She'd already put her bedding on the full-size bed, so she was able to pull him down beside her with no fear. Whether they would fit the bed without breaking it, that was a different story. Then his hands were on her again, and she forgot everything else.

Gods bless him, but he'd obviously learned a thing or two about pleasing a woman in four thousand years of living. He knew that every touch, every caress, every stroke along her bare skin was precious to her, just this side of overwhelming. She mirrored every touch, every stroke, with hand and body and lips, giving back to him everything that he gave her.

When the intensity had built to a do-or-die pitch, she pulled away from him. "Condoms. I didn't think about condoms. I know we can touch like this all we want, but I don't know what will happen with you inside me or if the, um, the issue of a four-thousand-year-old guy will trigger any sort of vision."

He rolled over, reaching for his pants. "That's what I call a definite buzzkill."

Heat burned her ears. "Well if you don't want to keep going, I can just go clean my blade."

Khefar grabbed her wrist before she could slide off the bed. "Where are you going?"

"I just said I'm going to clean my blade. Has your hearing gone the way of your erection?"

"My hearing and my erection are both just fine." He rolled back over so she could see for herself. "I just had to grab a couple of these out of my wallet."

Kira stared at the foil packets in his hand, relieved and nonplussed. "When did you have time to get those?"

"Back in Atlanta when I got the rest of my travel stuff. And before you say anything about it, no, I didn't assume you were going to sleep with me. It just made sense to be prepared, especially if we ever had another sparring match that ended like the last one."

The last one had ended with her sitting astride him, hungrily running her hands all over his bare chest. This would go much further than any sparring match. Her mouth watered. "I don't want to spar. And I don't want to argue anymore, either."

"Neither do I."

"Put it on. Now."

Like a good soldier, he knew when to follow orders.

If round one was good, round two was spectacular. Kira would never again claim that he didn't possess magic. What else could she call his talent for causing these electric sensations that zipped along her skin? Her hips lifted off the bed, incoherent words tearing from her as electric sensations zapped every nerve ending. The heat built, power built, stoked by velvet caresses. She wanted to hold on to the moment, the sweet sharp edge of pleasure, but it was just too much, he was

just too good. Pleasure blazed through her again, causing her to cry out in brilliant blue-white release.

"Kira."

"Hmm?"

"Just so you know, you can take advantage of me
any time you want to."

"What about right now?"

He laughed, reached for her. "Works for me."

Chapter 8

Warmth. The blissful warmth of being wrapped in someone's arms. A miracle Kira hadn't felt in six years, and had doubted she'd ever experience again.

She stared down at the arm draped over her waist. Dark and sinewy, capable of strength and tenderness. When was the last time Khefar had been with someone? Four thousand years was a long time to be without human comfort. Her six years of celibacy after Nico died had been hard, since she'd known exactly what she was missing.

Somehow she didn't think that the Nubian had gone without, not when she considered the very thorough attention he'd paid to her body. She couldn't get upset with him about that. She didn't think even his late wife would blame him.

One couldn't learn the perfect moment to move, to touch, to stroke, except from experience. So he must have had other relationships over the course of his incredibly long life. Had they been real relationships though? Had Khefar fallen in love again, married again, raised a family again? Perhaps more than once? Had he made attempts at being a normal man with a normal life, only to watch his loved ones grow old and die? Which was worse: to love and lose everything once, or to love and lose over and over for thousands of years?

Kira couldn't imagine it. Comfort, yes. That was as basic a need as food and shelter. But creating meaningful relationships, developing deep bonds, then having to leave before your lovers left you for death? She couldn't do it.

She didn't have to worry about that with Khefar, of course. They were both near the end of their time. Maybe that was what made going to bed with him easy. She knew some of his history and, for the most part, understood it. He knew hers.

Maybe he saw this as she did: there was attraction, yes, but more than that, each was uniquely qualified to provide comfort to the other.

Kira shook her head. It was a little too neat, too improbable, to be a coincidence. An immortal warrior and a superhuman Shadowchaser, blade-wielding champions of Light. Both in service to Egyptian goddesses. He the only one she could touch without harming. She—well, she wasn't sure what she offered him other than a challenge liberally laced with comfort, but perhaps that was enough.

Still the circumstances of their association would defy any oddsmakers. It was enough to make her wonder if the Powers of Light had a hand in it. She didn't want to believe it, but as Sherlock Holmes had fictionally said, "Once you eliminate the impossible, whatever remains, no matter how improbable, must be the truth."

If the gods had a hand in their meeting, the question was, why? Why bring them together? Why now? What was gathering on the horizon that necessitated the gods' involvement in mortal lives?

She'd ask Nansee about it, but she doubted he'd tell her. The normally loquacious demigod could be just as reticent as Khefar when he wanted to be. Obviously they were rubbing off on each other.

She snuggled back down under the covers, his masculine scent filling her nose. Later. She'd worry about the metaphysical whys and wherefores later. For now, nothing was more important than savoring the heat of another person's skin against hers.

Kira? I need to speak with you, Daughter.

Crap. So she hadn't been completely awake during all that heavy thinking, and now Balm wanted to talk. Had her time with Khefar been nothing more than a dream? No. She doubted she could dream of this kind of blissful lassitude. The interlude with Khefar had made enough of an impression on her that she'd reconstructed it in this in-between dream state. She wanted to hold on to it in case she didn't get the chance to experience it in real life again.

So instead of banishing the scene, she conjured up a sweeping Bedouin tent, then wrapped herself in a soft white cotton kurta and drawstring pants. Steeling herself, she lifted the tent flap and stepped out into the wadi she'd conjured, complete with watering hole and a pair of dromedaries. Mediterranean blue sky curved above golden white sands, with bright green bushes adding a splash of color. Here the temperature could be anything she wanted, so she made it comfortably warm.

Balm materialized out of the dream ether, wrapped in flowing earth tone robes and a pale beige head scarf as if she had been a Bedouin woman before becoming the head of Gilead. As always, Balm looked the same as she had fourteen years ago when Kira had first met her.

The older woman's gaze swept over the scene, settling on the tent. She frowned as if she knew what lay inside.

"Obviously I'm intruding."

Kira pulled the linen shift onto her shoulders. "Would you deny me this moment, Mother?"

"There are few things I would deny you, Daughter, without good reason," Balm answered, her expression stern. "I asked you once before if you trusted this Medjay. I would think that would be the least you should question before you give yourself to someone."

"He's the only person on the planet whom I can touch without killing," Kira retorted. "Most things are pointless after that. Still if you must know, I trust him as much as I trust anyone."

Balm nodded, though she hardly looked mollified. "It's not as if I can undo what's been done. I would just urge you to be careful, Kira."

"Balm. Mother. He's not Nico, and this isn't Venice. I'm not nineteen. My eyes are wide open, believe me."

That seemed to placate Balm. "Very well, Daughter. I suppose I should get to the reason for this dream-walk."

"What's happened?"

Two brightly striped beach chairs pushed up from the golden sand, a large umbrella to shield the sun sprouting up between them. Balm took one of the chairs. "It was apparently a good time for me to pay the London branch a visit. The office is in near-complete disarray. The section chief has resigned."

"Are you kidding? What's going on that the section chief quit?"

Balm made a sweeping motion with her hand. The air before her solidified into a screen, showing two men. One was blond, and looked as if he'd just graduated college. The second had reddish brown hair, and appeared to be about Kira's age. "Who are they?"

"The blonde is Pavel Gunderson, the Chaser responsible for most of Western Europe. The redhead is Adam Marshall, his handler. They've gone missing."

"Missing?" Kira frowned. "Chasers and handlers don't go missing. They get killed, but they don't disappear."

"I know. The section chief appears to be inept or unconcerned, neither of which is acceptable. I'll be taking him back to Santa Costa for debriefing. I know that you're on a leave of absence, but I need you to look into this. At the moment, you are peculiarly qualified for this Chase."

Kira's heart thumped heavily. "You're sanctioning a Chase? Not a retrieval?"

"Which it is to be will depend on what you uncover," Balm answered. "I'm also receiving word that a powerful artifact was stolen from a private collector a day or so ago. Something that wasn't documented, if you know what I mean. The collector doesn't want to go to the police for obvious reasons, but from the description he gave, it appears that Gunderson was the thief."

"Did someone in the London office botch a recovery?" Chasers often had to walk a fine line to ensure that Shadow objects didn't fall into the wrong hands, but the Commission's response teams always cleaned up any loose ends. In a case like this, they would have replaced the artifact or taken it and erased memories of the object from the owners' minds. For the collector to not only know his treasure had been stolen but also remember the Chaser who had stolen it from him was beyond messy. What in the world was going on?

"It wasn't a recovery, Kira. Gunderson never had orders to retrieve the artifact. Even if he'd come across it in the course of carrying out his Shadowchaser duties, neither he nor his handler reported the recovery to the section chief."

A blood vessel throbbed at Balm's left temple, a show of emotion Kira had rarely seen. The head of Gilead was deeply, royally furious. "Given the . . . disarray of the London office, I don't want anyone there to be involved in this case. Unofficially, I need you to do whatever it takes to discover where they've gone, what they're doing, and who's helping them accomplish it. They have dropped off my radar. No one in my organization is hidden from me, ever. For me not to sense them is . . . unacceptable."

It was more than unacceptable. It was unheard-of. Even though Balm had told Kira she could no longer see her path, the head of Gilead could still contact her. For Balm to be unable to reach any Chaser, anytime, went beyond unthinkable.

Kira's breath caught. "You think they've slid, don't you?"

Dark brows lowered. "Shadow is always after those who serve the Light, seeking to corrupt, and if not corrupt, then destroy. Chasers have been a prime target of the Fallen for centuries. You yourself know what it's like to be targeted. If one is able to turn one's enemy to one's side, one's power and standing instantly increase. I and the others on the Commission do what we can to prevent that, to ensure that Chasers are loyal to none but the Light."

Kira knew what Balm had done to ensure that she would be a faithful Chaser. She was able to eat, to function, to be reasonably sane, thanks to Balm. Kira owed the woman for giving her a life of stability instead of one of madness.

"Do you want me to come into the office?" Kira asked. "I mean, I'm here and all. I can interview some of Gunderson's colleagues, look into his handler's files, and generally make a nuisance of myself."

Balm managed a smile. "And enjoy yourself immensely while doing it, no doubt. Although it might do you and Gilead London a world of good to become acquainted during official business."

Kira had been in the London office fewer times than she could count on the fingers of one hand. On those occasions she'd found the beings working there brought a whole new meaning to the phrase "British reserve." If she ever decided to do so, Kira was sure Balm could stir the place up all by herself. But if Balm wanted some assistance agitating, Kira would be glad to lend a hand. "What about the Chaser and his handler? What do you want me to do when I find them, wherever they may be?"

"I would like them brought to Santa Costa to stand before the Commission and answer to the Light for what they've done. To undergo refinement if possible."

Refinement. In her years growing up on Santa

Costa, Kira knew of only one Chaser who had been brought back to the island for refinement. The process was reportedly as punishing as the process to become a Chaser in the first place, a deconstruction of the self and reconstruction as a being wholly dedicated to working for Gilead in spreading Light and taking on Shadow. That particular Chaser had never gone on a solo mission again. Her handler hadn't survived the procedure.

"Okay, bring Gunderson and Marshall in for refinement if at all possible. What if I determine that they've slid?"

Balm looked at her. "Justice and order must prevail, Hand of Ma'at. If they have turned from the Light, then they have chosen Shadow's embrace. There exists a path of forgiveness for humanity and even for some halflings to live in Balance, but Chasers have always walked a different way. You know this."

Yes, Kira knew. It was part of the reason why she didn't feel comfortable being truly forthcoming with Balm. Being elevated by Ma'at had moved Kira slightly out of Balm's sphere of influence and control. That didn't mean that Gilead wouldn't send a team after her if they felt Kira posed a threat to them.

"I'll need access to Gunderson's home base," she said then. "Marshall's too."

"Of course," Balm said. "They share a flat in Shoreditch, in Hackney."

"Okay. A satellite phone would be nice. Bernie has a laptop in his flat, so I can use that. I don't want to have to go through Gilead London for gear if I can help it."

"I understand." Balm's expression was stony. "If

they can neglect to apprise me of the problems with Gunderson and Marshall, they will be even less forthcoming with you. Still, I trust in your particular ability to find clues where none seem to be, and to use whatever methods you deem necessary."

"Are you serious?" Balm's giving Kira free rein was unprecedented. Of course, Kira did what she felt she needed to do anyway—much better to do first and seek forgiveness later. For Balm to actually give blanket permission boggled Kira's mind.

"I'm very serious, Daughter. It is obvious to me that a lesson needs to be learned."

"You're an excellent teacher."

"And you a most exceptional student. I'd like you to come to Gilead London in full Chaser gear first thing in the morning."

Kira folded her arms across her chest. "Like a lamb being led to slaughter or a lion entering the Coliseum?"

Balm leveled a glance at her. "As if you've ever been defenseless as a lamb." She chuckled softly. "For the mission overall, by the way, you will have backup. I have already sent for your friends from Atlanta."

Kira stiffened. "You mean Wynne and Zoo? They're humans."

"They're the best reinforcements a Chaser can have—even one as stubborn and hardheaded as you. They also still want to help you despite your attempts to push them away. At their request, I made them official members of Gilead East before we left."

"You made them *what*?" Kira shot to her feet. "How could you do that to them? How could you do that without telling me?"

"Did you not hear the 'at their request' part, or are you just ignoring it?"

"You just had to meddle, didn't you? Why couldn't you just leave well enough alone?"

Balm gave her another stare. "Because sometimes, dear daughter, it's not about you. Sometimes your pain is actually someone else's pain. More than that, those two people love you and you love them. My goal has always been to keep you anchored in your humanity. Your friends will help with that." She looked down. "And perhaps, since I took something away from you, I felt the need to give you something back."

Kira's throat tightened. Balm looked vulnerable. It wasn't a look either of them was comfortable with. Balm had always been powerful, a larger-than-life figure who guided the lives of hundreds, if not thousands, of people the world over. What in the world was happening that could put such an expression on Balm's face? Chasers dropping off the grid was bad. What more was happening in the Gilead Commission that Balm wasn't telling her?

"Balm, is everything okay back home?"

The head of Gilead drew herself ramrod straight. "Of course it is. Santa Costa is as it has always been."

"You'd tell me if it wasn't, right?" Kira persisted. "You'd trust me that far, wouldn't you?"

Balm's expression softened. "Are you not my daughter, though not my flesh and blood? Did I not raise you in a version of my own image?"

Kira sighed. That was as close to an answer as she was likely to get out of Balm, and it would have to do. "So Zoo and Wynne are on their way here for backup.

Does this mean that you would prefer me not to have Khefar and Nansee helping with this?"

"Well, I don't know if you can call what Kweku Ananse does 'helping,' but I am fine with the Nubian helping you. Bring him with you, if he is so inclined. He's also more than qualified for this particular duty."

"Really? Why?"

"Because he's killed a Shadowchaser before."

Chapter 9

Kira didn't want to let the dream state go. It was more peaceful, more quiet, more bright than what harsh reality could offer. Especially since that reality contained the cold fact that her new lover was a killer of Shadowchasers. Only one, Balm had said, but that was enough, wasn't it?

Trust the head of Gilead to disappear after delivering that bombshell, leaving Kira to decide for herself what to do with her newfound knowledge. Part of her wanted to feel betrayed, but that was a tiny, irrational part. The larger part, the controlling part, wanted to confront Khefar, wanted to know what had caused him to kill a Shadowchaser.

Gods help him if he didn't have a good reason.

Of course he has a good reason. The man doesn't do anything "just because." What she really wanted to know was whether it had been self-defense, or whether perhaps he'd killed the Chaser during his grief-stricken rampage. Or had it been someone like her, a Chaser in danger of sliding into Shadow?

One thing for sure, she wouldn't get answers hanging around in dreamland. She turned back to the tent, to use it as the doorway to return to the waking world.

The tent wasn't there.

"What the . . . ?" This was *her* dream state. No one other than Balm could disrupt the landscape she'd forged, and the head of Gilead had already departed. This was something else, someone else. Someone with a tremendous amount of power and access to her mind.

Her hand immediately reached for her Lightblade, but grabbed only air. Her heart thumped a nearly audible beat. *This is nuts,* she thought to herself. *Wake the hell up.*

Only desert remained of her dream place, hot, dry, endless. Kira fought to wake up, fought to touch her Lightblade, fought to banish the panic that threatened to seize her lungs. She could not be trapped here.

The feather tattoo at the base of her throat stung, then burned. Kira reached up to touch it. Agony blazed in her throat as if molten gold had been poured into her mouth, the pain knocking her to her knees. "Ma'at," she gasped, "Ma'at, preserve me!"

A dry scream shoved its way past her tongue as Ma'at's feather peeled away from her skin. It glowed golden fire as it hovered in the air, nearly blinding her with the magnificence that was the Eternal Truth.

Kira lowered her head, blinking to clear the tears from her eyes. Obviously Ma'at wanted her attention. The goddess certainly had it now. "Forgive me. I await Your Truth, Lady of Justice."

She cautiously raised her head. The feather began to float away, the ostrich plume straight and unwavering, brilliant white against the amber sand. Kira stumbled to her feet, then struggled to follow the incandescent plume as it crested a dune.

Her ascent was nowhere near as easy or graceful as

the feather's. She sank into the shifting sands, resorting to using her hands to climb the dune. Each dig into the toasty silica sent a flash through her extrasense: human, animal, vegetable lives lived and lost since the dawn of creation. By the time Kira reached the top of the dune, sweat drenched her clothes and her mental shields lay in tatters.

Desert stretched out before her, barren, endless, as if life was a long-forgotten concept. Nothing above except clear turquoise sky, nothing beneath except sand.

Something moved at the edge of the horizon, obscured by shimmering waves of heat. Kira shielded her eyes with one hand, straining to see clearly. Ma'at's feather hung beside her as if held aloft by an invisible hand.

As she watched, the shimmering heat resolved itself into two gleaming columns: a procession of people wrapped in white, skin gleaming gold and copper and black, wearing ornate headdresses. Not people, then, but the gods and goddesses of Egypt.

Between one blink and the next, the procession had traversed the distance from the edge of the world. Ra, the falcon-headed god with the sun disk crown, stretched forth his scepter, gouging a channel into the earth. From the midst of the deities stepped a bearded god with shimmering blue skin: Nun. He carried a palm frond in his right hand, and a smaller one rose from his hair. With him came a ram-headed god, a goddess wearing antelope horns flanking the crown of Upper Egypt, and another goddess wearing a tall headdress of reeds.

The gods waited, silent, as Nun, the embodiment of the primordial waters, reached inside himself, his hand disappearing beneath the liquid surface of his chest. He drew out an amphora of the brightest alabaster, its round body and long graceful neck symbolic of the union between male and female.

The blue-skinned god stepped forward, the amphora held high. Then he tilted the vessel. A river of water spilled out. No, not a river, but *the* river—the Nile. For a moment it formed the shape of a man, another god. A green-skinned god with a full belly, pendulous breasts, and a crown of papyrus flowers. Hapy stepped into the trench that Ra had made. Water instantly burst forth, flooding the channel, forming an island out of the land the gods stood upon. The river wound its way through the land. Greenery sprang up as it passed, life brought from the eternal water.

Nun handed the water vessel to Satet, the goddess wearing the white crown of Upper Egypt. He then stepped into the rushing river. It instantly stilled, becoming as smooth as a sheet of glass as it continued to flow. Ra stretched out his hand. What looked like a star fell from the sky, forming the shape of a river barge as it came to rest on the water. Ra and the rest of the gods climbed into the boat, leaving the three deities who had stood with Nun. They remained on the island as Ra's sun boat sailed away, carried by the waters of Nun, the waters of the Nile.

Many sunrises and sunsets passed. The goddess Satet emerged from the depths of the island—as she would once every year—and called forth Hapy. Using the amphora, the god poured the living water into the river, causing the annual flood that brought crops and life to the delta.

More years, the advancement of ages that saw the island grow and change.

The Aswan Dam sprang up across from the island, the flow of the Nile now controlled by human technology. Yet somehow Kira knew Satet and the vessel Nun had given her were still part of the river, still part of the ebb and flow of the Nile. Despite this knowledge, foreboding tightened her stomach.

The second dam, the Aswan High Dam, stretched across the river far south of the island that marked Egypt's ancient border with Nubia. Lake Nasser rose to full pool. But shadows filled the horizon like gathering thunderclouds. Darkness hung over the island. The land shook, the temple cracked. Satet appeared, her arms empty. The river ran and rushed, and then Kira noticed the level rising. Water swallowed the island, breached the dam, an impossibly high river of water, bursting free of the river's banks, inundating the floodplain, spilling across the desert. Rushing to Luxor, enveloping palm trees and the temple complex, flooding the Valley of the Kings.

And still the waters rose.

From Egypt west, drenching the Sahara, meeting the Atlantic. Merging north with the Mediterranean. Overtaking the Red Sea to the east, covering the Arabian Peninsula and beyond. Surging southward, devouring all of Africa. The Far East, the Old World and the New World. Everything—the entire world—succumbed to the flow of the Nile. No, not the Nile. The primordial waters of Nun.

"Kira!"

She jerked awake, her body drenched with sweat. Khefar leaned over her, his braids dripping water. She said the first thing that came to mind. "Oh, I guess that wasn't sweat."

"No, it's water." He pulled her upright, off the drenched bed. "Nile water."

"Nile wa—" She realized they were both still naked, then quickly rummaged through her suitcase for a couple of towels. She handed him one, then ran another over her own hair. It would take hours to dry out her braids. "You were there? I didn't see you!"

He ran the towel over his locks, then wrapped it around his waist. Water still glistened on his chest and shoulders. "I didn't see you either, but considering that you're not all that surprised about the water, I'm guessing you had the same vision I did?"

"The gods and goddesses of Egypt in a processional that created the Nile."

Khefar nodded. "Then the annual floodwaters, ages and ages of them, until the building of the dam."

"And then a flood that swallowed the world."

They stared at each other in silence, each digesting their vision. Kira cleared her throat. "Would you mind putting on something besides the towel? All that bare skin is distracting me."

"Like your bare skin doesn't distract me?"

Khefar found his boxers and stepped into them. He carefully sat on the edge of the bed. The sheets were already beginning to dry the way a nightmare slowly fades. Not that what she'd done with Khefar had been nightmarish. Far from it. In fact it had been downright heavenly.

"Kira, did you even hear what I said?"

Heat stung her cheeks as she caught Khefar's

all-too-knowing gaze. She forced all distractions aside. "What did you say?"

"I asked you if you've ever heard of something called the Vessel of Nun."

She frowned as she exchanged the towel for a tank top and yoga pants. "Sounds familiar. Maybe it's something I researched during my study at university. I think I've also heard it called something like the Bowl of Naunet. All I know is that Nun is the god of the primordial waters before the creation of everything. The creator gods sprang from Nun and even now his still waters lie at the edge of existence. There is a legend that one day Nun will return to destroy the world and start the cycle of creation again. What about this vessel thing?"

"There are plenty of stories that have been passed down. Many of them came to the northern part of Nubia after our generals gained the throne of the Two Lands. According to one reference, the Vessel of Nun takes a year to fill up at its source near what we call the First Cataract before spilling over."

"I thought the source of the Nile was somewhere in the highlands of Ethiopia or the mountains of Uganda," Kira said. "Besides, doesn't the Aswan Dam prevent the Nile from overflowing its banks?'

"It does. The Egyptian government controls the flow of the water through October, and the levels should be dropping off considerably now."

"What if they aren't?" she asked. "The vision was quite clear. The Vessel of Nun that Satet used to create the annual Nile inundation has been stolen. The water isn't going to go down."

"That will be a simple enough thing to check," Khefar said. "It would be all over Egyptian news reports by now. Somehow, though, I don't think Ma'at and Isis would bother giving us both this vision if we weren't supposed to stop it. The question is, where in the world to start?"

"Here."

"Here?" Khefar frowned. "If we're looking for a recently missing Egyptian artifact, we should probably head to Cairo."

"Yeah, but there's more."

"What more could there possibly be?"

"Before Ma'at gave me that vision, I had a dreamwalk," she explained. "Balm came to me."

His expression blanked. He'd be an awesome poker player, she thought. "I see. What did she have to say?"

"Quite a bit, actually." She moved in front of him. "Apparently the Chaser that operates out of Gilead London has disappeared. So has his handler. It's entirely possible that he's gone rogue."

"Rogue?" Khefar stood so quickly she had to back up a step. "What leads you to make that determination?"

"No one's seen or heard from the Chaser in a couple of days, not even the section chief," Kira explained. "Balm can't tap into either the Chaser or the handler. And a private collector has reported that a recent addition to his collection has gone missing. This particular collector has a penchant for Egyptian antiquities but doesn't necessarily care where they come from."

"So you think this Chaser has stolen the Vessel of Nun from a private collector?"

Kira checked her braids. Surprisingly dry, as if she hadn't almost drowned in her vision or awakened drenched in river water. "The timing's a bit too coincidental, don't you think?"

"I don't believe in coincidences, do you?"

She shook her head. "Not even a little."

"So we have a Shadowchaser and handler who are missing, an Egyptian artifact that's also missing, and a pair of goddesses who tell us that if Satet doesn't get her jar back, the Nile will flood the world."

"That's pretty much it," she agreed. "Well, there might be a little more."

"A little more? Like what?"

"Oh, just that Balm made Zoo and Wynne official members of Gilead East, they're on their way here as backup, and she wants you to help me with this Chase because you've killed a Chaser before."

To his credit, he didn't try to deny it. "She told you this?"

"With all the brevity and bluntness that the Balm of Gilead possesses."

"Does this upset you?"

"Which part?"

"Kira." He captured her hand, dragged her closer. "For what it's worth, I think having Wynne and Zoo at your back with the full might and money of Gilead behind them is a good thing. Remember, they were military before you knew them. And sometimes when you've been at this a while, fighting what we fight, it's easy to lose your humanity. I think your friends can help you retain it. And we can help each other, if you wish."

She grinned. "Sorta like we helped each other last night?"

He returned her smile. "Something like that." He sobered. "It's probably best to take each day as it comes."

She knew exactly what he meant. "No promises, no expectations."

"Exactly."

"You're right. It's just that I don't want things to be awkward."

He gave her a wry smile. "Not as awkward as you discovering the man you've just slept with killed one of your coworkers."

"There is that," she admitted, glad that he didn't seem inclined to dismiss it. "I'm hoping, for once, that you'd like to actually be forthcoming with details."

To her surprise, he was. "It was about two hundred years ago. He was a double agent, and then he went rogue. A lot of people died because of him. My only regret is that I didn't stop him sooner."

"Wow." She relaxed. "Thanks for telling me."

He looked taken aback. "You don't want to know more?"

"Don't need to." She squeezed his fingers. "I got all I need to know. One, you actually came right out and told me without me having to hold a blade on you. That means a lot to me. Two, you didn't kill him because you wanted to, but because you had to. It means when the time comes, I can trust you to make the right decision and stop me before I go rogue."

His expression shuttered. "If."

"All right. *If* the time comes, I know you'll do the

right thing." She kissed him on the cheek. "I can't tell you how much of a relief that is. But we don't need to worry about that right now. Right now we need to come up with a plan, then make some noise at Gilead London. First though, I'm going to go take a shower before Anansi gets here and starts telling tales about that wet spot in the bed."

Chapter 10

If Gilead East in Atlanta was all high-tech sleekness, Gilead London was European chic at its most aristocratic. It occupied a gleaming eight-story building not far from the stock exchange in the City of London, one square mile of London proper surrounded by the thirty-two boroughs that comprised Greater London. The world's fortunes had been made and lost in "the City" for centuries.

"Are we going to have any issues entering the building?" Khefar asked as the hired car pulled away from the sidewalk.

"We shouldn't," she answered. "Balm's in there somewhere, and she knows we're coming. I guess we'll know for sure when we go inside."

Just as Balm had requested, Kira had donned her Chaser's gear: khaki cargo pants, black work boots, black long-sleeved T-shirt, black leather vest. She also wore her trusted trench coat. It not only protected her from the elements, but also helped to conceal her weapons. Besides the Lightblade, she had daggers in both boots and her favorite gun in a left shoulder holster. Crossing the Atlantic in Balm's private plane definitely had some advantages.

Khefar had dressed the part too: dark denim,

rugged boots, and a charcoal gray trench. Besides the Dagger of Khefaratum, she'd seen him tuck two guns into quick-release holsters at the small of his back. He wouldn't carry a blade other than his dagger, but he didn't need to.

He surveyed her with bottomless dark eyes. "These people are going to think we're terrorists, Goths, or Milli Vanilli impersonators."

"Milla-who?"

"Never mind. Are you ready?"

"Sure. Why don't I go in first?"

Kira approached the entrance. A discreet sign embedded in a stone column to the right of the double doors announced the building as being occupied by Light International, London. A stylized lighthouse was etched in the stone next to the lettering, identifying the structure as part of the Gilead Commission. The logo was used by a plethora of hotels, restaurants, and other establishments. Whenever Kira was on a Chase in unfamiliar territory, she simply had to look for the lighthouse logo to find a member of Gilead's massive network.

Balm?

Come in, dear. Whatever you do, don't kill anyone.

Kira paused. *What are you up to?*

Just a little experiment. I'll see you soon.

Wrapping her gloved hand around the vertical brass handle, Kira pulled open the heavy glass door, then stepped inside, Khefar following. Silence, total and absolute as a tomb, greeted her. It was an amazing feat considering that there were at least fifteen people in the multi-level lobby in various stages of motion—going through the security checkpoint, walking toward the elevators, headed out for a break. The Chaser and the warrior's entrance froze them all in place, eyes wide, jaws slack, as if disbelief and shock had caused a chemical chain reaction resulting in suspended animation.

Khefar stopped beside her, his coat settling so heavily about him Kira wondered if it had been reinforced. "It's almost like a time-dilation field," he said.

"You're a sci-fi fan?"

"I'm a fan of many things."

Kira surveyed the mix of people in business attire, wondering where Balm was. She hadn't seen so many tense people in one place since her university finals. "You know, it should be the other way around to have any sort of tactical advantage. They're moving so slow we could have picked them off by now."

"True. From their collective expressions, I'd say Balm neglected to tell them we were coming."

As soon as Khefar said Balm's name, the spell broke. People scattered like cockroaches in bright light. A security team spilled out of the left corridor, the sound of their boots echoing through the large chamber as they pounded across the polished granite floor.

"Get on the ground, get on the ground now!"

"I will not." She kept her hands at her sides, trying to appear nonthreatening. They were coworkers, after all. "I belong here."

The guards didn't seem to share her sentiment. One strapping bruiser of a redhead stepped forward, the barrel of his rifle inches from her face. "I said get on the ground. Now!"

Khefar ignored the guards pointing weapons at him. Instead, he glared at the one holding his rifle on Kira. "Take that out of her face," he said. The lethal tone of his voice was unmistakable to anyone with half a brain.

The bruiser evidently lacked that half. "Or what?"

"Or it's going to get very messy in here and you will be very dead."

Kira had had enough. "I am a Shadowchaser, as my Lightblade should prove to anyone monitoring your surveillance systems. My name is Kira Solomon and I'm based out of Gilead East in the States. We are here at my mother's invitation."

The other guards stepped back at the mention of her title. Bruiser chose to assert his authority. "I don't care who your mum is."

Khefar moved. Kira's Chaser-honed senses could barely follow his movements as he disarmed the redhead and took the guard to his knees. "You should be more polite," the Nubian said, his tone still even. "I'll be happy to provide some pointers for you."

"I think that's enough." Balm's voice, as soothing as a gentle rain, wafted through the sweeping vestibule, cutting the tension. The other guards quickly lowered their weapons. Several stepped back. Kira scanned the area but couldn't see her mother anywhere. A dark-haired, thirtyish man in a navy blue suit skidded to a stop before them, two other suited men close behind.

"Stand down," he said, waving at the guards. "Back to your posts, except for you two. Jensen, I want the head of surveillance in my office in five minutes."

"Yes, sir."

The man gestured to Khefar. "If you would be so kind as to release Stephenson, sir, I need him taken to my office as well."

Khefar took his time freeing the guard. He turned to Kira. "Did she give you a heads-up about this?"

"Not unless you consider a warning not to kill anyone when we walked through the door a heads-up." She looked at the dark-haired suit. "Terry Steinmueller? I thought you were in charge of the sweepers, in the Shadow-magic division."

"Hi, Kira, er, Chaser Solomon. I was. I'm acting section chief now."

"Congratulations, then, Acting Section Chief Steinmueller."

"You should probably hold off on the congratulations." Steinmueller looked as if he'd rather be anywhere else, preferably somewhere with lots of sun and drinks with umbrellas in them. "The housecleaning isn't over by a long stretch."

Again Balm's voice came, soothing and gentle yet with an edge to it, quite like a blade wrapped in silk. "Agent Steinmueller, if you'd bring my daughter and her guest to me?"

Terry ran a finger along the inner edge of his collar. "How is she doing that?" he whispered. "We don't have a paging system."

"She's Balm," Kira said, which was explanation enough. Balm could probably do whatever she wanted as far as Gilead holdings were concerned.

Steinmueller guided them through the security checkpoint and to the elevators. He swiped his key card and the doors immediately opened. Once inside, he swiped his card again. The doors closed silently and the car began to rise.

"I heard about Mr. Comstock," Terry said then. "My condolences on the loss of your handler."

"Thank you," Kira said. "Did you know him?"

"Not very well. Like the other handlers affiliated with this branch, he preferred to work outside the office. Still, from what I knew of him, he was a good man."

"Yes, he was."

Steinmueller glanced at Khefar, then hurriedly looked away. Kira couldn't blame him. The Nubian had been silent since asking her about Balm, but it wasn't an easy silence. Anger swarmed around the man like a disturbed hive of bees looking for a target.

The elevator slid open onto a pristine white hallway. The overhead fluorescents emitted a soft blue glow. "They were standard white lights before she arrived," Steinmueller whispered.

Kira smiled, then spoke in a normal tone. "You know, if she can talk to you, she can hear you too."

Steinmueller tripped, then caught himself. "Right," he stammered, straightening his tie. "Of course. To the office, then?"

The corridor opened onto a wide expanse of glass, white granite, and sunlight, with a few plants to soften the harsh effect. The reception desk was a curved structure of glass blocks and white laminate. Two slate fountains flanked the executive office doors, the soft gurgling the only sound on the floor.

A soft blue glow emanated from the executive

office, swamping the reception area. "Balm's in full show mode," she whispered to Khefar.

The Nubian nodded, his expression grim. "I feel sorry for everyone working in this building, right down to the janitors. Your mother's been known to 'soothe' people to death."

Balm's assistant sat at the reception desk. He smiled and waved them in. The double doors leading into the office swung open on their own.

Khefar stalked inside, followed by Kira, then Steinmueller. An oak conference table stood to the right of the doors, ringed with twelve hunter green high-backed chairs. A glass and oak desk sat deeper in the large room, with a beige conversation set beyond that. Balm stood at the massive wall of windows, dressed from head to toe in winter white. At least Kira thought it was winter white. It was hard to tell other colors from the blue aura the Balm of Gilead kicked out.

Her voice carried across the large room, as tranquil as the fountains beside the doors. "Thank you, Mr. Steinmueller. If you'll wait a moment outside, I'll contact you as soon as we're ready."

"Yes, ma'am. Of course, ma'am." The acting section chief made a hasty retreat.

"What was that all about?" Khefar demanded as soon as the doors closed behind the other man. "That little setup in the lobby?"

"A simple test."

"Simple? You put Kira's life in danger!"

Balm turned away from the windows. "My daughter was never in danger," Balm said, a hard edge creeping into her serene tone. "I for one have a healthy respect for Kira's ability to protect herself. Secondly, I would never allow Kira to come to harm in *my* presence."

"No, you'd turn your back first."

"Whoa." Kira held up her hands, stepping between them as Balm's eyes flared blue. "As curious as I am about whatever this is between you two, time is not on our side."

Khefar's jaw worked, but he nodded, took a step back. Kira turned back to her mother. "I sure hope you need more from me than that little show in the lobby."

Balm drew herself up. "Yes, I do."

She crossed to the desk, her eyes still sparking. "As Steinmueller explained, I'm cleaning house here in Gilead London. The systematic failures that led to Gunderson and Marshall going rogue are unbelievable. The section chief and several levels below him are being reassigned. I have our psychics filtering through the human data but it's taking some time."

She picked up her smartphone, scrolled through it. "I have a couple of people I'd like you to interview, beginning with Shanti Singh. The psychics received several impressions of evasiveness from her. I need you to find out what she knows."

Khefar folded his arms. "I can interrogate her."

Balm turned a stony expression his way. "I'm sure you can. However, Ms. Singh has a high clearance level that enables her to work directly with Chasers. Because of that, she's . . . resistant to standard interrogation techniques."

Kira dropped her hands. "You want me to read her." She'd figured that was what Balm needed her for, she'd just hoped she was wrong. "All right. Take me to her."

"Wait a minute." Khefar grabbed her shoulder. "You can't do this. It isn't right."

"The normal rules don't apply when a Chaser's gone rogue, Eternal Warrior," Balm said evenly. "You know this well."

A vein throbbed in his temple. "I know. I also know what this 'reading' will do to Kira. Have you forgotten?"

Balm lifted her chin. "I think you've forgotten yourself, Khefar, son of Jeru, son of Natek. Kira is a Shadowchaser. She will do what is necessary for the Light."

"Doing what is necessary for the Light doesn't include being your attack dog."

"Enough!" Kira looked from one to the other. "This stopped being amusing when you both forgot I was in the freakin' room! I've got a brain and I know how to use it, including knowing when to be an attack dog and when to be a trained investigator. If you both would like a reminder of my abilities, I suggest you come with me to see Ms. Singh, or you can stay here and duke it out with each other. I really don't give a damn."

She headed for the door, so angry she could feel her power tingling along the surface of her skin. Dammit, she was hardly a damsel in distress!

"Kira." Balm's voice wrapped around Kira as softly as a cashmere sweater. But Kira had grown up with the head of the Gilead Commission, and the attempt to soothe didn't work on her as it did with Gilead's employees.

"Yes, Mother?"

"Steinmueller will take you to the interview room. I'll monitor from here."

"All right." She headed for the door again. "Khefar, you coming or are you going to continue your glaring contest with her?"

"I'm coming." He didn't sound happy about it though.

Kira jerked the office doors open. Steinmueller took one look at her, then jumped to his feet. "Is everything all right?"

"Fine. I need to interview Shanti Singh. Will you take us to her?"

"Of course." He took them back to the elevator hallway, then called for the car. "Will Her Serenity join us?"

"Her Serenity?" Kira echoed. "You mean Balm?"

"Of course. That's what everyone calls her, or the Serene One." He stepped into the elevator. "What do you call her?"

"I call her 'Balm' or 'Mother' when I'm talking to her." She stepped in, followed by Khefar.

Steinmueller tried to engage the Nubian. "And what do you call the Serene One?"

"That's not important," Kira interjected before Khefar could speak. "Tell me about Shanti Singh."

Steinmueller handed her an employment folder. "She graduated Fordham University two years ago, scored extremely high on aptitude tests, which flagged her for us. She cleared all the rigorous protocols and was granted Level Eight status."

"Someone with no track record was granted status

to assist Shadowchasers right out of the gate?" Kira shook her head.

"We were short on analysts at the time we brought her on," Steinmueller explained. "At least, that's how the former section chief made it out to me. And she made it through every periodical psychic review she'd been tagged for. We had no reason to suspect her of anything."

"Something must have been the trigger," Kira mused. "I'll see what I can find out."

The interview rooms were in the bowels of the building, which didn't surprise Kira in the least. With so many different types of creatures brought in for questioning, Gilead had to make sure their employees—and their suspects—remained protected.

Shanti Singh looked to be just out of college, equal parts false bravado and true apprehension dancing across her brown face. She sat huddled in her navy business suit, half a glass of water before her, fingers twirling her shiny dark hair.

Kira slipped into the molded plastic chair opposite the woman. "Ms. Singh, this interview is being recorded on audio, video, and extrasensory scanners."

"Who are you?" the woman asked, defiant.

Kira decided to let her have the point. It would be the last the girl would get to make. "My name is Kira Solomon. I'm a Shadowchaser, and I'm here to find out what happened to Chaser Gunderson and his handler."

Singh jerked her chin at Khefar, lounging near the door. "And who's he?"

"Just an observer." Kira flipped through the folder

Steinmueller had given her. "So you worked closely with Pavel Gunderson and Adam Marshall?"

The young woman folded her arms. "I was already interrogated by Gilead psychics. I do not see why I need to answer any of your questions. I have rights."

Kira nodded. "You do indeed. I'm assuming you read your employment contract and handbook thoroughly when you agreed to work for Gilead?"

Singh fidgeted. "I did."

"No, you didn't," Kira said softly, folding her gloved hands together before leaning across the table. "If you had, you'd know that as a condition of being employed by Gilead, you agreed to be interviewed during the course of any investigation, especially when your work directly supports or intersects with that of Shadow-chasers and their handlers. That means polygraph, psychics, or even someone like me."

The woman's chin lifted. "Are you some sort of super psychic?"

"Psychics get flashes or impressions from your aura or from touching you or objects belonging to you," Kira explained. She made a show of propping her elbows on the heavy plastic table, then tugging at the glove covering her right hand. "When I touch your belongings, scenes of your life unfold for me like a movie. But when I touch you . . ."

"What?" Shanti asked when Kira fell silent. "What happens?"

"Chaser Solomon has a unique ability among Shadowchasers," Khefar said. "When she touches you, everything you have ever experienced—from one second ago to the moment you were born—gets downloaded into her brain. All your thoughts, actions, emotions—all of it becomes hers. She can examine your life as if she's looking at a DVD. Fast forward, reverse, section by section, your entire life will be hers. Of course for her to take your life experiences requires energy, so she takes about a year off your life too."

Singh's dark eyes widened, then bulged. "Is he—is he telling the truth?"

Kira caught her gaze, held it. "He is. I would rather not go to such extreme measures with you. My goal is to find out what's happened to Gunderson and Marshall. Will you help me?"

The other woman stared at Kira's bare hand for a long moment. "All right. I've run some queries for Gunderson before. You know, simple support things while he and Marshall were out in the field."

"When was the last time you spoke to him?"

"Two days ago. He asked me for a list of known collectors in and around London. He particularly wanted to know if any had a penchant for Egyptian artifacts."

"You gave him the names."

"Yes."

"Did you ask Gunderson why he wanted the list?"

"No, I just assumed it was part of a Chase he was on."

"I see." Kira closed the folder with her gloved hand. "Were there any hybrids on the list?"

"No."

Kira leaned forward again. The other woman backed away. "Tell me, Ms. Singh, what does Gilead require for a Chaser to retrieve an artifact from a human collector?"

"It doesn't matter if the collector is human or hybrid, a formal request for retrieval has to be made," the analyst replied. "Unless the object is an imminent threat, one of several standard plans is approved by the section chief and coordinated with the Shadowchaser and a retrieval unit."

"Did Chaser Gunderson request a retrieval?"

Singh dropped her gaze. "No."

"Did you follow procedure and suggest a retrieval when the Chaser neglected to?"

Singh remained silent, but the silence was answer enough.

Kira pulled her glove back on. "Thank you, Ms. Singh. The Commission appreciates your assistance."

"That's it?" Singh asked, surprise raising her eyebrows. "There's nothing else?"

"What were you expecting?" Kira climbed to her feet. "Torture?"

The other woman scooted forward in her chair. "So, I can go back to work?"

"No, I'm sorry, that isn't possible."

"But . . . why?"

"You deliberately withheld information from an ongoing investigation. You're compromised now. I don't know if they're going to fire you or not. That's up to the acting section chief and the Balm of Gilead. I can tell you that your clearance has already been revoked and you'll never work with another Shadowchaser again. No one can trust you now. Next time, don't try to hide. Everything eventually comes to Light. And I do mean everything."

Chapter 11

Kira sighed with relief as they finally stepped out of Gilead London and back onto the street. A few pedestrians heading back to work from their lunch breaks gave them curious glances as they passed by. Their boots and trench coats were a little out of place among the suits and Burberrys of the financial district.

She'd interviewed four others after Ms. Singh. Only one of them had checked out. The others would be reassigned if they were lucky, or completely scrubbed of all knowledge of their sensitive duties with Gilead and placed in clerical positions with Light International.

"Thanks for your help in there," she told Khefar. "I wasn't looking forward to reading any of the suspects. Thanks to you, I didn't have to."

"Glad to help."

"Do you mind telling me what that confrontation with Balm was about?"

"I do mind." He looked up and down the street for their hired car.

"You know I don't care if you mind, right?" She pulled her coat closer about her. "I just want you to tell me what's going on between you two."

"I just don't appreciate Balm sending you in to do her dirty work, that's all."

"It's not dirty work, it's my job. It's part of what I do as a Shadowchaser."

"It doesn't have to be part of your Chaser duties," Khefar retorted. "The interrogations inside just proved that. You can do your job without resorting to reading people."

"I think I'm supposed to be flattered. I am, kind of. But I'm also a little ticked off." She stabbed a finger at his chest. "I know you don't want me to hurt those people—"

"I don't care about those people, I care about you!" He captured her hands in his. "Reading people takes a toll on you. I know it. Balm knows it, but she told you to do it anyway. That's what hacked me off." He leaned in close. "I just don't want you endangering yourself for the greater good. What if you had to read all of those people? What would that have done to you? Especially after what happened in Atlanta?"

Khefar was afraid for her, she realized, truly worried about her and her well-being. It was a heady realization that caused Shadow to beat a hasty retreat in her spirit.

Kira kissed his cheek. "Thank you for that. But seriously, taking on Balm in her own stronghold? Suicidal, much?"

His expression lightened. "I wasn't thinking. Seems to be a common occurrence where you're concerned."

Their car finally pulled up to the curb. "Okay," Kira said, "we just ended on a sweet note. You might want to be quiet so it doesn't go sour."

He opened the car door for her. "Good point.

Maybe we should go back to Bernie's and de-arm before you head over to the lawyer's offices?"

"Now that's good thinking."

A few hours later—after Kira had finalized her business with Cooper, Johnstone, and Braithwhyte, at least for the time being—she, Khefar, and Nansee made their way to a quiet section of London where, at a light-favored hotel frequently used by Gilead personnel, they were to meet Wynne and Zoo.

Kira didn't expect Wynne and Zoo to be all that thrilled with her, and she wasn't disappointed.

They filed into the living area of the Marlowes' hotel suite. Khefar and Nansee sat down on a dark green couch; Wynne and Zoo remained standing in front of club chairs, matching expressions of defiance coloring their faces. Both wore black paramilitary uniforms capable of stowing an arsenal of firepower with a magical boost. In their cargo pants, dark shirts, and jackets, they couldn't have looked more military if they'd been dressed in camouflage. She hoped they hadn't worn the clothes all the way from the States. Even if they'd made the trip on a Gilead Commission plane, those kinds of outfits were sure to raise eyebrows around London.

Kira folded her arms as she regarded them. "So, Balm made you guys members of Gilead East."

"Balm didn't make us anything," Wynne said, her chin high. Her bright pink hair had been toned down to a deep russet red, making her look like a fire elemental in human form. "If you recall, you left us at her house with her, Sanchez, and Nansee. Zoo asked me why I was upset and I told him."

Zoo stood next to his wife, his shaven scalp with its horned owl tattoo hidden beneath a black cap. His eyes, usually a soft, mossy green, seemed as hard as emeralds now against his light olive skin. Then again, he was a walking contrast, a witch trapped in the six-foot-plus body of a rock show bodyguard, a healer who'd served as a sniper in the military. "We decided then and there to ask Balm to make us members of Gilead. Sanchez mentioned our military experience and how we'd helped in Atlanta, how we've been helping you all along. She actually recommended us, said that since we'd been doing such a good job as support personnel for a Shadowchaser, we might as well get paid for it."

"The section chief said that?" Kira couldn't decide whether to be impressed or upset. Sanchez recognized talent above all, and knew how to leverage her people to get the results she wanted. Having Wynne and Zoo under her command was like having a professional on your neighborhood pickup softball team.

"So you answer to Sanchez now?" Kira asked, trying not to feel ill at the thought. Even though they had worked together to stop the Fallen, Kira didn't think she and the section chief would be fast friends anytime soon.

Wynne looked disgusted. "You should know better than that. We agreed to sign on if and only if we got to support you. We report to you. When you're done, we're done."

"When you're on a mission, you need backup," Zoo said. "I don't give a damn how many demigods and ultimate fighters you have with you. We're your backup. Whether you want us to be or not."

She heard the hard edge in his voice, so unlike the Zoo she was used to. There was wariness to both of them, an edge to them, and she knew she'd put it there. She'd been harsh with Wynne in an effort to protect her friends from her dangerous life. Instead, they'd signed up as members of Gilead's goon squad. They might as well have painted bull's-eyes on their backs.

She tried to dissuade them again. "What about your shop? Charms and Arms is your baby, and it's important to the metaphysical community in Atlanta. How can you just leave it like that?"

Wynne's scowl deepened. "How do you leave your archaeological work behind? How do you tell the Carlos, or the British Museum, that you can't work for them anymore?" She dropped a hand to her hip. "You don't. You do your job—you do both jobs. We still own Charms and Arms, and we still have our work there. Katie's been with us from day one; she knows how to run the shop better than we do. Zoo and I still get to concentrate on special requests like we want to anyway. There's no reason we can't do that and back you up."

Kira looked to Khefar and Nansee, but knew they wouldn't be any help. "Guys, this isn't right. You know it's not."

Zoo got in her face. "Look, Kira. I know you're still thinking about what happened in the cemetery back in Atlanta, but you need to shut it out. It was combat, friendly fire. Yeah it sucks, but it happens. When you go Chasing there's always a chance of things going wrong. When we were in combat, we always knew there was a chance we weren't coming back in one piece, if at all.

But you do what needs doing and keep going as long as you can because that's your job."

"All right." Kira unfolded her arms. "Are you guys done reading me the riot act, or do we need to keep going?"

They looked at each other, then Wynne spoke. "You're not going to say anything about us joining up with Gilead?"

"Just one thing: when the Chase is on, the Chaser's word is law. Understood?"

They snapped to. "Understood."

"Good. Take a seat." Kira rubbed her hands together, eager to move on to the Chase. "We need to come up with a plan. Two big things have happened, and we think they're related. Khefar, you want to start?"

Khefar nodded. "Ma'at and Isis came to both of us. We were shown a vision of the first flooding of the Nile, caused by the Vessel of Nun. I don't know if this is supposed to be some sort of metaphysical vessel or a real vase handled by the primordial water god. Either way, an artifact that fits its description has been stolen. How that works in the make-up of the universe is beyond our understanding. What we do know is that without it in place, the Nile will allegedly release the waters of Nun, the ancient waters from before creation. That flood not only will devastate Egypt, but is pretty much guaranteed to inundate the world."

"I sent some feelers out along my various webs," Nansee said. "Looks like there's been some unusual weather in the Ethiopian highlands. Record-breaking rain for most of the summer flooded the Nile. Apparently, the downpour keeps coming. Aswan Dam is measuring record water levels."

"Are you shitting me?" Zoo breathed. "Stopping a flood is our first mission?"

"Actually, recovering the Vessel of Nun isn't the focus of our Chase," Kira told them, "but something that I have to do as the Hand of Ma'at. What Balm has asked, unofficially, is that I track down Pavel Gunderson, the Shadowchaser for Western Europe."

Wynne's eyes widened. "We're Chasing a Chaser? That's what we get right out of the gate?" She shook her head. "I should have known better. Kira and the mundane don't exactly go hand in hand."

"Both Gunderson and his handler have been incommunicado for the last several days," Kira said, ignoring Wynne's comment. "Gunderson is believed to be the one who stole the Vessel of Nun. Gilead London hasn't seen the Vessel or Gunderson and Marshall, and isn't quite sure exactly how long they've been silent. Things are kinda wonky there, and the section chief has been removed. It's part of the reason we're not going through the London office and why I'm doing the Chase. The goal is to find them, find out what's going on. If they're still alive, and we believe at least Gunderson is, we need to see if it's at all possible to bring them in for refinement."

"And refinement is . . . ?" Zoo prompted.

Kira hesitated. Like it or not, her friends were now a part of the Gilead Commission. They needed to know what they'd signed themselves up for.

"I suppose now is as good as time as any to provide a little background information on what the Gilead

Commission is all about. Granted, even though I lived in the main stronghold on Santa Costa for nearly seven years, even I don't know all there is to know about Gilead."

She paused to gather her thoughts. "You guys already know that there are two fundamental sides to the Universal Balance: Light and Shadow, or Order and Chaos. There are hierarchies on both sides: Fallen and Guardians of Light, angels and demons, Shadowlings and Shadowchasers, then the assorted mix of hybrids, humans, and other magical mutations and elementals that don't fit either side of the Balance.

"When the War of Being occurred, some of the sons and daughters of Chaos and Shadow fell through the Veil and came here, losing their corporeal forms in the process. Children of Light and Order also fell. Most of them are the gods and goddesses you know of today. Others blended with man, mutating into hybrid beings like mer-people, the different varieties of vampires, were-folk.

"The Gilead Commission began as a Light-sanctioned human organization dedicated to fighting Shadow. For as long as there have been humans, there has been a group Commissioned to stand as a beacon to guide any and all to the Light.

"There are seven Commissioners who serve as the elders of Gilead. The head of that body is Balm. The saying goes, 'There has always been a Balm in Gilead,' and that's more or less true."

"So which came first, the Bible or Gilead?"

"The Gilead Commission was first," Kira told them, and Zoo's smile vanished. "The prophet Jeremiah wasn't speaking in allegory. There was a time before

Gilead moved to Santa Costa, when it was headquartered in what's now Jordan, and there was a period of unrest when there wasn't a Balm in Gilead. No one really talks about what happened, and I was never able to find records of the era. My best guess is that the Balm of that time was killed, turned, or somehow forced out. The Gilead Commission then moved to the island of Santa Costa in the Aegean Sea, a place they could easily fortify and defend. Since then there's always been a Balm. Some say the current Balm is that Balm, but again, I haven't been able to find any information about how many Balms there have been, how she's chosen, or how the elders are chosen for the Commission."

"What about Chasers?" Wynne wondered. "You've never really told us about how you became a Shadowchaser. And what's this refinement thing you talked about doing to the missing Chaser?"

"Shadowchasers tend to be orphans or children abandoned because they're different." Kira cleared her throat. "Any type of extrasense or psychic ability would make a child a prime candidate for Chaser training. For example, Zoo would have been a target if it weren't for the fact that he's part of a close-knit family of natural-born witches comfortable with themselves and their abilities. Gilead will also take teens or recruit college-age acolytes, but no one over the age of twenty is usually chosen for Shadowchasing."

"Why?"

"Because it's easier to rewire a young brain," Kira said bluntly. "That's what Shadowchaser training is. It's entirely reconstructing a person mentally and physically, enhancing their magic and extrasense, to hone them into an instrument of Light. General education and training happen first, along with magical enhancement. Around age fifteen or sixteen, Chaser training begins in earnest. By eighteen, a Chaser has been assigned to a handler, who trains them to survive the Crucible."

"Do we even want to know what the Crucible is?" Wynne asked.

Kira noticed that neither Khefar nor Nansee was adding to the questions or supplying any answers. Probably because they already knew, which wouldn't surprise her in the least. "Think of what Spartan boys had to go through as a rite of passage, then toss in some magic and a couple of demons. That's the Shadowchaser Crucible. Only about seventy-five percent of acolytes actually survive."

"You don't mean they die, do you?" Zoo asked.

Kira remained silent for a moment, but it was enough. "Anyway, bringing a Chaser in for refinement means putting them back through the deconstruction and reconstruction of the Shadowchaser mind-set, bringing them back to Balance, then back to Light. The older a Chaser is, the more difficult it is to successfully complete refinement."

She reached into the packet Wynne and Zoo had brought with them, extracting several copies of the same photo. "Fortunately for Gunderson, he's relatively young. He can make it through the refinement, if the only problem is him being a little confused about his duties. If he's abandoned being a Chaser or gone rogue, then it becomes a real Chase."

Wynne and Zoo looked more uncertain by the

moment. Unfortunately for them, it was too late to change their minds. "Before you ask, a real Chase means the Shadowchaser's goal is to send her target back to Shadow. If I'm after another Chaser, and it's been determined that he's beyond refinement, then the goal is to eliminate that Chaser. There's no redemption for a Chaser who slides into Shadow. The Commission elders are quite adamant about that."

She looked at each of them in turn. Both her friends looked dismayed. Nansee's gaze was way too understanding for her comfort, and Khefar just seemed irritated. It wasn't what any of them wanted to hear, but they needed to know the truth.

"Look, I'm hoping that this will be easy. I'm hoping I'm not going to have to use my Lightblade on a fellow Shadowchaser. I'm really hoping there's a very good reason why Gunderson took the Vessel of Nun, if he even took it."

"How do we find that out?"

"We start at their flat. It's in Shoreditch."

Chapter 12

Shoreditch lay in the borough of Hackney, northeast of London proper, just north of the infamous areas of Whitechapel and Bishopsgate. When Kira had left to assume her Chaser duties in Atlanta, the area had been undergoing revitalization, with a slew of technology companies and the creative arts taking up residence. It was a perfectly trendy area for a young Shadowchaser and his handler to set up a home base. Shoreditch also had a large multicultural human and non-human population that made it easy to go unnoticed, something Kira and her team used to their advantage.

Gunderson's flat was in a modest and modern conversion, unobtrusive to the Normals. The layers of protections on the entryway, however, were anything but mundane.

"Zoo, hang out down here and keep a lookout," Kira ordered. "Give us a shout if anyone who fits Gunderson or Marshall's description approaches the flat."

"I'll keep watch with Marlowe," Khefar suggested. "I can subdue the Shadowchaser if necessary."

Right. He certainly could. Kira nodded. "Okay then, Wynne, Nansee, you're with me."

Kira made her way up to the third level, Wynne

and the demigod in tow. After Nansee verified her suspicion that no one was home, Kira stripped off her gloves and called her extrasense. A blue-white sheet of power coated the door and two feet of the walls surrounding it, a rather crude shield. Shields and protections were some of the first things learned during Shadowchaser training. Gunderson should have been better at it . . . unless he'd had to leave in a hurry.

With her extrasense providing a layer of protection, Kira placed her palms flat on the door. The pale blue shield throbbed. Kira sent a soothing pulse of power into the layer so that it flowed around the door much like a jellyfish surrounding its prey. Her power consumed the other, dissipating it. Then she drew her power back, leaving the door as just a door.

"Okay, Wynne, you're up."

Wynne made short work of the lock. They slipped inside. It was obvious from the interior that Gunderson considered the flat more of a stopover for a frequent traveler than a home. The austere apartment consisted of a small main room with a kitchen area tucked into a corner, one bedroom, and a tiny washroom. Minimalist as it was, they made a quick search of the flat, turning up nothing that could provide clues to Gunderson's or Marshall's disappearance.

Kira stood in the center of the main room. "I'm going to have to use my extrasense. I'd rather not have any accidents, so I just need you guys to stay put, in case there are any metaphysical traps I haven't sensed yet."

"I don't sense anything," Nansee said.

"I don't either, which means there probably is something hidden," Kira told him. "A Shadowchaser lives here. We always have something we have to keep secret."

She held up her hands, breathed deep, then called her power. Her friends disappeared into their energy fields, Wynne's a rainbow of color, the demigod's almost all white.

Again, she sent her extrasense beyond the Veil, searching for any magical blank spots. Something pinged at the edge of her awareness. She followed its trail down the short hall to the bedroom, then the closet. The back of the closet wasn't a wall, but a door. Blue, green, yellow all swirled around the edges, the colors of Light, Shadow, and Balance. What lay on the other side of the door?

She reached out a hand, trying to get a sense of what awaited them on the other side.

"Kira!"

A hand clamped down on her shoulder, disrupting her extrasense. She turned to face Nansee. "Why in the name of the Light did you stop me?"

"Because there's a difference between using your extrasense to reach through the Veil of Reality and walking through yourself," the demigod said. "Humans cannot go where the gods tread."

"Oh, really? Then do you mind telling me why there's a Veil doorway in a Shadowchaser's closet?"

He looked grim. "I don't know, but I don't like it. There's no telling what's on the other side. It could be something, it could be nothing, or it could be Shadow. No matter what, you *cannot open that door.*"

The urgency in the demigod's voice was enough to convince her to leave it alone. "Why does a

Shadowchaser have a door beyond the Veil hidden in his bedroom? A door he hasn't told anyone about?"

"You know I don't have the answers for you, Kira Solomon," Nansee said sadly. "I would suggest, however, that we attempt to find your fellow Chaser. Something or someone constructed this door here specifically for him. If the doorway is still active, that means he hasn't traveled through it from this side yet. We have to find him and get this cut off."

"And if we don't?"

Nansee just looked at her. "Do you really want an unknown door to an unknown place to keep hanging around, used by who knows what?"

He had a point. "Can you do something to keep it contained for right now?"

He shook his head. "I say it's better to leave it than to tamper with it. Evidently it takes a Shadowchaser to trigger it, since even I didn't notice it the first time we searched through the flat. It may even be intended as a trap for a Chaser. But now that it's been enkindled, it would be best to keep everyone away from it. If you put one of your special blocks on the front door, that should prevent anyone from entering the flat while we track down Gunderson."

Wynne entered the bedroom. "Just heard from Zoo. Target's been spotted, headed this way."

Crap. "Okay. Douse the lights while I reinstall his shields. Nansee, tell the guys not to crowd Gunderson until he gets to the door."

Nansee's eyes flared blue, and Kira knew the demigod was relaying the message. She quickly returned to the front door and reset the original shields, adrenaline surging through her system. Gunderson had to be really green or really confident to return to his home base. Then again, he probably figured that Gilead had people watching the airports and ports. The only way he could get out, short of using smugglers or magically altering his appearance, was through that portal to who-knew-where.

Nansee placed a hand on Wynne's shoulder, effectively shrouding her life signature. Kira kept a small tendril of her extrasense out, but she couldn't feel Gunderson even bothering to scan. How in the name of Light had he managed to survive the Crucible and win his Lightblade?

The front door swung open. A lone figure stepped inside. He shut the front door before he snapped on the overhead light and placed his backpack on the coffee table. He fumbled it open, then shuddered with relief as he examined the contents. He was whisper-thin, pale blond, with ears too large for his head. In his leather bomber jacket and jeans, he looked as if he'd just gotten home from a hard day at Uni.

Aw, hell. He's just a kid.

Kira stepped forward. "Pavel Gunderson, I'd like to talk to you for a moment."

Gunderson froze, blue eyes widening in his pale, sweat-stained face. "Wh-who are you? What are you doing in my . . ." Belatedly he palmed his Lightblade. "Get out."

Kira raised her hands, her power dialed back to the lowest level she could manage. The male Shadowchaser didn't seem to be drenched in Shadow. If anything, fear poured off him. He looked desperate, and if he was desperate, one wrong move could make him dangerous. He was still a Shadowchaser, after all.

"You know I can't do that, Pavel," she said, deliberately using his first name. "People have been looking for you, and I've come here to get some answers."

Nansee removed the glamour that hid him and Wynne. Gunderson jerked in surprise, then crouched, his blade at the ready. "No! I won't let you stop me!"

"I don't want to fight you," Kira said, pulling her own Lightblade and ramping up her magic. "But I will if I have to, to protect myself and my friends. I'd rather we try talking, though. After all, Shadowchasers should stick together, don't you think?"

Gunderson stared at her blade, the blue glow concentrated in her hands. "Who are you?"

"Kira. Kira Solomon. Balm sent me to find you."

The blond-haired man laughed, and there was something desolate, hopeless, in the sound. "You? The Balm of Gilead sent the infamous renegade Chaser after me? That's irony for you. Not that it matters. I know there's no coming back from this."

Kira frowned. He certainly didn't sound like a man who'd completely turned his back on the Light to walk in Shadow. "There's always a chance." She had to hope there was. If not through Gilead, then through Khefar upholding his promise to her.

She dialed back her power again. "Look, there's no need for this. You're outnumbered. I just want to know what's going on, see if there's anything I can do to help. There's no need to spill blood."

Surprise slackened his jaw. "You're not here to kill me?"

"Dude, if I wanted to kill you, you'd be dead already. You didn't scan for intruders before you barged in, and it took you way too long to pull your Lightblade. You dropped off the radar with Gilead and you didn't think they'd send someone to your flat looking for you?"

He flushed scarlet. "I didn't see anyone looking for me. And I wasn't planning to stay long, I just needed to—" he broke off. "Are you sure you're not here to kill me?"

"Geez, take down one Fallen and a handful of halflings and people think you're bloodthirsty."

"So it's true?" Gunderson stared at her, then looked at Nansee and Wynne, who'd produced a pair of 9mm guns and had them trained on the male Chaser. Something filled Gunderson's eyes, something very close to hope. "Did you really Chase one of the Fallen back to Shadow?"

It was Nansee who answered. "She did."

Gunderson's shoulders slumped. "Sweet Mother of Light, maybe there's a chance!"

Kira frowned. "A chance for what?"

"You can help me." He reached for the backpack.

"Stop!" She aimed her Lightblade at him. He froze, hands above his head. "Gunderson, I think you can understand why I'm a little wary of you right now. You dropped off the grid. No one knows what you or your handler are up to. That makes people think the worst."

"I haven't slid!" he exclaimed, flushing bright red. "I didn't have a choice!"

"I want to believe you. I want to help you. For me to do that, though, you need to calm down, stop with the sudden moves, and tell me what the hell is going on." She gestured at the bag. "Did you take the Vessel of Nun from that collector?"

"Yes." Tears streaked his face. "It's there in the bag."

Yes! Kira tamped down her elation. She had to keep her emotions in check. Gunderson was on the verge of losing it. She didn't want to be the one to kick him over the edge. "Why did you steal it?"

"Adam. I took it for Adam. And now that you're here, you can help me get him back."

They had the Vessel of Nun.

It was a graceful alabaster amphora, perhaps twenty inches long, with a slender base, oval-shaped body, and curved mouth. Sweeping curved handles attached to the neck, enabling the vessel to be carried. It looked like many of the containers she'd seen used to carry wine, except this one was engraved with the likenesses of three separate gods, their names carved above them: Nun, with his palm frond as staff and waved rippled skin; Satet, with her crown of Upper Egypt adorned with a pair of antelope horns; and Hapy, the personification of the Nile, with full breasts and belly and his head adorned with papyrus plants.

Kira handed the jar to Khefar. Even through her gloves, she could feel the power of the container, the ancient magic that still imbued it, waiting for the right person to call it forth. "I know you'll keep it safe," she said as she passed it over. "I need to handle the Shadowchaser."

Khefar had seen a number of Shadowchasers over his lifetime, but he didn't think he'd ever seen any like

Pavel Gunderson. For one thing, the male Chaser seemed young, far younger than the twenty-two he claimed to be. There was a greenness to him, a lack of experience that Khefar had seen in recruits many a time over the ages. They were usually the first ones to die in battle.

Gunderson sat on his sofa, chewing on his fingernails. Wynne and Zoo flanked him, standing at the ends of the couch, their weapons down but ready. Kira stood on the other side of the coffee table. She still had her blade out, but it hung loosely in her hand. "Okay, so why don't you tell me what's going on."

"I was only trying to set everything right again."

He reached for Kira, but Khefar blocked him. "The time for plain speaking is now, Shadowchaser."

Gunderson looked up at both of them. "Adam," he said. "I did this for Adam."

Khefar looked at Kira. She stared at the other Chaser, equal parts anger and disgust wreathing her expression. "He means Adam Marshall. His handler."

"He's more than just my handler," Gunderson interjected. "He's my everything. I'd give my life for Adam. If you had a handler, you'd understand."

Kira flinched, but remained silent. Wynne broke the silence. "Dude, that's so not the way you ask for help."

"I know. I know, and I'm sorry." He bowed his head. "But everybody knows about Kira Solomon. Even when I was going through training on Santa Costa, you were the one everybody talked about. When someone said 'the Chaser,' you knew they were talking about Solomon. She's the baddest and the best, so tough that she doesn't need a handler, so dangerous no one wants to work with her."

"Again, not helping," Wynne said.

"It's okay, Wynne," Kira said. "I already know what they say about me." She sheathed her Lightblade.

"Kira . . ." Khefar warned. She might trust her fellow Chaser, but the rest of them didn't.

"It's all right, Khefar." She looked at the Nubian, then turned her attention to the male Shadowchaser. "Pavel understands that I don't need my Lightblade to kill him, don't you, Pavel?"

The blond man nodded, then ran his hands through his hair. "You might as well go ahead and do it. If I don't get the Vessel of Nun to Cairo tomorrow, they're going to kill Adam."

"And 'they' are?"

"Shadowlings."

Kira looked at Khefar. He shook his head. He didn't have any idea why Shadowlings would want an ancient water jug, but he wanted to find out. "Why would Shadowlings want the Vessel of Nun?"

"I don't know. They didn't tell me, and I didn't ask."

"How did they get to you?" Kira asked.

"We were ambushed during a Chase in Lisbon. They took Adam and told me that I had to steal the Vessel and bring it to them or they'd kill him. I thought it was in Cairo but then I found out it had been stolen. I did some research and discovered that it had somehow made its way here and was in a private collection. The collector has a history of buying stolen artifacts. He has all the Normal security, but I had no problem breaking into his place and taking the jug back. I contacted the people in Egypt and they told me to bring the Vessel to Cairo tomorrow."

"How long have you been a Chaser?" Kira asked.

"What?" Gunderson frowned. "Why? What does that have to do with anything?"

"You've got to be a new Chaser," Khefar said, agreeing with Kira. "Not that it's much of an excuse."

"Excuse? Excuse for what? They've got my handler. I want him back. You have to help me!"

"I don't *have* to do anything now that we've got the Vessel of Nun back," Kira retorted. "You had your handler snatched right from under your nose, if I'm to believe you. Instead of contacting Gilead London, you took it upon yourself to become an agent of Shadow. You know the Commission doesn't take kindly to Chasers who slide. Any other Chaser would have killed you first, and then where would your handler be?"

Khefar shifted beside her, not wanting to step on her toes, but wanting to deflect some of her emotion.

"I don't want to work for Shadow, but they've got Adam! All we have to do is take the Vessel through the portal."

Then he does know of its existence. What more will he tell us? "What portal, Gunderson?" Kira asked.

"It's like a doorway. They made a portal between here and Cairo so I wouldn't get detained when I left the country." The young man's exasperation was mounting. "I *have* to get to Cairo and save Adam! You said we Chasers have to stick together. Are you so cold that you'd just let someone else's handler die?"

Kira settled her hands on her hips and closed her eyes for a long moment, reining in her anger with visible effort.

After counting to ten, she opened her eyes and looked at the Chaser again. Khefar spoke before she could.

"Where is it?" Khefar asked.

Gunderson's gaze shifted. "They said it's not far."

The truth, but not the whole truth. There is a chance Gunderson is unaware the portal is in his closet. But it is slight. Kira leaned forward. "Are you telling me the truth, Gunderson, or do I have to sift through your memories?"

"I'm telling you the truth," he answered, lifting his chin and managing to hold her gaze. "I know what you can do. If you think you need to read me, go ahead. As long as you get Adam back, I'll do whatever you want."

Kira looked at Wynne and Zoo. "Watch him for me. He makes a move, shoot him." She moved away from the male Chaser, then motioned for Khefar and Nansee to join her. "Nansee, can you shield us?"

"Done," the spider said. Kira, Khefar, and the demigod could no longer be heard by Gunderson or the Marlowes.

Kira sighed. "Idiot. Stupid, clueless idiot."

"You're angry with him."

"Damn right I'm angry. Not just anyone can or should be a Shadowchaser. It takes a special type of being to be molded into a Shadowchaser. Training is grueling and takes every bit of mental and physical stamina a body's got. It takes years of preparation and even then, most people wash out during their final exam."

She glared at Gunderson's back. "I don't know how this guy managed to survive to claim his Lightblade, but he should be made of stronger stuff than what I've seen so far. If this is the type of Shadowchaser that Gilead's putting out these days, the world is in serious trouble."

"He's suffering the loss of his handler, Kira," Khefar said quietly, though he did agree with her about the caliber of Chaser. "You are each different, and you express that suffering in different ways."

She ran her fingers through her braids. "So what do you think?"

Her question surprised him. "You seek my advice?"

"Any reason why I shouldn't?"

Plenty, beginning with the fact that they were dealing with Shadowlings. "You've never asked my advice before, certainly not for anything dealing with Gilead business."

"We're still in the early stages of knowing each other. I think I can manage a few more surprises for you." She sobered. "What do you think of Gunderson?"

"I don't think he's telling us everything he knows," Khefar said. "But I think his concern for his handler is very real. You're thinking of helping him, aren't you?"

She nodded. "A Chaser without his handler is almost like a Chaser without her Lightblade. We're bonded to our blades through a trial that not everyone lives through. Our handlers train us for that trial and are there to help us heal and come back from the extreme mental and physical exertion. We have to trust them even as they send us out into danger. We are lost without our handlers. It's devastating."

He knew she was talking about Comstock as much as Gunderson's handler. Of course, she hadn't bonded to Comstock during her Shadowchaser training, but during her time at university. She'd bonded with him as daughter to father, and that made his loss all the more devastating. And, like Gunderson, Kira had lost her first handler. Nico. She had been young, in love, and she'd fallen apart after his death. Gunderson's relationship with Adam seemed similar. He'd lost more than a handler—and he did not have Kira's personal inner strength.

"Gunderson is obviously in love with his handler."

Kira nodded. "Which means he'll do whatever he can to save Marshall, damn the consequences. We should at least try to manage those consequences."

"We're going to try to save his handler from Shadowlings?"

"I don't know if Marshall is still alive, but I think Gunderson would know if he was dead. I don't know if the Shadowlings holding Marshall will keep their word and give the handler back if they get the Vessel of Nun."

"Neither do I," Khefar said, "but I guess that's not going to stop you from trying to help."

"Balm asked me to get to the bottom of this, and that's what I intend to do." She lowered her voice. "Besides, we should at least recover Marshall's body. Gunderson will need that sort of closure."

Khefar hadn't thought she'd do otherwise, though he would have preferred putting the Vessel of Nun in a safe place before going after Shadowlings. Yes, Kira had a duty to Gilead, but she had a duty to Ma'at first.

"Khefar. We recovered the Vessel. We've done what we were asked to do. Do you know where we're supposed to take it?"

"No." He had to admit that he didn't know. The

vision had contained no clue. In all his time on the planet, he'd heard precious little about any amphora capable of holding the primordial waters of the universe. He'd heard no direct references; seen no images, no wall paintings, nothing. "But we should probably go to Cairo until we hear something definite. Wherever the Vessel of Nun is supposed to go, it's got to be somewhere in Egypt."

"Which is where Gunderson says he was supposed to take it," Kira reminded him. She turned to the demigod. "Nansee, is there any way to know for certain if the portal we found will get us to Cairo?"

Nansee's expression soured. "I can try to check it out. But a portal made by someone else, especially if it's made by Shadow, might not be a good thing for me to get involved with. In fact, this entire endeavor may need to be off-limits for me from here on out."

"Right. There's no telling what they'd bring to Balance you. But there are already Shadowlings involved, and whoever's coordinating them. Maybe it would be all right if you created a passage to get us to Cairo. That's not interference, it's merely providing transportation. Can you do that?"

The old man looked thoughtful. "I travel that way all the time, of course. I've taken our Nubian through when we've needed to move quickly."

"I don't really think that's a good idea, Kira," Khefar interjected. "It's not a pleasant experience."

"Why not?"

"It's not unlike being turned inside out," Khefar explained. "You're neither here nor there, you're somewhere in between."

"Okay, so we won't be flying the friendly skies." Kira looked at the other Chaser, still huddled between Wynne and her husband, then turned back. "Somehow we've got to get to Cairo by tomorrow. Obviously Gunderson is planning to use the portal to get there, but I'm not too keen on us going through a portal we don't know anything about."

"You and me both," Khefar said, barely suppressing a shudder. He always threw up after that sort of travel. The natural mind just wasn't able to handle something so out of the ordinary. "Let's book a commercial flight, or better yet, see if we can use Balm's plane instead. We don't have to be in Cairo tomorrow."

"Khefar." She wrapped her fingers around his wrist. He wondered if she had done it deliberately or if she'd already gotten used to touching him. "We *do* need to be in Cairo tomorrow, and not just for the sake of Adam Marshall. We need to find out who's behind this. Whoever it is expects Gunderson and the Vessel to come through that portal. Getting on a jet with our ancient pot might get us to Cairo, but it won't get us closer to finding any answers. We have someone who organized Shadowlings into taking on a Chaser and kidnapping his handler. Not 'just because,' or for fun, but to coerce the Chaser into doing their dirty work for them."

She leaned closer to him. "This wouldn't have happened to most Shadowchasers. I know a few who went into the field while I was growing up in Gilead and a couple of others who were part of my graduating class, so to speak. None of those Chasers are pushovers. None of them would lose their handler without a life-or-death struggle. Someone targeted this guy. This particular guy, to get this particular object. We've got to find out why."

A chill skittered down Khefar's back, that sense that he'd relied on from his very first skirmish. "You suspect there's another Fallen out there, someone planning something big."

She nodded. "Someone who's been around long enough or who's old enough to know about these ancient Egyptian artifacts. Someone sent Shadowlings after this vessel, just like someone sent Shadowlings after your dagger."

The implications of her words were hard to wrap his mind around. "You think it's the same Fallen? This Enig?"

"I don't know. Maybe." Something painful slid through her eyes. "Or it could be someone he was working with or for."

"Someone more powerful than one of the Fallen? Like who?"

"I've got some suspicions, but I really don't want to think about it, and I certainly don't want to speak it into being." She rubbed her hands along her arms, trying to dispel a sudden chill. If whoever was calling the shots on the other side was who she thought, they were in serious crapola. "Like you, I'm not interested in risking the Vessel of Nun to find out who's been playing Gunderson. Even if it wasn't used to hold back the Nile, it's an authentic artifact of ancient Egypt. We'll keep it safe until we find out what Ma'at and Isis want us to do with it."

"Then what do we do with him?" Khefar asked, nodding toward Gunderson.

"I have an idea." She turned to Nansee. "It's been a while since you've played a trick. Think you're up for one now?"

The old man's eyes twinkled. "Absolutely."

"Good. Here's what we're going to do: Khefar and I will stay here with Gunderson so he can lead us to whoever is calling the shots."

"You're betting our lives on the hope that Gunderson's portal will take us to Cairo," Khefar pointed out.

"I know. But Gunderson's got to get there. The portal has to be a direct connection. It's the only logical explanation."

"It takes a singular mind to use logic to explain the magical." He shook his head. "What about the Marlowes?"

"That's up to Nansee." She turned back to Nansee. "I need you to get Wynne and Zoo and our gear to Cairo as painlessly as possible. I don't know if Balm can provide air transport there quickly enough, but if you think you can convince her, go ahead."

The demigod blanched. "I will have the Marlowes ask first. If that fails and they refuse to travel my way, I will ask the Balm of Gilead for her plane. But you should know that will make me beholden to her, which means that you will be beholden to me."

Kira nodded. "Understood. And I have one more request to add to my tally."

"What's that?"

"Normally when Chasers have to retrieve an artifact, we work with the closest section office to switch out the real magical artifact with a replica, or wipe the owner's memories of the object. I need a replica Vessel of Nun. It doesn't have to be perfect. All we need to do is convince Gunderson that he has the real one. His knowledge of ancient Egypt is practically nonexistent. If he hadn't been provided a description of what to steal and stolen it, you could probably slap an ankh on a bamboo salad bowl and he'd think he had the real artifact."

"Harsh," Khefar murmured, "but no less true."

Kira turned back to the demigod. "Can you do this? Can you make me a replica of the Vessel of Nun?"

The demigod considered it. "Well, it's just weaving together a few molecules, isn't it? Nothing I can't handle."

"Good. We'll switch it out while you, Wynne, and Zoo take your leave. You guys get the real artifact to Cairo while Khefar and I take on whatever Gunderson's mixed up with. We can meet at the main entrance to the Cairo market when we're done. Sound good?"

"It's the best thing we've got," Khefar said.

"It's the only thing we've got," Kira corrected. "Let's do this."

Anansi dropped his sound shield.

Chapter 13

Kira crossed the room to Gunderson. "Hey, Pavel?"

The young Chaser stopped chewing on his thumbnail and looked up. "Yes?"

"I don't suppose you have some tea? Making plans always goes a lot smoother over a proper cup."

"Oh. Of course." He rose to his feet, movements unsteady, then made his way to the kitchen area.

Kira gestured at Khefar. The Nubian stood in front of the coffee table to block the view as Anansi sat on the couch. "Do you have something other than Earl Grey? Maybe a Darjeeling?" he asked the male Chaser.

"I'll look." He took the kettle to the sink to fill it.

Kira cautioned the Marlowes to silence, then nodded at Anansi. The demigod took an earthenware vase off the table beside the sofa, then tucked it into his coat. For a brief moment his eyes flashed multifaceted blue. When he pulled his hand back into the open, she saw that he held a stunningly precise duplicate of the Vessel of Nun. In his quick-handed way he made the exchange, tucking the true artifact into his coat pocket against all known laws of physics.

The old man stood. "You know, Kira, perhaps I should skip the tea. I need to take the Marlowes back to get the rest of our gear."

"Good idea," Kira said as Gunderson rejoined them. "If we're going to help Gunderson take on Shadowlings and get his handler back, we need to be prepared. Khefar and I will stay here with Gunderson and come up with a plan. We'll see you guys back here in a little while."

They left.

Gunderson seemed relieved the others had gone. He managed a wan smile and looked at Kira. "Thank you, Solomon. I appreciate what you're doing."

"No problem, and please call me Kira."

"All right then, Kira." He sat on the couch, staring at what was apparently the Vessel of Nun sitting on his coffee table. "Hard to believe that Shadowlings would kidnap a Chaser's handler for some old jar they could have stolen themselves."

"That jar isn't just any old Egyptian artifact."

"Well, I figured it had to be special in some way, considering the trouble they've gone through to get it." He looked like a sullen teenager being grounded for staying out past curfew again.

"This amphora is called the Vessel of Nun," Kira said, lightly touching a finger to it. "How familiar are you with Egyptian mythology?"

He shook his head. "Not very. I'm more into Greco-Roman history."

"This is Nun," Kira said, carefully turning the urn so that Gunderson could see the image of the god on the amphora's surface. "He's the deification of the primordial waters of creation," she explained. "This is Satet. She's a fertility and flood goddess. In her hands, the Vessel of Nun is used to call Hapy, the personification of the Nile, who makes the annual flooding that brings fertile soil to Egypt. We're not sure how it works, but apparently the amphora can also be misused to cause drought or ravaging flooding. And if the Vessel of Nun were missing for too long or destroyed, the primordial waters of Nun would break free."

"What would happen then?" Gunderson asked.

"A great flood of more than biblical proportions," Khefar answered. "In other words, there wouldn't be an ark capable of saving anyone."

The male Chaser scoffed. "Nobody believes that though, right? I mean they have dams and irrigation systems in place in Egypt that control the river. There's no danger of uncontrolled flooding, and certainly no danger of this Nun thing breaking free."

Kira stared at the young Chaser until his smile faded. "No one would believe that your job is to police half-human, half-demon hybrids between here and Central Europe," she said quietly. "No one would believe that all of the world's myths are anchored in reality. Shadowlings from another dimension have kidnapped your handler and demand this amphora in exchange for his release, and yet you want to deny the power this vessel represents?"

He blushed. "That was wrong of me. I apologize."

"Apology accepted." Kira shrugged to hide her disdain. She was more than ready to be done with the young Chaser. He shouldn't have been sent out into the world. A researcher, perhaps, but not a Chaser. What the hell was going on with the quality of recruits in the Gilead Commission?

The kettle whistled. Gunderson returned to the kitchen area to gather tea supplies.

"Don't worry about the tea," Kira called out. "Especially since the others won't be back for a while."

"Sure." He rejoined them. "Is that old man your new handler?"

"Who? Nansee?" She started to shake her head, then caught Khefar's gaze. "Why, yes, yes he is. Gilead figured that it would do me good to have someone with a bit more, uh, maturity to offset my rebelliousness."

"And what about him?" He jerked a thumb at Khefar.

"Khefar's a living encyclopedia," she answered, keeping her face straight with effort. "You'd be surprised at the amount of history he knows. It's almost as if he had been there."

"You have a whole team around you," Gunderson said with a sigh. "It must be nice."

"After you've been out in the field for a while, you learn who will have your back and who you can depend on," she said. "I've learned that it's hard to do this job without people you can trust."

"Like Adam." He shifted anxiously. "He's the best. So smart and patient. I miss him."

"We'll get him back. I promise."

He nodded, his gaze on the jar. He looked incredibly young, his emotions broadcasting all over his face. "I know."

Khefar stirred. "It would help if you told us more about the Shadowlings who approached you. Where was it and how long ago? How do you contact them?"

The blond Chaser fidgeted, his hair catching the

light. "I think I told you that Adam and I were in Lisbon. We'd just finished with a minor Chase involving drug smuggling and had decided to take a quick break before coming back here and completing the mountain of paperwork the Commission seems to love. No offense."

"None taken," Kira murmured. "It's a lot of paperwork. I hate it too. Go on."

"Well, it was very early in the morning and we were heading back to our hotel, the Anjo Azul in Bairro Alto. We were just two guys out having a bit of fun coming back from a club. I didn't think anything would happen."

"You didn't have your Lightblade on you," Kira guessed.

Gunderson's flush was answer enough, but he said, "I didn't think I'd get into the club with it."

"And you obviously didn't think you would be bothered by any Shadowlings or hybrids," Khefar added.

"I wasn't even in my Chaser gear," the blond man said, his ears bright red. "One night. All we wanted was one normal night. That's all."

"Go on," Kira prodded, torn between commiseration and exasperation. She could understand Gunderson's desire, but she couldn't excuse it. She'd never excused herself after she'd lost Nico, why would she pardon him? "What happened?"

"We were ambushed," Gunderson told them. "There was hardly anyone about at that time of morning. A group of hybrids and Shadowlings literally came out of nowhere. Adam and I fought them as best we could, but they outnumbered us. And then they took him."

"Took him where?" Kira asked.

"I don't know! They just opened up some sort of doorway or something and took him through. He vanished. If I knew where, don't you think I would have gone after them and tried to rescue him already?"

"Which would have been a suicide mission, and done neither you nor your handler much good," she reminded him. She only had a few years on him, but she felt far older. He was just too green to be a full-fledged Shadowchaser, and it didn't sound like his handler was all that experienced either. "Who told you to take the Vessel of Nun?"

"Their leader." Gunderson shuddered. "She's the one who can make the portals. She looked human, but a bit off, you know?"

Khefar leaned forward. "Describe her."

"Brunette, slender, with yellow-green eyes that glowed sometimes. A little shorter than Kira, Eurasian, I think, maybe Armenian. But when she smiled, all you could see were pointed teeth, shark teeth. The other hybrids and Shadowlings did what she said without question. I think they were scared of her."

Kira looked at Khefar. He looked as unhappy with the news as she was. Shadowlings were offspring of Chaos. Power was all they recognized, all that they feared. For them to gather, to organize, hinted at someone with considerable power and intellect. Someone dangerous.

"Does she have a name?" There were a few named agents of Shadow, but the fact that the Fallen could simply burn through their parasitic use of a human Avatar and claim another made maintaining and updating a database cumbersome.

"Marit. She didn't tell me a last name."

"She's the one who told you to steal the Vessel of Nun?"

Gunderson nodded. "She showed me a picture of it. It was in Egypt up until about three months ago. Still don't understand why they wanted me to take it instead of them going in themselves. If they can make portals and knew where this jug was, why didn't they just make a portal in this guy's gallery, grab the thing, and go?"

"It's an object of high magic, god magic," Khefar said. "Humans can hold it with little to no ill effect, provided they don't try to tap into its power. Someone attached to the temple of Satet would be able to hold it, but it's probably too dangerous for anyone or anything claimed by Shadow."

I hope Satet's all right with those claimed by other Egyptian goddesses, Kira thought, staring at the Vessel of Nun. Nansee had made an excellent substitute, duplicating the original's beautiful simplicity and the ancient style of the figures etched into its surface.

Khefar gestured to the amphora. "What time are you supposed to meet your accompli—ah, the others—tomorrow?"

Gunderson dropped his eyes, then chewed on a ragged fingernail. "They said they'd meet me here and get me to Egypt. I'm guessing they're going to tell me to go to the portal that Marit made." He concentrated on the floor.

"Why don't you turn in, Pavel?" Kira suggested.

"If we're going to rescue Marshall, we need to be in top form."

"Oh, okay." He jerked to his feet, full of nervous energy. "I—I just wanted to say thanks again. I know this goes against Gilead protocol. I appreciate you taking a risk like this for me."

"I'm just maintaining my rebellious reputation." She smiled. "Go get some rest."

With a last look at what he thought was the Vessel of Nun, Gunderson headed toward his bedroom, softly closing the door behind him.

"No click," Khefar mouthed to her.

"I know," she mouthed back. "He knows the portal's in his closet."

Khefar spoke too softly for the Chaser in the adjacent room to overhear. "If he didn't before, he probably saw it or sensed it as soon as he entered the bedroom, especially if it's keyed to his energy signature."

"Nah. He knows," Kira whispered. "The fact that he didn't tell us about it makes me think he's going to try to make a move without us."

"We're not going to let that happen."

"No, we won't. So now we wait." She raised her voice. "Wanna thumb-wrestle for the couch?"

"No, I'll let you take it. I'll take the chair." Khefar's reply was also loud enough for Gunderson to hear.

Kira stretched out on the couch while Khefar took the large stuffed chair, carefully propping his booted feet on the coffee table, the Vessel between his heels. "A living encyclopedia? Did you really go there?"

"I didn't lie. I just didn't elaborate."

"You know how to live on the edge, Kira

Solomon," he said, his voice a mixture of awe and envy. Khefar resumed whispering. "You think this is going to work?"

"Yeah." She pulled her coat snug, then carefully settled against the cushions, making sure her skin was completely covered. "He all but telegraphed his intent. All we've got to do now is get on with the fake sleeping."

"This wasn't how I envisioned sleeping with you tonight."

Her eyes popped open. "Did I hear you right?"

He gave her a quizzical glance. "What, are you content with sharing only one night together?"

"No." Not with her drought of touch. "I was just planning on taking each day as it comes, like you said. I don't want there to be any weirdness between us."

"Me either. I just enjoy holding you, though at times I think it's like holding a live grenade." He glanced toward the bedroom. "Maybe we should talk about this at a later time."

"Sounds good. In Cairo?"

"In Cairo. It's a date."

Kira settled down on the couch again, forcing herself to breathe deeply and evenly. Hard to do when her mind was racing like a cheetah. While she had figured Khefar, being a guy, would want more than one night, she hadn't expected him to come right out and say it. She wasn't sure how to handle that and, with Wynne and Zoo now with them, how to handle her friends' knowledge of her private life.

She couldn't worry about that. Being able to touch anyone, especially Khefar, was a gift. She intended to cherish it and enjoy it as much as possible because soon enough the gift would be taken away again.

Less than half an hour later, she felt the air pressure change. Gunderson had opened his bedroom door. Kira kept her breathing regular. She heard Khefar gently snoring as the male Chaser crept over to the coffee table and retrieved the impostor Vessel of Nun.

She cracked her eyes open, watched the slim form creep back to the bedroom. A flash of green, then silence.

Khefar switched on the side lamp as Kira sat up. She quickly pulled out her satellite phone, put it on speaker, then tapped a number. "Hey, Zoo. He's gone. We're getting ready to go through."

"Looks like you were right," Zoo said. "Nansee's getting ready to transport us to Cairo. Says he doesn't want to take the time a flight would need." He paused. "This is gonna hurt, isn't it?"

She looked at Khefar, who nodded. "Probably."

"Have no fear," Nansee said, as if he were in the room with them. "I'll treat the Marlowes as if they were my own children."

"I'd rather you treat them better than that."

"Cheeky girl." Nansee coughed. "Kira, make sure that Khefar calls to me if you need me to get you out of there," he admonished. "Go in with blades drawn."

"We will, Nansee, no worries."

"I'm serious, Chaser. I don't trust that Gunderson boy. This tale only ends well if we all meet again in Cairo."

Kira let Khefar pull her to her feet. "I understand, Nansee. Don't worry about us. We'll look before we leap. And if we end up somewhere other than Cairo, we'll give you a shout. Zoo, take care of Wynne and everything else, all right?"

"You got it. See you on the flip side."

Kira disconnected, then tucked the sat phone into her coat pocket. "I think your demigod fancies himself a handler for real."

"Mother hen is more like it," Khefar said, making no move to release her hand. "It's probably a good idea for you to go through with your gloves off and your Lightblade in your hand. I'll keep the Dagger of Kheferatum sheathed for now and just have my guns."

"Sure. But I need you to let go."

"Oh. Yeah." He dropped her hand as they entered Gunderson's bedroom and stopped in front of his closet. The blue, green, and yellow lights still swirled along the edge of the door.

Kira stripped off her gloves, then pulled her Lightblade. She nodded at Khefar, as ready as she could get. The familiar kick of adrenaline swept through her, a Chase hitting its stride. Action of some kind lay on the other side of that door, and she craved it. She was more than ready to leave London behind.

Khefar jerked the door open. Something lay beyond the swirling, changing doorway, some place that looked at lot like the Giza Plateau. "You ready?" he asked.

"Nothing to it but to do it," she replied, then stepped through.

Chapter 14

Light flared around her, bright and flickering. Her body felt wrenched and twisted in a hundred different directions, and it was all she could do to keep her grip on her Lightblade. Just when she thought that her body would rip itself apart, that she'd be reduced to screams and pieces, she broke through to the other side.

Kira hit the ground hard, gasping, her stomach threatening to empty as she gagged on a mouthful of sand. A surge of pressure squeezed her eardrums, then Khefar dropped to the ground beside her. He sucked in a huge rush of air as if he'd been suffocating, then rolled over.

"By the left eye of Horus, that hurt," he groaned. "But still less painful than what Nansee takes me through—for his own amusement, I believe. Did you make it through all right?"

"I'll let you know when I find the rest of my insides." She considered it a small victory that she could sit up beside him. "So it looks like Gunderson was right, and we're somewhere across the Nile from Cairo."

He straightened to a sitting position, surveying their surroundings. His grimace froze. "We're not."

"What do you mean, we're not?" Kira asked. "I'm

sitting in a pile of sand and rocks. I see pyramids. Where else could we be?"

"Look."

She looked. The city lay to the east across the river, the Giza Plateau stretching to the west behind them . . . except it wasn't quite the plateau she'd visited with Comstock a few years before. This Cairo didn't seem to have sunlight, just a late-day sky that couldn't make up its mind whether it wanted to be green, blue, yellow, or choked with golden brass clouds. But most of all, there were no people. Anywhere. Giza was one of the most popular tourist destinations in the world. But there was not a soul in sight.

She surveyed the replica of the Giza Plateau. The more she looked, the more wrong it became. There were the three main pyramids of Khufu, Khafre, and Menkaure and their respective mortuary temples with causeways separating them from the valley temples; the smaller pyramids for the various queens; the legendary and awkwardly shaped Great Sphinx, whose face seemed so different from its body, though she couldn't place this face on this version.

Surrounding those were the eastern and western cemeteries of nobles, the mastabas dotting the landscape. But there were walls bounding the entire complex, making the plateau seem even higher above the surrounding area. Further to the west lay a structure that looked like a temple, except no temple existed there in real life. Where the city of Cairo encroached in the real world, here it shimmered in the distance, far on the other side of the river that ran blue-black in the odd light.

Cairo, the real Cairo, was stuffed with more than sixteen million people who were out and about at all times of the day, especially at night. Yet she and Khefar seemed to be the only living beings in this world. Nothing moved in the twilight landscape, as if someone had built a movie set of Cairo to scale but forgotten to call the actors in.

"What in the world . . . ?"

"That's the problem," Khefar said, offering her a hand up. "I don't think it's in the world. Not our world, anyway."

"That's just peachy." She slapped away most of the dusty, gritty not-quite-sand. "Something else you know about that I don't. I expect a full explanation when we're done here."

He nodded. "Of course."

"So we aren't in Kansas, Cairo, or Oz. How are we supposed to find Gunderson now?"

As if in answer, a shout cut through the still air of not-Giza. Khefar lifted his guns. "That sounded as if it came from Khafre's temple."

Khefar took off at a brisk trot, weapons ready. Kira followed cautiously, not sure what to expect. Being in this twilight place felt like reaching through the Veil. It felt like a place of magic, ancient magic, unknown magic. It made her glad that the original Vessel of Nun was safe with Wynne, Zoo, and Anansi.

As for who wanted the Vessel of Nun, they were about to find out.

They came around the grit-covered hill and cautiously approached the southern entrance of Khafre's valley temple. The archaeologist in Kira wanted to pause and marvel at the inscription dedicating the entryway to Hathor, to touch the huge stone slabs that served as the wall. Even in this strange landscape the vestibule was an impressive display of pink Aswan granite and white alabaster floor. They entered another doorway to find themselves in a T-shaped hall populated by more than a dozen pillars of the same pink granite. The strange swirling sky was visible through the columns, casting the entire complex into darkness punctuated by flashes of blue and yellow light.

Gunderson screamed again. It was a scream more of rage than pain. Sounds of struggle, the clang of a Lightblade.

Kira and Khefar stopped at the entrance to the temple, pressing their backs against a granite column. She touched Khefar's weapons, charging them with Light magic. "Don't know if this will work here or not, but Gunderson needs help."

Khefar nodded. "Ready?"

Kira held up her Lightblade, then counted to three on her other hand. On three, they entered the temple.

Gunderson faced three Shadowlings dressed in flowing desert robes. He stood in the far corner of one of the rooms, a still form on the alabaster floor behind him. He held the amphora dangling in his right hand and his Lightblade, an hourglass-shaped Roman Pugio dagger, in the other.

"You said if I brought you the jar you'd give me my handler back!"

One of the Shadowlings laughed, sharp pointed teeth crowding her mouth. She must be the leader,

Marit. She pointed to the still form on the ground. "And there is your handler."

"He's dead!" Gunderson screamed.

"You did not say you wanted him back alive," Marit sneered. "You should have been more clear in your negotiations."

"You're going to pay for this!" Gunderson threw the amphora down. Even though she knew it wasn't real, Kira's heart still plummeted as the Vessel hit the hard alabaster floor. A sharp crack cut through the charged silence as one handle and the bottom third of the amphora snapped clean off.

"Bastard!"

Gunderson laughed, the sound clearly proving he was beyond help or care. "You didn't say you wanted it whole. Guess you should have been more clear in your negotiations."

The leader of the Shadowlings struck Gunderson hard across the jaw. To his credit, the Chaser didn't fall. He swung his Lightblade in a wide arc, catching the female across her sternum. She stumbled back, then turned to the other Shadowlings. "Attack him!"

Kira and Khefar swung into action. Khefar fired two shots, dropping the two males. Kira advanced with her Lightblade blazing. Bullets, even bullets infused with Light magic, didn't keep Shadowlings down for good. Only Lightblades could send the creatures back to Shadow.

The wounded Shadowlings struggled to regain their footing, their jaws unzipping into saliva-dripping snarls. Kira plunged her blade into the second Shadowling's chest as Gunderson broke away from the female. Kira called her power, wrapping her hands around the wrists of the second being as the third one swiped at Gunderson again. The male Shadowchaser cried out, dropped his blade.

Khefar dove in, grabbed Gunderson's blade. Blue-white light flared, almost blinding as it arced through the chamber, bouncing off the granite walls. A thudding sound, another shriek of pain. By the time the light faded, the two male Shadowlings were down, disappearing into the dust. The female and the shattered amphora were nowhere to be seen.

Gunderson sank to the ground, cradling his handler in his arms. Marshall's pale, still face was young, so painfully young, too young to be that of a handler for a new Shadowchaser. Neither of these boys should have been sent from Santa Costa so unseasoned. Balm and the Council had a lot to answer for.

Blood welled across Gunderson's cheek and down his left arm. "You followed me. You knew I'd steal back the jar and bring it here."

"We figured you'd try to exchange the amphora for Marshall," Kira explained, unable to quell the sadness, the memory. A few weeks ago she'd been in the same position, kneeling beside Bernie after he'd been killed by a seeker demon.

"But he's dead. He's dead and the Vessel is broken." He lowered his head.

"It's time to go, Gunderson," Khefar said, grabbing the man by the back of his shirt and hauling him to his feet. The Nubian's face was set in stoic lines. Someone had to be cold, Kira knew. Someone had to keep it together, at least outwardly. Who else but a man who'd seen tens of thousands of deaths in four thousand years?

Kira sheathed her Lightblade, then touched the fallen handler. Images slammed into her, pounding her mind's eye. Questions, denial, pain, poison, sorrow. It took her a moment to separate herself from the vision, from the conflation of Marshall and Comstock. "Marshall killed himself. All handlers are equipped with fast-acting poison to be used in event of capture so they can't be tortured into providing information. Marshall died with honor. And the real amphora is safe in the real world."

"You knew. All along you knew." A sob choked him.

"I wanted to be wrong, Pavel," Kira said softly. "I'm sorry."

"We've got to get out of here," Khefar urged, helping Kira to her feet. "I doubt they were the only Shadowlings in this place. The female probably went for reinforcements."

"Agreed. Can you get Marshall? I'll watch your back."

"All right." Khefar lifted the handler's body onto his shoulder as Kira retrieved his guns, then sent a pulse of power into them, charging the bullets with her extrasense.

The male Chaser stared at the spot where his handler had lain, tears streaming down his dirt-stained cheeks. Kira knew that look well, knew that utter loss and desolation. "Gunderson. Pavel." She waited until he looked at her. "You need to honor your handler's memory. You don't do that by dying in some gods-forsaken alternate dimension. Take him home, bury him, then live to fight another day."

"You're right." Something bleak and resolute slid across his face. "He wouldn't have died if I was a better Shadowchaser."

"Then get better," she said, making her voice deliberately harsh to get him moving. "Get better, then come back and get revenge. It's what Shadowchasers do for their handlers."

Tucking one of the guns into her belt, Kira pulled on her left glove so she could physically drag Gunderson back to the portal if necessary. He moved clumsily, shock beginning to set in. She kept the second gun in her right hand, still glowing with power. She didn't trust this strange place. There were too many Shadows lurking for her liking, the Light a pale imitation of itself.

Balm. Can you hear me, Mother?

Kira? You sound so far away. Did you find Gunderson and Marshall?

Yes. And the missing artifact. The handler's dead, and Gunderson's wounded by a Shadowling. Not seriously, but I think losing his handler is the greater injury. He'll need healing and refinement. Can you send a team to Shoreditch? We're bringing them through a portal in Gunderson's flat, and it's going to need to be sealed.

Electrified silence on Balm's end. *Did you say a portal? Where are you?*

Not sure. Kira scanned the landscape as they scurried down the causeway. She could see the outline of the portal, the faint image of Gunderson's bedroom, and the real world, beyond. Not close enough for comfort, especially with some of the shadows moving, gathering shape and form. *We thought we were traveling to Cairo, but the light's all wrong. It's somewhere else.*

Get out of there, Kira. Get out now!

She'd never heard Balm sound so . . . fearful. *We're trying, but it looks like we've got company. Gotta go.*

"We've got Shadowlings at three o'clock," she informed Khefar, transferring the gun to her left hand so she could draw her Lightblade. She looked over her shoulder. "And at six."

Khefar stopped, handed Marshall's body to Gunderson. "Get your handler through the portal."

"But—"

"Don't argue, just do it!"

The blond-haired man, gulped, nodded. "I'm sorry." He stumbled down the slope toward the portal.

"You too, Kira." Khefar turned back toward the temple as the ground rumbled beneath them. "I'll cover your retreat."

"Like hell you will! I'm not leaving you behind to face that alone!"

"My duty, my vow, and my desire is to protect you," he declared, using his body to block hers. "Your duty is to get your fellow Chaser back through the Veil, then restore the Vessel of Nun."

"Not without you!"

He grabbed a handful of her braids, tugged her closer. "You die, you stay dead! I can come back. I will come back."

He was right. She knew it, but she still didn't want to let him go. "You'd better come back."

"Of course. We have unfinished business, you and

I." He kissed her, a hard, bruising kiss that she'd feel for a long time. Then he shoved her away. "Now go!"

He plunged down the dune, screaming a battle cry, his blade flashing bright blue in his hand. Shadowlings skittered like crabs across the sand. Kira counted at least two dozen heading toward the Nubian. At least it would be a fair fight.

She turned to look at the male Chaser. He'd stumbled beneath his burden. A Shadowling broke from the others, heading toward him, but he made no move for his Lightblade. Had he dropped it again?

Dammit! Khefar's sacrifice would be for nothing if the Chaser got himself killed on this side of the Veil.

Screaming, she threw herself down the slope, sliding and rolling until she landed between the Chaser and the Shadowling. She lowered all of her mental barriers, allowing her power to fill every fiber, every cell, of her being. A minute relief to see the purple-blue of Light suffusing her skin, not the yellow of Shadowmagic or the green of a mix. Perhaps helping Gunderson had helped her.

"Get your ass through that portal now, Chaser!" she screamed. "That's an order!"

She fired the gun, emptying bullets into the Shadowling all but galloping toward the male Shadowchaser. Puffs of blue-white flame danced along its back as the bullets struck home, sending the creature rolling. It scrabbled to its feet, yellow blood leaking onto the sand. A snarl curled its lips.

"That's right, you slimy piece of Shadow shit," she taunted, throwing the first gun away and pulling the second free of her belt. "You want some? Come get it."

The Shadowling leapt at her. All she could hear was her heart pounding in her ears as she raised blade and gun to follow the creature's trajectory. She could feel her mouth stretched in a scream, could feel the recoil of the gun firing, yet nothing registered but the pounding of her heart.

Her blade swung up, bright and true, piercing the creature's skull. She spun with its momentum, flinging it off her blade as it began to disintegrate. A heartbeat, then a breath, then a sob.

The portal vanished. Gunderson must have made it through. Now she had no choice but to go after Khefar. As if there had been a choice in the first place.

The ground rumbled beneath her feet again. The entire landscape of the Giza Plateau began to change as the sand shifted, sending rocks and hewn slabs from the temple complex sliding down the sand toward her. Grit swirled into eddies, signifying an approaching sandstorm. She tried to sheathe her Lightblade in order to use both hands to climb the dune. The tip hit something solid, metal, sending a wave of power through her body and almost causing her to stumble. She dug her heels in, then looked down at her hip.

Another blade already filled her Lightblade's leather sheath. Her throat closed on a hard knot of panic as she recognized Khefar's blade, the ancient Dagger of Kheferatum. *Oh, gods, no.*

Gunderson didn't have his dagger because Khefar had scooped it up during their fight in Khafre's valley temple. Khefar must have shoved his blade into the sheath when he'd grabbed her, when he'd kissed her before going off to face a horde of Shadowlings armed with a weak Chaser's Lightblade. If you were going on a suicide mission, you didn't take the chance of the ultimate weapon falling into your enemy's hands.

"Ah, no. Sweet Mother of Justice, please, no."

Kira exploded into action, shoveling handfuls of sand as she powered up the hills toward Khafre's valley temple. The wind increased, tossing sand and debris into her face, clogging her eyes, nose, and throat. She coughed, but that only made it worse. It didn't matter. Nothing mattered more than getting to Khefar—not Gunderson and his dead handler, not Balm screaming in her head. She had to get the Dagger of Kheferatum back to its rightful owner. If she did that, he'd be all right. If she did that, he'd live.

She finally crested the top of the dune. If the sandstorm hadn't stolen her breath, the sight before her certainly would have.

Shadowlings littered the sand. Khafre's temples were completely obscured. Even as she held up her arm to block the brunt of the sandy wind, the ground around the Sphinx filled in, swallowing up the Shadowlings. She couldn't see anyone or anything that looked like the Nubian.

"Khefar!" She screamed into the wind and got a mouth full of sand for her trouble. "Where are you?"

Silence answered, thick and absolute.

He's not gone. He can't be gone. He said he'd come back, dammit. He said he'd come back. But what if he's hurt? What if he's under the sand? He needs the sunlight to touch him or he won't come back.

I gotta dig him up.

Noises sounded in her head, but she wasn't sure if it was Balm or her own mind screaming.

Suddenly the sands rocked, shifted, elevating the ground around her. It seemed as if the pyramids themselves groaned. A sandstorm swirled behind the Great Pyramid, heading straight at her. Earth dipped beneath her feet. She tumbled down the incline head over heels, stopping hard. Mastabas began to crumble around her. Something very large and very solid slammed into her, stealing her breath and causing spots to dance before her eyes.

As Kira watched, the sandstorm condensed, contracting to human height. The sand dervish spun to a stop in front of her, taking on a distinctly human form. A woman, dressed in flowing robes of a deep rust color, stepped from the shifting sands.

Kira struggled to regain her feet, but her brain and body wouldn't comply. She blinked to clear her vision. "Balm? What are you doing here?"

The voice in Kira's head fell silent.

The woman lowered her head scarf. No, not Balm. Well, almost Balm, so much like Balm it was eerie. The main difference was the streak of silver in the deep auburn hair, the gleam in those green eyes.

"Hello, Kira Solomon. I am Solis. It's a pleasure to finally meet you."

Chapter 15

"K hefar!"

Kira jerked upright and immediately wished she hadn't. She grabbed her head, groaning, as she waited for her brain and her stomach to decide to stop fighting.

"That hard head stands you in good stead, I see."

Kira dropped her hands. "Balm, quit ribbing me and just tell me where. . . ."

Her voice faded as she realized she wasn't home, wasn't on Santa Costa. Wasn't in London or Cairo. And the woman leaning over her in robes the color of dried blood was not her guardian.

Kira's fingers tightened on her Lightblade. "You're not Balm."

The woman smiled, the skin around her eyes crinkling. "No, I am not. Not really. I told you before, Kira, my name is Solis. Of course, that was just after a slab of granite tried to flatten you, so you can be excused for forgetting."

"What? Wait." Kira shook her head, trying to clear her mind to accept what she saw versus what she knew. This woman did look like Balm, or rather like Balm would look if she'd ever hit her late forties or early fifties. The hair was still a riot of mahogany curls, but strands of silver accented the rich color. The eyes twinkled with humor instead of Balm's stern glint, and the creamy skin around the eyes and mouth was softer.

Kira took stock of her surroundings. She was on a pallet of some sort, sand still beneath her, but in the shelter of one of the few intact temples. She still had her Lightblade, and Khefar's dagger still lay in the sheath at her hip. Though her face felt clean, grit still covered every inch of her. She hadn't been out for long, then.

"How do you know me? Do you know Balm? Why do you look like her? What's going on here? And what happened to Khefar? Is he—is he—"

"I know you have questions, Kira," Balm—Solis— said. "I can even answer some of them for you. But yes, I know you, and you can even say that I know Balm. And no, the Eternal Warrior isn't dead, though he may well wish to be."

"What does that mean? Is he in danger?" Kira tried to sit upright, only to be stopped by a wave of dizziness.

"Take it easy, Kira. You can't go off half-cocked after the Medjay." Solis folded herself into a lotus position on the floor beside Kira's pallet. It was so reminiscent of waking up in Atlanta after defeating the Fallen to find Balm staring down at her that Kira felt dizzy again.

"You shouldn't be here, either of you, but I can offer you a bit of protection for a while."

"Just what is your protection going to cost me?"

"Smart girl," Solis said with admiration. "I ask for nothing more than a little conversation with you. Is that too much to ask?"

"Conversation is all well and good, but I'd appreciate information even more," Kira told her. She could be charitable. The woman had saved her life, after all. But she had to get to Khefar, had to get the Dagger of Kheferatum back to him. She was resisting its call for now, and she figured she could continue to do so as long as she didn't touch the ancient blade.

"I need to find out who's behind stealing the Vessel of Nun, who took Khefar. I really need to know what they're planning so I can stop it if necessary. Can you help me with that?"

"Not asking for much, are you? And what possessed you to come here in the first place with those blades," Solis demanded, "other than a Shadowchaser in over his head? I swear, I don't know what that woman is thinking at times!"

Kira bit her lip. She had a pretty good idea who "that woman" of whom Solis spoke was. Her brain began to pound. It sounded so much like Balm being critical of herself that Kira's mind was having difficulties wrapping around it.

Kira finally answered. "We have a mission given to us by the goddesses of Truth and Life themselves, a mission that affects the Universal Balance. We needed to find out who wants the Vessel of Nun. A known enemy is better than an unknown enemy."

"You sound like the Nubian." The older version of Balm shook her head again. "That god-struck idiot. I suppose you now realize your presence was noted as soon as you stepped through the Veil. You let that female Shadowling get away to report back to her master."

"Hold up." Kira rolled to her feet. Nothing like anger to clear the mind. So much better for her brain than confusion, or fear. "Blaming me for stuff I don't even know about isn't fair!"

"You know better than to go into an unknown situation, and now the Shadowling is holding the Eternal Warrior as bait for you."

"You know, I could have stayed at home if I wanted some incarnation of Balm to chew my ass," Kira shot back. "This isn't helping me get Khefar back. If you want to give me information, then give it to me!"

"Fine." Solis released an impatient sigh as she smoothed the folds of her robes. "That portal you came through was a temporary passageway through Logic's Veil. You normally use your extrasense or dreamwalking to push beyond, which tends to protect you."

"This is what happens when Nansee travels, isn't it?" Kira asked, biting back her impatience. Like Balm, Solis would give information when she was good and ready, not a moment before. "When he steps between one place and another, he comes through here."

Solis smiled. "Good girl. Because you're from there, you change here just by coming through. This side of Logic's Veil has the capacity to mirror your side, colored by your perception of reality."

"Excuse me?"

Solis looked exasperated. "Every plane of existence has a mirror. Hello? The Universal Balance?" She *tsked*. "Did they teach you nothing on the other side?"

Kira rubbed her forehead. "Are you saying that you really are a mirror of Balm?"

The older woman *tsked* again as she shook her head in barely concealed disappointment. "She really hasn't told you anything, has she? Perhaps you should wonder, my child, if Balm is a mirror of me."

Kira groaned. There wasn't an aspirin large enough to knock out this headache, this universal shift in her beliefs. Solis appeared entirely too satisfied with Kira's discomfort. "Enjoying yourself?"

"Absolutely," Solis replied. "The expansion of the mind can be a painful thing, but necessary. It's your time now. Balm should realize that."

"I'm pretty sure Balm wouldn't have been pleased with us coming through the Veil," she said, conscious of the silence in her head. "I'm betting that she didn't want me to meet up with you."

"That's probably true." Solis displayed a pronounced lack of concern. "Balm can be a bit . . . overzealous about what she sees as hers."

"You make it sound as if Balm owns me."

Solis cocked her head. "Are you telling me you don't feel that way, like an indentured servant forever unable to repay the debt you owe?"

Acid churned in Kira's stomach. The strange woman made Kira uneasy with her astute observations. Balm had saved her life, taken her in when her family gave her away, taught her how to control her extrasense and her killing touch. She knew she'd never be able to even the score despite being a Shadowchaser. "For someone I've never met before, you seem to know a lot about me and about Balm."

"I know quite a lot of things, Shadowchaser," Solis told her. "Including the fact that you carry a touch of

Shadow and you have yet to tell your beloved guardian about it."

Tension sang along Kira's nerves. "How do you know about that?"

"As I said, I know a lot of things. You reach through the Veil all the time. Do you think you're the only one who can, or that it only goes one way?"

Kira had to admit that it made sense. Calling her extrasense, her innate magic and extrasensory perception, required her to push beyond the Veil of Reality often. She knew Balm could do it. Balm could probably do a lot of things she hadn't bothered to mention to Kira. Especially if she were some sort of reflection of Solis.

She regarded the mysterious woman. "Are you going to tell Balm about my Shadow problem?"

"Why do you think it's a problem?"

Kira jerked back in surprise. "Hello? I'm a Shadow-chaser. I hunt down Shadowlings and hybrids that get out of line."

"But only the hybrids that get out of line," Solis observed. "Meaning you leave them alone if they're not causing problems. Sounds to me like having a little Shadow in you isn't a bad thing."

"Of course it's a bad thing!" Kira spluttered.

"Why?"

"Why? Why?" Kira stared at the other woman in disbelief. Why did Solis make it seem as if there was nothing wrong with being a Shadowling? Of course Kira didn't have a problem with most hybrids. Demoz and most of his staff were okay, and so were the band members who'd helped get innocents out of the DMZ while she fought the Fallen. And Comstock's solicitor was a hybrid. Hybrids weren't the problem—most wanted to be left to their own devices living their lives, and she was content to let them do it. But none of them had gone on a killing spree through downtown Atlanta because Shadow had gotten the best of them.

"I don't want Shadow infesting me. I want it gone."

"That's not possible, Kira," Solis said, her voice soft. "Shadow is a part of you. It always will be."

Kira's heart thumped heavily. She didn't want to believe Solis, but she could feel the taint spreading tiny vein-like roots throughout her psyche. It was as if Shadow had grafted itself onto her cells, mutating them. She'd never be able to get it out, not completely. If Ma'at Herself hadn't excised it, what chance did she have? All Kira could hope was that she'd be able to keep it in check and not let it control or overwhelm her.

She looked at the anti-Balm, so smug and serene in her rust-red robes. "You seem pretty nonplussed about my Shadow infection. You mind telling me which side of the Balance you're on?"

"Neither."

"Neither." Kira balanced on the balls of her feet, ready to fight if necessary. "What do you mean, neither? Is this some sort of trick?"

"Ease, Shadowchaser. I mean you no harm."

"Uh-huh. Don't think I'm going to implicitly trust you just because you look like Balm. Heck, I don't trust Balm all that much, and she raised me."

Solis beamed. "Well said, Shadowchaser."

"So tell me what you meant about being on neither side of the Balance. Everyone has a side. Even not choosing is a choice. There's no such thing as being a metaphysical Switzerland."

"Isn't there?"

Kira gritted her teeth. "Look, I'm trying here. I'd think you'd be glad that I'm taking names before I kick butt, but I've only got so much patience or time. So give me the highlight reel. Tell me what I need to know about this side of the Veil."

"What should you know about this side of the Veil? First, there is Light. There is Shadow. And in the sliver of existence that separates the two is Between." Solis gestured at the swirling sky. "That's where we are now. Between is the Veil and the Veil is Between. Between measures Light and Shadow, and Light against Shadow. There's more to it than that, of course, but, as you mentioned, you don't have a lot of time." Solis smiled.

Kira ground her teeth. At last she'd found someone willing to give her information, and she didn't have time to digest it. "Okay, what else?"

"Here is almost like there, with a few differences. I'm sure you've noticed a distinct lack of humans?"

"Yeah, kinda noticed the whole no-human thing. Not much of anything on this side, actually. Any particular reason for that?"

"The Fallen can exist on this side. So can hybrids and Shadowlings. What you don't find here are humans—not naturally—on this side. And they don't seem to do well over here when they do come through the Veil. Their minds don't handle the trip with ease, and neither do their bodies. The other Shadowchaser and handler weren't here as long as you and Khefar have been."

"So, there have never been humans on this side?"

"No, no humans on this side," Solis said, her eyes glinting in anticipation. "And yet, here you are, hale and hearty."

Kira knew this other Balm wanted her to make some intuitive leap, but jumping to conclusions went against her training as a Shadowchaser and archaeologist. "If I were to posit your statements as fact, then I would have to conclude that either a long-held tenet of Universal Law is mistaken, or Khefar and I aren't human."

Solis lifted her hands, palms up, as if cupping a bowl in each one. "Two conclusions. Which would you choose?"

"Well obviously, someone misinterpreted Universal Law. Khefar is human, and so am I."

"Was," Solis corrected, her tone gentle. "The Medjay *was* human. Then he died, only to be brought back from death by Isis. How many humans do you know who die, yet are called back to life with the rising sun?"

"None."

"Ergo, not human." She raised one of her hands higher than the other, as if weighing them. "How many humans do you know who can channel both Light and Shadow through their bodies, and survive?"

Kira's heart pounded. A precipice loomed ahead of her and she had no other way to go but over its edge. How did Solis know that she carried Shadow? She hadn't even told Balm. Did Balm know, but kept it to herself? "I know of one. Me."

"You." Solis cocked her head as she regarded Kira. "But what are you?"

"I'm human." Kira could hear the lack of conviction in her voice. She tried again. "I am a human being."

"Then why can't you touch another human without hurting them?"

Kira looked down at her hands. She still had on her left glove from helping Gunderson get through the portal, but her right was lost to the sands. Here, in this in-between place, her hands looked as if they were enveloped in a dense blue fog with occasional flashes of green.

"Kira?" Solis prompted.

"I don't know." The precipice loomed closer. "Is there a point to this exercise? How does this help me find Khefar and get back home?"

"Oh, but there is a point, Shadowchaser. Your epiphany has been a long time in coming. I do not profess to understand why the Keeper of Light decided to hinder it, but Ma'at now claims you for Her own purpose and there's precious little Balm can do about that. Truth is neither good nor evil; truth simply is. Who are we to interfere in the course of the Universal Truth?"

Kira bowed her head. She could touch Khefar, had touched him intimately. He was the only human she'd ever been able to touch without downloading all of his memories or hurting. Or, worse, killing. Just after puberty, she'd accidentally hurt her adoptive sister before being sent to Balm. Her sister had spent several days in a coma, then was institutionalized.

She'd never tried touching another human again. Not until her first handler, Nico, had found a serum that blunted her powers. That serum had been

Shadow-magic, born of Chaos. It had shut off her Light powers, her extrasense, her touch ability. A couple of weeks ago she'd been injected with Shadow-magic again, and this time it had stayed inside her, melding with her own Light-given ability.

What did it mean? What did any of it mean?

She squared her shoulders, then stared at Solis, her chin high. "Truth has always been what I've sought, what I've wanted. Knowledge is truth, and truth is power. I want to know."

The older woman nodded, cupped palms still raised. "Another question for you to ponder. How many non-humans can you touch, just touch, without calling your power with the intent to harm?"

Kira struggled to find words, to force her mouth to work. Difficult to do when her entire body seemed trapped in quicksand. "I—I don't know." Why would she have tried? Hybrids and Shadowlings were the enemy.

Weren't they?

"This doesn't make any difference," Kira said, feeling the need to be stubborn. "I can touch Khefar just fine!"

Solis remained unruffled by her outburst. "We've already established that the Nubian no longer fits the definition of human. One has to wonder, however: did you ever fit it?"

"I did," she insisted, the protest weak to her ears. "I do. I'm human."

"Who are your parents?" Solis asked, her soft voice relentlessly hammering away. "Where were you born? Why were you separated from the other trainees on Santa Costa? Why was your training so much more brutal than the others'? Why has Balm kept such close watch on you out of all the Shadowchasers she's sent out into the world? Why have you not told her about the taint of Shadow that grows in your body?"

Solis clapped her hands together. The sharp sound echoed like a thunderclap in Kira's brain, throwing her mentally and physically off-balance, rocking her world to its foundations. Everything seemed awash in shades of green.

A chasm opened beneath Kira's feet, threatening to drag her under. Balm had withheld so much from her. She was still doing it. Why? What didn't the head of the Gilead Commission want Kira to find out about herself?

Who was she? What was she?

"Stop! Just stop. There is no point to this."

"Isn't there?"

A tremble swept through her. She looked down at her Lightblade, still wrapped tightly in her fist. It glowed brightly in her grip, its blue sheen reassuring.

Did it matter? Whatever the truth about herself and her history, it made little difference in the here and now, to her duty. Duty. Yes, when all else failed and fell away, duty remained. No matter what she was, she was a Shadowchaser. She was the Hand of Ma'at. The goddess had charged her with a sacred duty, and she intended to fulfill that duty, come Shadow or high water. But dammit, there was still so much that she didn't know!

"If your goal is to make me question Balm, question my place, congratulations," Kira told the other woman. "But questioning who I am is something I've been doing for most of my life. It ain't nothing new."

"If you haven't found answers yet, Kira Solomon, then I must say that you haven't been asking the right questions."

"You really are like Balm," Kira said, "and I don't mean that as a compliment. Both of you dribbling out information in bits and pieces, never being straight with an answer. I'm over it. I don't know your game, nor do I understand your motives, but I will not be your pawn."

Solis appeared unruffled. "What do you think you have been for the past few years, Shadowchaser? Though it is not I who aim to control you, and the stakes are so much higher than the outcome of a game!"

"You know what? I don't want to hear any more." Kira stripped off her remaining glove, threw it into the sand. "I can't do this right now. Right now, I have to find Khefar and get us out of here. Where is he?"

Solis took her time answering. "The female Shadowling took him to the Temple of Set."

Kira frowned. "There's no such thing as a temple to Set."

"Not where you're from," Solis agreed, "but you are not the only one who can impact what is reality here. Here there is a temple dedicated to Set, and that is where you'll find your Eternal Warrior."

"Fine. Then where is this temple of Set?"

"Take the road west of Khufu's tomb."

Kira headed for the open air, the strange sky in the strange place.

"Kira Solomon."

She turned back. "Don't try to stop me."

Solis raised her hands. "Not I, Shadowchaser. Not

I. I merely wanted to warn you that to find yourself, you may have to lose yourself, or what you think of as yourself. Remember, truth is neither good nor evil, Light or Shadow. Truth simply is."

"Now that sounds just as cryptic as Balm."

"I'm sure it does." Solis inclined her head. "When you return, be sure to give my regards to the Lady of Light."

"Trust me, when I see Balm, your regards won't be the only thing I give her."

Kira stepped out onto the plateau. The absolute silence of the plain reflected the shocking transformation that lay before her. The renovation by the sandstorms and landslides had rendered some familiar landmarks all but unrecognizable. All of the queens' pyramids were covered over by millions of cubic feet of sand. Only the top of the Sphinx's nemes headdress could be seen. Even the three great pyramids seemed smaller than they should have been.

Out of the western plain rose what must be the Temple of Set, unmarred by the ravaged landscape behind her. It was grand, as grand as most temples in their prime. Statues of the stylized animal form of the desert god, a cross between a jackal and an aardvark—Egyptologists called this unknown creature the Typhonic beast or, simply, the Set animal—lined the processional, more than two dozen of them. Beyond that stood two towering obelisks that flanked a boundary wall, carved with the names of Set: *His Majesty, He of Great Strength, One Who Shines.* Obviously Set or his followers were intent on reclaiming his original place in the Egyptian pantheon.

Several things clicked into place. Now she knew why someone had sent Fallen and Shadowlings after ancient Egyptian artifacts. Enig probably was supposed to bring the Dagger of Kheferatum back to Set, but had decided to keep it for himself. And as a god of the desert, of storms and darkness and chaos, why wouldn't Set want to flood the entire world in the ancient waters of pre-creation, to start the cycle anew?

Now Kira knew why she'd been elevated by Ma'at, why Khefar had been claimed by Isis. The goddesses of Life and Order knew of the storm brewing on the horizon, the imminent return of Set. All They could hope was that the dormant god had not yet awakened. If He could marshal the Fallen and other Shadowlings to do His bidding, though, the world was in serious trouble.

She stopped on the processional way a short distance from the huge pylons that marked the entrance to the hypostyle hall. Beyond the granite pillars lay the sanctuary. She knew they were waiting for her inside, but she didn't care. Khefar had sacrificed himself so she could get Gunderson and his late handler back through the Veil. If she'd come to an unknown land to recover a handler's body, there was no way she'd leave Khefar behind.

She tucked her Lightblade into her belt, then pulled off her coat, dropping it to the sand. Keeping her senses fanned out for any sign of Shadowlings, she pushed the long sleeves of her black T-shirt up past her elbows, then pulled her Lightblade free of her belt with her left hand.

"Lady of Truth and Justice, be with me," she prayed. "Give Your blessing to the one You called to

Your service. Help me save the one claimed by the Mother of All so that together we may complete the work You have set before us."

The feather symbol at the base of her throat tingled. Every shield she used to rein in her power melted away. She could feel power rolling over her and through her, swirls of blue, green, and yellow light pulsing in time to the light churning in the sky above her.

Very slowly and carefully, she slid her right hand down to grasp the Dagger of Kheferatum. The first time she'd touched the dagger, she'd thought it nothing more than a well-preserved artifact of ancient Egypt. That was before it had shown her the Nubian's bloody past and his attempts to set things right. It had almost burned out her extrasense with that "conversation," and had lured her with its power ever since.

Khefar had given it to her because he'd trusted that she would get it through the portal safely. And she would have, if the portal hadn't closed on her. If she'd believed Khefar would make it back through safely. If she didn't think that leaving him over here would give him a fate far worse than death. If she didn't care so much about him.

Her fingers wrapped around the hilt of the ancient blade. Energy lifted the small hairs on her arms, swept through her braids like an invisible wind. Sand whirled around her, billowing as the pressure around her increased. Her vision shimmered, coloring everything in shades of teal. So much power, more power than she'd ever known. It threatened to fry her synapses, but she relaxed into it, into the sensations that hovered on a dagger's edge between pleasure and pain.

Could a human handle this much power?

At that moment, it didn't matter who she was, what she was. All that mattered was reclaiming Khefar from the female Shadowling, getting him back through the portal. He'd saved her life. She damn well could return the favor.

She held the magical blade at eye level, too full of power to worry about the deepening green of her extrasense as it mixed with the yellow of Shadow-magic. "I need your help," she told the dagger before it could swamp her with images of Khefar's life. "I need to borrow your power so that we can take back the one who truly wields you. Help me bring him back, and I will give you plenty to drink. Will you help me?"

The blade vibrated in her hand, a sensation eerily like a heartbeat. It was ready, and so was she. With her Lightblade she was a force to be reckoned with. With both blades, not even hell would stand against her fury.

Squaring her shoulders, she trudged her way through the sand, toward the inner sanctuary of Set, toward Khefar.

Chapter 16

So many times over the centuries Khefar had wished for death, but Anubis would not claim him. Those instances paled in comparison to what he now endured.

There had been more Shadowlings and hybrids than he'd anticipated, breaking through the shifting sand like scorpions. With only the Lightblade dropped by the male Chaser, Khefar had switched from offense to defense, hoping to give Kira enough time to get the Chaser, the dead handler, and herself safely back through the portal.

He'd thought he'd die beneath a pile of Shadowlings. It had been part of his plan. To wake in this strange place, call Anansi, and join the others in Cairo. He'd never died in this Between place before, but he'd never seen Cairo and the Giza Plateau behind the Veil. He had faith that Isis, the Giver of Life—She who'd bestowed a form of immortality on him, She who'd claimed him for Her service—would not abandon him in this place with his task for Her unfulfilled.

Unfortunately, the female Shadowling had not wanted his death—at least, not at the outset. Instead, he'd been captured, beaten, dragged through the sand. Taken to a temple on the plateau that he'd not noticed before. A temple with two soaring statues standing guard outside—Anubis? No, not the jackal-headed god, but a man holding a *was* scepter, with the head of an animal with a long, sharp face, downturned snout, and long squared ears that stood up.

Set. He was being taken into a temple dedicated to Set.

Dread filled him. A temple to Set here, in this space Between, had to mean that a cult of Set had been resurrected. Was the ancient god gaining power by further aligning himself with Shadow? Set was originally a god of chaos, after all. If so, it brought home to Khefar just why Isis and Ma'at had claimed him and Kira. Their jobs had just become that much harder.

He struggled, trying to free himself from the bonds that held him. He'd lost the Chaser's Lightblade beneath the swarm of Shadowlings who'd overpowered him. It had been a poor choice of weapon anyway, not charged with power as was Kira's. For a brief moment, he regretted sending the Dagger of Kheferatum back through the portal with her. But no, better for the dagger to be safely on the other side of the Veil under the watchful eye of Nansee or even Balm than close to the ancient Egyptian god of Chaos.

"Don't bother to struggle to free yourself, immortal one," the female Shadowling said, dragging her golden-hued dagger along his forearm, slicing it open. "You're going to be used as bait. I already have the Vessel of Nun. How much better for me to present my master with the Dagger of Kheferatum and the Shadow-touched Chaser as well."

"And just who is your master?" Khefar asked. "Your side finally got someone with brains to take the helm?"

She laughed, the tip of her blade slicing through his shirt. "That's not how this works, Nubian. I'm not going to stand here like some bad movie villain and tell you all my secrets. I'm just going to amuse myself with your immortal carcass until the Hand of Ma'at returns."

"You won't have her," he declared, hissing through the pain. How did she know that Kira had become the Hand of Ma'at? "She's gone back through the Veil."

"If you say so. But I have to think, if she'd come through to retrieve a dead handler, why would she leave you behind?"

He wanted to believe that Kira wouldn't be foolish enough to try to rescue him, but it was a senseless notion. Of course she'd try to find a way back. He'd do the same thing if their roles were reversed.

They passed through the temple opening, revealing an open sanctuary. Its walls were covered in bright paintings. Pictures of Set in His various animal forms, the hippopotamus, the black boar, even a hybrid blend with Apep, in the form of a crocodile. A grand painting of Set at the helm of the Solar Bark of Ra, striking down Apep in His form as the demon serpent attempting to prevent Ra from making His journey through the underworld each night.

The ancient Egyptians had done a disservice to Set, stripping Him of His ambivalence and His role as protector of Upper Egypt, probably in some dispute between the Two Lands. Khefar wasn't sure exactly what had happened, but it had started before his own birth. By the time the Persians ruled Egypt, the Egyptians had recast Set in the role that had been Apep's—the bringer of Chaos, the destroyer of Order. If enough of your people believe you to be a thing, then you become that very thing. Set had obviously decided to embrace his new role with fervor.

The few Shadowlings Khefar hadn't killed dragged him into the center of the sanctuary, bound both his wrists with rope, then hung him from a granite cross lintel. The rope stretched so tightly that he had to hold his weight by standing on his toes. Blood ran from the cut the female had given him, a gash above his eye, and the slashes he'd received from the other Shadowlings. At least the female Shadowling didn't have a seeker demon with her.

She stood before him, a pleasant smile on her face, if you could call crocodile-like teeth on a human pleasant. Like Gunderson had told them, the female Shadowling looked Eurasian, as if her ancestors had roamed the steppes of Mongolia or Siberia. She had a compact frame, standing five-five in her sand-colored tunic and pants. Her eyes glowed a steady amber yellow beneath her head scarf.

"You're wasting your time." What had Gunderson called her? Marit. "Marit, you won't curry your master's favor today, only his wrath. The Shadowchaser is gone and won't return."

She looked at him, yellow eyes flashing in the dark interior. "Nice try, Medjay. You'll forgive me if I don't take your word for it."

"You don't have to take my word for it," Khefar said, smiling now. "Take a look at the Vessel of Nun."

Marit flicked a glance at her remaining helpers. "Bring the Vessel of Nun to me."

A pair of Shadowlings brought the pieces of the

amphora to her. She wrapped long fingers around the neck and bowl, held them up to Khefar. "The power will be restored once the pieces are rejoined."

"I suppose if you had some Super Glue you'd be able to use it again. I wouldn't put it in the dishwasher though. The color might fade."

She turned the pieces over, stopping when she noticed the imprint on the bottom of the jar. "China? Made in fucking *China*?"

"Anansi had to make a duplicate in a hurry," Khefar explained, not caring that his grin caused his busted lip to sting anew. "Luckily for us, Gunderson had a cheap stoneware vase the spider could use."

Marit stared at the shards in disbelief. "You lie. This is a trick!"

"The real Vessel of Nun is safe and protected in the real world," Khefar told her, unable to hide his satisfaction. "Kira will return it to where it belongs. And you will have nothing to show for your plans but dust."

Marit shrieked, tossing the useless pottery to the sandstone floor. She swung her dagger up, then plunged the blade deep into his thigh. Pain lanced through him, causing him to grunt with it, but he refused to cry out.

"You'd better hope you're mistaken, Medjay," Marit declared, raising her dagger again. "Or else you're going to spend an eternity in pain."

The Shadowling decided to amuse herself while waiting for the Shadowchaser by experimenting, with him as the test subject. The first test: how many knife wounds he could bear before he cried out. She became bored with that soon enough, and instead tried seeing how many bones she could break before he passed out.

Time became elastic, a looping thing, powered by pain. His clothes hung in ribbons. Thirst beat into him, so much so that even blood welling on his lip was a relief. He had no idea of how long he hung, how long he suffered. All he knew was that each moment he hung on was another moment he was sure that Kira would not come, that she, his dagger, and the Vessel of Nun remained safe.

He tried to fight back when she touched his warrior's braids. The ropes, stiff with his blood and sweat, held him fast.

"Still have some fight in you, huh?" Marit smiled. "Good."

Rolling pain, rolling blackness. Awareness that his braids lay draped on his shoulders, stuck in the dried blood, piled at his feet. Some had been hacked off, some pulled out. And still the she-demon continued.

In his agony, he dreamed. His wife, Merire, with her bright smile and soft skin, proudly presenting him with Henku, his firstborn son. Moving them farther north so that he could join other Medjay in service to the pharaoh and move up in the world. Fighting for the honor of the god-king and the glory of Egypt. Merire giving him their daughter, precious Meri, followed soon after with his second son, happy little Seneb.

"No," he croaked out, knowing what came next.

A decisive battle, chaos all around, saving the life of the second prince. Being chosen as worthy to bear the Dagger of Kheferatum, elevated in rank, and being awarded an estate of his own. Coming home with some of his fellow Medjay, eager to share the news with Merire. Seeing the smoke, dark and sinister, staining the bright turquoise sky. And the bodies, all the bodies, the precious broken, bloody bodies.

That pain slammed into him anew, that blistering, agonizing loss. Grief, raw and total, yawning like a maw of darkness. Guilt, overwhelming guilt, guilt so bitter it choked him, that while he was away protecting the son of the king, no one had protected his family.

It was suddenly too much.

Emotional torture did what physical pain could not. Something inside him cracked, then shattered. *My Lady Isis. Divine One, Giver of Life, You who preserves one such as me. If it be Your will, give me strength to endure, allow me to continue to serve. But if it be not Your will . . . take back Your favor and give me over to Anubis. Allow me to stand again before the great Osiris.*

The ankh at the base of his throat burned. Immediately he thought of Kira. At least the fiery Shadowchaser was safe on the other side of the Veil. He'd known the moment he'd given her the Dagger of Kheferatum that he'd made an irrevocable decision, that he wouldn't be returning to her.

Of the many regrets he had, that was the most poignant. He hadn't felt close to human in years, perhaps decades. She had given that back to him. It had been his goal to return the favor, to keep Shadow from stealing her humanity away. It was the least he could do for her. Gods willing, she'd find someone who would be able to fulfill his promise to her in his stead.

"She comes, she comes!"

Khefar heard the excited whispers, the clicking

of claws. He managed to lift his head, turn so that he could see out of his good eye.

Light spun and danced at the entrance of the temple, a column of controlled fire. Except he'd never seen fire that burned such a brilliant green. In the center of the spire of flame he could just make out a figure, two daggers ready to strike. Her eyes glowed brighter than the power that surrounded her.

Surely this was Sekhmet, drawn by all the blood he'd shed. The lion-headed goddess. Lady of Slaughter, sent by Isis to finally end his torment. "Thank You, Great Lady."

Laughter. "So you finally decided to show yourself, Shadowchaser?"

Shadowchaser?

The figure in the glowing column of light spoke, her voice echoing in the temple. "You know who I am. You know why I've come. And you know what I hold in my hands."

Not Sekhmet. "No, Kira, by the Light."

The female Shadowling laughed. "You cannot wield the Dagger of Kheferatum," she sneered. "It is just a knife in your hands. Only those born of the gods can master its power."

"Bitch, please," Kira said. She stepped further into the temple, and even in his condition Khefar could see the grim smile pulling her lips back from her teeth. "If you think I can't control it, come and take it from me. No really, I want you to try. That way they can say it was a fair fight when I unmake your ass."

"Don't do it, Kira." He struggled then. Not because Kira was in danger from the Shadowlings, but because he knew that Kira could wield his dagger, could unmake the Shadowling who'd tortured him. She would destroy them, and she'd laugh while doing it. He could feel the power of the dagger, his dagger, wrapped around her power like a lover's embrace, strengthening her.

The Shadowlings were doomed, but too cocky to know it.

"What are you waiting for?" Marit demanded. "There's only one of her and a dozen of you. Take her. Get me the dagger and then you can have her body!"

"Ooh, super happy fun time," Kira all but cooed. "Bring it on!"

Power thickened the air pressure inside the temple, causing the walls to groan. Light danced off the granite and sandstone walls as she moved, a whirling dervish of blades. His blurred vision couldn't make out much more than a dazzling play of green, yellow, and blue Light, Light and Shadow, Order and Chaos, flowing from the same source. Screams, shrieks, thudding of bodies, and laughter as the Dagger of Kheferatum drank Shadowling blood.

Something sharp pressed into his neck. "Shadow-chaser!"

The temple fell silent. "Hey, you got any more Shadowlings hiding around here?" Kira called. "Looks like these are tired of playing. They're like, dead and stuff, and my dagger still wants to play."

Even in his pain, Khefar knew she didn't mean her Lightblade. Somehow he summoned the energy to try and free himself again. A wrenching pop, and his shoulder dislocated, putting an end to his attempt. The blade dug deeper into his neck.

"Take another step and he dies," Marit said.

"That's not how this works," Kira said, her tone chiding. "You see, how this works is that I hurt you just like you hurt him. I have just as much fun doing it as you did with him. Then, when you are nothing but a lump of useless Shadowling flesh, I'll use the Dagger of Kheferatum to very slowly and very painfully unmake you. I'm going to send you back to Shadow in disgrace, knowing that your fellows don't look kindly on those who've failed. I'm going to laugh while I'm doing it, and when I'm done, I'm going to take the Nubian out of here."

The Shadowling beside him faltered. He couldn't blame her. This wasn't the Kira he knew, not really. This Kira was different, dangerous. Deadly.

Shadow-touched.

"What sort of Shadowchaser are you?"

"The pissed-off sort."

A ball of blue-green energy streaked toward him, so fast he didn't have time to instinctively close his eyes and await the impact. A howl of pain let him know the bolt of power had struck the Shadowling instead.

"Be glad it's only an arm." Kira's voice held a strange amusement. "If you want to run, I highly suggest you go ahead. I'm more concerned with getting Khefar out of here right now, so I'll even let you escape. I can always find and kill you later."

"You haven't seen the last of me, Shadowchaser."

"Oh, I hope not." Another bolt of light. "The name's Kira. Kira Solomon. And I am more than just a Shadowchaser."

The light dimmed. Silence fell, filling the cavernous

temple. "Kira?" Her name came out as less than a whisper. He tried again. "Kira!"

"I'm . . . here, Khefar. I'm going to get you out of here and back home."

"You shouldn't have come."

"I had to come. The portal closed after Gunderson went through. Besides, we have unfinished business, just like you said."

He turned his head, trying to find her with his good eye. "You shouldn't have done this. I would have escaped after I died and came back."

Color swirled, blue and green and yellow. The air around him thickened as Kira stepped closer, power rippling off her. "You come back when the sun hits you. Our sun, in our reality. There's no sun here. I didn't believe you could come back, and I need you to come back. You are my fail-safe, Khefar. More than that, you're my friend, and . . . someone I care about. If I refuse to leave someone else's handler here, why would you think I wouldn't come back for you?"

"Kira, Kira . . ." He couldn't seem to push past the pain, the despair. She'd come back for him, but she'd yielded to his dagger and Shadow to do it. He couldn't have failed her more if he'd tried. "I'm sorry."

"You have nothing to be sorry about, Khefar." His left arm dropped, then his right. He could tell by the change in his stance, not because he could feel it. She thrust her shoulder beneath his, taking his weight.

"Yes I do," he tried to tell her. "You sacrificed too much on my behalf. Your life is more important. Mine has run its course repeatedly, and I . . . I am tired."

One of her hands slowly came up to cradle his

face. He tried not to flinch, he really did, but his body betrayed him. Somehow he managed to bite down the groan of pain. He wanted her touch, needed it almost as badly as she needed his. But even though he had no innate magical ability, he could feel the power that thrummed through her body, changing her.

"I know." Her voice shook with sorrow and understanding. "I know that of all the beings involved in this cosmic tug-of-war, you have done much, too much. You've done more than has been required of any human, any deity. If anyone deserves rest, you are the one."

Kira rested her forehead against his. "But I'm selfish and scared and I—I need you. I need you with me, Khefar, son of Jeru, son of Natek. I need your help to keep Shadow at bay, to make me feel human when so many people seem to think I'm not. I need you to take your dagger away from me once we leave this place. I need your strength to drag me kicking and screaming back into the Light and keep me there, or unmake me instead. Please don't make me go back through the Veil without you. Don't do that to the unsuspecting world. Stay with me. Please, Khefar. I need you to stay with me."

Somehow he managed to lift his head, stare at her through his good eye. She was so beautiful, even with blood, so much blood, and dust and tears staining her cheeks. Even with her eyes glowing a steady green. He could see her determination, her fear, and a deep abiding caring . . . for him. She needed him, more than Isis, more than his long-lost family, more than anyone ever had. Because of that, he would keep going. Because of that, he needed her too.

"All right, Kira. I'll stay."

She smiled, a shaking, tremulous curve of her lips that beat back some of the Chaos from her eyes. Carefully she placed a kiss on his forehead, the only part of him still undamaged. "It's okay to rest now," she whispered. "I'll take care of you."

His chest tightened. "In four thousand years, no one's ever said that to me before."

"Then I'm glad I was the first."

He could feel the inevitable failure of his body's ability to continue. "I have to go. Just for a little while, then I'll be back. You will wait for me."

"I will. Sleep now, Medjay. That's an order."

"Yes, ma'am," he said, and promptly obeyed.

Chapter 17

Kira caught the Nubian's body as he died, gently lowering him to the sandstone floor. Rage boiled inside her, feeding the power engulfing her, more power than before she'd entered the temple.

Khefar. She knelt beside him. Marit had inflicted horrible damage; Kira didn't understand how he'd lasted as long as he had. Could he come back from this? She had her doubts. Surely Khefar had survived worse than this, had come back from worse injuries than this. He'd been in fierce battles before, been gravely injured before. This, however, was torture, designed to systematically break body, mind, and spirit.

He'd sounded so . . . despondent when she'd cut him down. Had he ever been taken to such darkness mentally and physically before? When she got him through the portal, would the rising sun be able to bring him back?

They need to pay for what they've done, a savage voice in her head whispered, a voice not wholly her own. *We can start with that Shadowling bitch. Make her pay for what she did to Marshall and especially to Khefar. Won't be hard to find her. Just let the magic take control, let me do what I do best.*

"No." She shook her head, trying to fight the words,

the voice. The perfectly reasonable, if brutal, tone. "You let me borrow your power, Dagger. I've given you blood. Our bargain is done."

We need to get them back. Get them for Khefar. For Marshall. For Comstock. For Nico. Make things right, be the true Hand of Ma'at and establish real Order in this sad, pitiful world. . . .

Pressure and power and anger and pain intensified, crystallizing her fury into diamond-hard rage. She screamed, needing to let it out before it burst her skin open. The sound cut through the voices, pummeled the very air. The walls of the temple groaned, then began to buckle.

It was enough to spur her to action. Extra power gave her extra strength, and she was able to drape Khefar's lifeless body onto her back, his arms dangling over her shoulders, his head tucked to the left of hers. The need to escape drove her to her feet, but after several strides toward the opening, she faltered.

Khefar was dead. Marshall dead, Comstock dead, Nico dead—and several innocents whose names she didn't know. All those losses could be placed at her feet. In the real world there would be nothing but reminders of her failures, her shortcomings, her deadly abilities. Why go back? If she returned through the Veil, she'd take the new powers with her. The concentrated fury barely locked inside her would return. The Dagger of Kheferatum would be bared in her hand, and with Khefar dead, there would be no one alive who could stop her. Here she could control it, mostly, simply by choosing not to pass through the Veil. Here at least, there were no innocents to harm.

She stumbled again, sinking awkwardly to her knees. Khefar's body shifted on her back. Something touched her back: the fetish necklace he wore around his neck.

Images slammed into her. *Pain, wrenching pain and pressure, screaming through the pain as she squatted, bore down. A rippling tearing bolt of agony as her body seemed to turn itself inside out, the pressure easing. A squall cutting through the smoky dimness, the sound of a newborn's cry. Pride, such pride and joy as she held her son for the first time, knowing Khefar would be proud to have a male as their firstborn.*

Three times more the pain, one daughter lost but then Meri and Seneb. Khefar promising a move to the golden city of the god-king after the next battle, when he was sure to move up in rank. Secure in this knowledge, her love for him, his love for his family, sad though to be leaving her own family behind but wanting a better life for their sons and hoping their daughter would catch the eye of a merchant's son.

An attack without warning, fire and arrows, and spears. Trying to hide, to protect the children, to stifle their cries long enough for rescue to come. No rescue, no help, no Khefar, just pain and blood and screams, so many screams, then finally, finally, silence.

Kira awakened to grit clogging her eyes, throat, and nostrils, and the overriding power contained. Sand danced around her, biting at the exposed skin on her face and arms, burying her legs. Keen loss ripped through her. Everything was gone, only the eternal sand as shifting ghosts of what had been, might have been.

Suffering, so much suffering, and the overwhelming urge to give up, to surrender to the darkness and the void. Perhaps that was as it should have been. He was tired, tired of bearing a four-thousand-year-old burden. She was tired, tired of wondering who she was, what she was, tired of never touching except to defend, to catalogue, to kill. If she just stopped, here and now, the sand would cover her as surely as it had buried the Great Sphinx centuries ago. The sands would cover them over and nothing would remain.

Why hadn't she thought of it before? Instead of asking Khefar to stay with her, she should have gone with him instead.

But he'd made her promise, promise to wait for him. Her word was important to her. He would expect her to be waiting for him when he arose at sunrise. She had to push the past away, just as he had to, and be in the moment.

At that moment, she wanted away from sand. The problem was, she didn't know if the magic, the dagger, would let her get away.

She looked at his dagger, still somehow clenched in her fist. "If I asked you to reveal the secrets of unmaking, would you tell me? Would you tempt me with that knowledge?"

The Dagger of Kheferatum thrummed in her hand. It didn't show her how to uncreate herself. Instead, she saw herself lying partially concealed by sand, the dagger clutched in one rigid hand. Someone reached down, casually broke her fingers to pull the blade free. A shout of triumph as Marit held the ancient dagger aloft.

Oh, hell no. Kira coughed a laugh, spitting out sand

in the process. "Good job," she told the dagger, surging to her feet again. "You showed me the one thing guaranteed to make me want to get out of here."

The dagger hummed again. "All right, Dagger. You're supposed to be all powerful and stuff. If you want out of here so badly, how about opening a portal to the real Cairo? Better yet, take us to wherever Anansi the Spider is. Can you do that?"

In answer, her right hand moved of its own accord, holding the dagger aloft. Power sang along her skin, concentrating in her fingers, making her shiver in pleasure. The tip of the blade glowed yellow-blue-green as it sliced into the grit-clogged air, carving a human-sized doorway. Light flared along the edge of the frame, dark against the red-gold air. She pushed on the edge, moving aside the Veil.

The air separated, revealing a dark slice of another reality. For a moment she doubted the blade's intentions. Then she saw a nighttime sky, city lights. Heard the sounds of people in a city that rarely completely slept.

Cairo at night.

"Kira!"

That was Nansee's voice, urgent, calling. Multiple hands reached through the doorway, prying it open for her. With a last surge of her legs, Kira shoved through. The transition from shifting ground to hard surface was too much for her overworked muscles. She buckled, trying to keep her grip on the blade, on Khefar, on herself. "Don't touch us yet. I'm not sure all the power's gone."

"She's holding the Dagger of Kheferatum." Zoo's voice, a hushed whisper.

Zoo. She wouldn't hurt him again, couldn't hurt

him again. Trembles shook her as she balanced on her elbows and knees, Khefar still slumped over her shoulders. "I had to ask the dagger to open the portal. It was the only way. Khefar is—is dead. She tortured him to death but he tried to hold on for me. I took her hand off but I didn't kill her. I will, though. I'll find her and kill her for what she's done."

"Kira?" Wynne called her name, her voice tight, worried. "Are you . . . you?"

Was she? She didn't even know if she was the same person she'd been in London, much less before her bout with the Fallen. So much had happened to her since she had gone through the portal that she barely knew which way was up.

"Yeah, Wynne." She pushed down the power, conscious of Khefar's bulk against her back. She sat up, easing him down until he lay across her lap. "Just . . . just give me a moment to breathe something other than sand. This is the real Cairo, right? What time is it?"

"This is really Cairo, Shadowchaser," Nansee said soothingly, his tone at its most jovial. "It's five hours until sunrise, but you've been gone two days."

"Two days? How is that possible?"

"We don't know," Nansee answered. "But we've created a safe place here; we have the rooftop to ourselves and the first apartment down. Balm notified us when Gunderson brought Marshall's body back through the London portal, but we were worried when we didn't hear from you or Khefar."

"I'm sorry, I didn't know it was that long. I didn't know she had him for two days. I don't have my gloves, and I lost my coat. I pushed Gunderson through the portal with Marshall, but a Shadowling attacked me before I could reach it."

Light flashed before her eyes; Zoo holding a lantern aloft. "Good Lord, Kira, where are you hurt?"

"I . . . I'm not. I don't think. Am I hurt?"

"You're covered in blood and other stuff."

"It's Shadowling blood. And Khefar's . . . She—Marit—had a bunch of Shadowlings with her. Khefar took Gunderson's Lightblade and went to face about two dozen Shadowlings. I didn't know he'd shoved his dagger into my sheath. I still had my Lightblade in my hand and a gun in the other, I think. He made me take Gunderson and Marshall to the portal but I couldn't leave him behind, and once I knew what he'd done I knew I couldn't come back without him."

She looked at each one of them, faint silhouettes in Cairo's ambient midnight light, hoping they understood. "She said I wasn't human, but I am. I would have left him behind if I wasn't human, right? It's inhuman to leave behind the person who saves your life. You don't leave your fail-safe behind. He wanted me to go but I couldn't leave him. I couldn't leave him."

"And you didn't leave him, my child," Nansee said gently. His form shimmered, became that of a younger man. "You brought him back to us. Why don't you give me the dagger and then we can take care of him?"

The blade thrummed as she raised her arm, pointing the dagger at the demigod. "Uh-unh. The dagger does not want your touch, Spider. I will hold it until the Medjay takes it from my hand."

"Back off, Nansee," Zoo urged, "before she sees you as a threat."

"I'm not a threat, Kira," Nansee said. "I can take care of Khefar while you get cleaned up."

"I don't want to leave him." It was important that they know that. "He was devastated when he found his family. He felt so alone. He shouldn't be alone."

"Kira." Wynne knelt in front of her. "You know who I am, don't you?"

"You're Wynne. You're my friend." Was she still? "Aren't you?"

"Of course I am. Which is why I'm going to tell you that you so don't want Khefar to wake up and see you like that."

Kira looked down at herself. The gore was plain to see, even in the lantern light. It stiffened the heavy fabric of her cargo pants. Everything was beginning to hurt now, her brain, her body, her heart. "I'll probably be more myself once I've cleaned these Shadowling bits off of me."

"No doubt," Wynne agreed. "Let Nansee take care of Khefar like he always does, and I can help you wash that gunk off."

She shrank back in case Wynne tried to touch her. "But I can't touch humans. You know that, right? I don't have any gloves. I don't want to hurt you, Wynne. You can't . . . you can't help me."

"It's all right." Wynne held up a hand, a wad of plastic gloves clenched in her fist. "I brought plenty of gloves. Let me help you."

Wynne was right. Khefar would need to see that she was herself, in control of herself. He couldn't wake up and find her looking like a hot mess and decide she was beyond hope.

"See?" She smiled. "I must be human if I'm caring how I'll look when Khefar wakes up." She turned to Nansee. "He will wake up, won't he? Even if he died in that other place?"

The demigod nodded.

Zoo knelt down beside his wife. "You know we'll do everything in our power to make sure he does."

"You're not afraid? Of being so close to me?"

"I'm not afraid of you, Kira," the witch said, his voice thick. "I'm afraid *for* you. You need this guy, more than you need the rest of us. Let me and Nansee take care of him, while Wynne takes care of you. All right?"

She lowered her head, suddenly so very, very tired as the last of the power mixture seeped out of her pores. "All right."

Chapter 18

The clash of wooden staffs and metal blades rang throughout the practice area. From beyond the palace walls came the sound of construction, workers busily erecting the stacked pyramid–shaped mortuary complex of their queen.

He stepped from beneath the shaded walkway. Brilliant white sunlight poured down on the smooth-swept courtyard, but most of those practicing in their loincloths ignored the heat. The Kandake of Meroë did not look favorably on any man who couldn't keep up with her in war or practice.

He waited until the queen noticed his presence. She gestured to him and he stepped forward, bowed low. Up close or far away, Kandake Amanirenas was an impressive, almost larger-than-life woman, full of life and drive and courage. Strikingly tall and solidly built, with beauty in her strong features, she'd inspired her people and led them in a five-year war against the hammer that was Rome.

"So, Medjay." The tip of her staff hit the ground, the sound loud in the sudden silence. "You are leaving, then?"

"Yes, Exalted One."

She laughed, leaning against her staff. She had a

habit of tilting her head when she talked to those close to her, an adjustment made for the diminished sight in her left eye. "We are beyond those formalities, are we not?"

"I suppose we are, Amanirenas."

The kandake nodded to one of her attendants. The eunuch clapped his hands. Immediately the guards and courtiers withdrew to the interior of the palace. A servant girl helped the queen into her elaborate fringed robe while another came forward with a goblet of cool wine.

She folded herself onto a waiting chair beneath the shaded overhang while her attendants buzzed around her. "Khefar, son of Jeru, son of Natek. You have done a good thing for my family, and for Meroë."

"The treaty is a good one. You have nothing to fear from Rome."

"Kandake Amanirenas *never* had reason to fear Rome," she corrected him.

"Of course not, my queen," he said, inclining his head. "My most humble apologies."

She laughed, a rich, deep, and booming laugh that shook her large frame. "You have never been humble, Medjay. There is no reason to begin now."

"I suppose not, my queen."

"Where will you go?"

Good question. He looked out at the golden-bronze pyramids that dotted the landscape, the burial places of so many. Egypt had lost much through its subjugation by foreigners, but here beyond its borders, the spirit and even some of the gods remained. Isis remained.

"I don't know," he finally said. "Egypt as I knew it is gone. Perhaps it's time to say goodbye to this land. I'll follow the Nile, see where it begins."

"You already know where it begins," she chastised him. "At Abu, beneath the temples to Khnum and Satet."

"Of course. I simply mean to say that it's time to move beyond the Two Lands. There are no more pharaohs."

"There is Meroë."

"There is Meroë," he said, nodding in agreement. "Meroë can safeguard what I could not. Perhaps Balance is restored."

"You must always have balance," Amanirenas observed. "You failed to save Cleopatra's get, yet you were successful in saving mine."

"Yes, Exalted One." He lowered his eyes. He would have saved her son, Akinidad, regardless. He'd not been able to save Cleopatra's son, Caesarion. The boy's tutors had convinced him that Octavian meant no harm—when all proof pointed elsewhere—and that he should return to Alexandria. Losing Caesarion was a bitter drink to swallow.

Another servant stepped forward, bearing a small basket. "I have something for you," the queen said, reaching into the basket. "A small measure of thanks." A beautiful gold arm cuff, richly inlaid with an intricate pattern of blue and red glass, gleamed in her hands.

"It is more than I deserve."

"You saved my life, and that of my son Akinidad, who will rule when I am gone," she said. "Though I still wish that you had been able to save our King Teriteqas, who gifted me with this when we became betrothed, you have preserved our future, and perhaps, some of your past."

She pressed the armlet into his hands. "One day, when your journey is near its end, you will come upon one who can walk with you. When you find her, gift this to her."

"All the more reason to refuse so precious a gift, my queen," he said. "Such is not my fate."

"I may be blind in one eye, but that doesn't mean that I do not see," Amanirenas replied. "Such an old soul bearing an old grief. So much weariness. I tell you true, you will find her. You will give this to her, and your grief will ease."

He had no choice but to bow again and accept the gift. "Thank you, Kandake. I will treasure this gift until the time comes to pass it on."

"Then I hereby release you from your service to me and to Meroë, Khefar," Kandake Amanirenas intoned. "May the sun always rise for you."

"And with you, Kandake Amanirenas."

Tucking the gold armlet into his pouch, Khefar took his leave of the most powerful woman along the Nile. Surely the history books would take note of the Golden Flower of Meroë, who had accomplished what Cleopatra VII could not. Just a few short years ago, Amanirenas had taken on Rome and won.

He was alive.

Khefar took a moment to allow the pure simple joy of that fact to seep into his pores. He was awake, without pain, without his insides outside his body, without a she-devil taking joy in his suffering. All he knew was warm sunlight, the scent of cloves, and a hand—warm, gentle, soothing—stroking his jaw.

Golden light crept across the mist-draped bowl of the sky above him, chasing away the sapphire velvet in the west. A woman in a white veil leaned over him, her bronze cheeks streaked with moisture. His head lay pillowed in her lap. For a moment he forgot where he was, *when* he was. Then he saw the flash of green in the red-rimmed eyes, and he knew.

"Kira."

"Hi there, Sleeping Beauty. Here."

She tilted a bottle and straw for him to sip a bit of lemon water, the most delicious water he'd ever tasted. It was a testament to his physical and emotional weakness that he didn't try to sit up. "Thank you."

"I would give you something stronger, but figured if you wanted it, you'd get off your lazy duff and get it."

"I'm good with the water. It seemed like I've been thirsty for years." He drank more, savoring the sweet and acidic taste. When he'd had enough, he stared up at her. "Please tell me we're in true Cairo."

"We are. In Old Cairo, actually. Nansee managed to find an unoccupied rooftop and secured one of the apartments below for himself and the Marlowes."

"Good." He frowned, dismayed by the green still flashing in her eyes, the tears on her cheeks. "Do you weep for me?"

"No." She sniffed. "Not anymore."

He wanted to reach up and touch her, but his arms still felt like lead. Memories swam hazily through his mind. "Was it bad?"

"Yes." Her fingers trembled against his jaw, then resumed their stroking. "Marit did a lot of damage to you before you died. It was . . . I'd never seen anything like that. It was—it was inhuman."

"Then don't think about it."

"This is the second sunrise since we came back through the Veil. Nansee said that two days passed here while we were over there, so it's been a total of four days since we entered the portal." She sniffed again. "I'm so sorry I left you to suffer for so long."

She'd been worried. He could see it in her eyes, crouched beside the Shadow. He'd have been worried too. He *was* worried, for her. "You took on more Shadow for me."

"Yes," she said again. "I had to ask the Dagger of Kheferatum to help me. I didn't know what else to do to save you and get us out of there. It lent me its power, and amplified my own. I think it amplified the Shadow in me too."

"Kira . . ."

She brushed her thumb across his lips. "Don't argue with me. It was worth it. I'd do it again in a heartbeat. I was not going to leave you there, not like that. Not with what that Shadowling did to you."

"What happened to her? To Marit?"

"I convinced her to keep her hands off you," Kira answered, a ghost of a smile bowing her lips. "I let her escape after I took out the rest of the Shadowlings."

"I remember. You were like Sekhmet, dancing in a rain of blood." It had been amazing and awful at the same time.

She dipped her head. "Maybe there was a little bit

of Her there," she admitted. "I'm grateful that She allowed me to borrow a bit of her strength."

"I'm grateful too. I just wish the cost hadn't been so high."

"I'd pay the price every time, if it meant rescuing you from torture like that." She smiled at him. "It's what Shadowchasers do, you know."

He lay on some sort of pallet. He could feel it as well as the sun seeping into his body, empowering him, and this woman's hands touching him in a way it seemed they both needed. A canopy stretched high above them, angled so that it provided shelter as the sun moved westward, making it seem more like a Bedouin tent than a rooftop in Cairo. "Did you tend to me the entire time?"

She nodded. "I couldn't sleep, and I . . . I wasn't fit for normal company. I channeled a lot of power over there, power from both sides. Add the dagger's power to that, and I knew it would take a while to come down from it. I didn't want to take the chance of hurting anyone."

If she was that aware, then she hadn't given herself over to Shadow. "You did a good thing. A foolish thing, but a good thing. Thank you for getting me out of there. I can honestly say that I have never experienced anything like that before in all my life, and I hope never to have to again."

"Me too." She stroked his cheek. "I saw them."

"Saw who?"

"Your family."

His mouth went dry again. "When? How?"

"In the desert, after I got you out of Set's temple. Your necklace touched my skin, and I . . . I felt Merire."

"Merire. My wife."

Kira nodded. "I experienced her giving birth. She was so thrilled with each of them, loved them, grieved the daughter she lost. She was proud of you, too, and looked forward to joining you."

He stared up at Kira, at the understanding in her now-hazel eyes encouraging him to ask the question to which he desperately needed the answer. "Did they suffer?"

"No," she said, her gaze steady on his. "It was very quick. She held no enmity toward you, Khefar. She loved you very much."

He covered his face with his hands, inhaling the pain, the memories. He felt her hand, so sure, so real, so gentle on his face, bringing him back. He opened his eyes, staring up at her, grateful. "Thank you for that, for telling me. It must have been hard."

"It was but it wasn't. Having that vision, knowing what you carried, motivated me to get you out of there. I know you've been around for four thousand years and all, but you can still use more good days, happy days. You wouldn't have gotten them if you had stayed there. So I brought you out. I owed you that."

"You deserve good days too, Kira. Balance helps."

"I know. It will happen."

"Where's the dagger, Kira?"

Her fingers stopped again. "Hmm?"

"The Dagger of Kheferatum. You still have it, don't you?"

"Yes. I was just going to hold it until you got back on your feet."

"I appreciate that." He kept his gaze locked to hers.

"But you asked me to take the dagger back from you once we made it back through the Veil, remember? You made me promise to keep you in the Light. You brought me back to make sure. I intend to help you do just that."

"Okay, I just need to know one thing."

"What's that?"

"Are you human?"

He frowned. "What?"

"Are you human?" Anguish filled her eyes. "I can touch you like this, more than this, and it doesn't harm you. Is it despite the fact that you're human, or is it because you're something else?"

"I'm human, Kira."

"Even now? Even as someone who dies, yet comes back thanks to the rising sun? You still think of yourself as human?"

"Yes." He reached up, wrapped his fingers around her wrist, not understanding the distress pouring off her, but needing to do something about it. "I have always considered myself human, and always will."

She shifted carefully, sliding from beneath his head to stretch out beside him. "Thank you."

She kissed him then, pressing her entire body against his. The sun had warmed him; this contact heated him, energized him. His hands slid over her curves, found the hilt of his dagger beneath the hem of her blouse. He relieved her of its burden, and she sighed, relaxing into him.

"Do you think the others are awake yet?" he asked, pushing her braids back over her shoulder.

"Nansee most likely is," she answered. "But then

I don't know if gods—even demigods—ever sleep. Wynne and Zoo tried to keep watch with me, or over me, but they sacked out. I promised that I'd wake them if there was any change. And I know you're going to want lots of food."

"Sounds good," he said, stretching, settling his muscles and joints into place. "Right now, though, I don't want food."

"What do you want?"

"You." He gazed up at her. "I suppose that's selfish of me, but right now, I don't care."

She smiled. "Neither do I."

Then she moved over him and against him, and he thought of nothing else except purging the shadows from her eyes as the sun rose above them.

Chapter 19

A while later, with the sun higher in the sky and the temperature warming, Kira let Wynne, Zoo, and Nansee join them on the rooftop for their morning meal.

"Good to see you upright, my boy!" the demigod said, greeting Khefar with an enthusiastic slap on the back that almost sent the Nubian tumbling.

"It's good to be here," he said, accepting a hug from Wynne and a fist bump from Zoo. "Kira tells me it was a bit trying."

"You and the spider are experts at understatement," Wynne told him. She nodded at Kira, who'd given them maneuvering space by leaning against the wall overlooking the city. "Our girl was in pure shock when you guys came through the portal. And she wouldn't let anyone else tend to you."

Kira folded her arms. Shock had been the least of what she'd felt once she'd come back to reality. "I'm just glad you guys remembered to bring our clothes with you. I can't imagine trying to get through this city without my gloves on."

"And I can't imagine going another moment without something to eat," Nansee piped up. "Let's dig in, shall we?"

Kira settled down with the others, barely paying attention as they dug into the meal of fresh-baked bread, fruit, *fuul*—a surprisingly delicious cross between a spread and a stew, made of fava beans—*t'aamiyya*—the Egyptian version of falafel—sweet Koshary tea, and more. The rooftop was one of thousands that had been turned into living spaces by Egyptians who couldn't afford or didn't want to live in the apartments below—or who, as they had from ancient times, simply used the roof as a cooler place to sleep at night. Somehow, Nansee had managed to find one in Old Cairo free of tenants and had also procured one of the smaller apartments below by putting the family up in one of the local hotels for a while. Tucked in among a hodge-podge of mosques, palaces, red brick apartments, new construction, and ruins from the pharaonic age, the rooftop served their purposes as a place to hide in plain sight while Khefar recovered from his wounds and they decided their next moves.

Coming back through the Veil was a hazy event in Kira's mind. The need for retribution had warred with the need to get Khefar back home. On top of that had been the power—so much wonderful, heady power channeling through her. It had been like being in a vortex of pure energy, like the product of two cyclones coming together.

She remembered half-dragging, half-carrying Khefar out of the remnants of Set's temple. Experiencing the life of Khefar's wife, Merire. Using Khefar's dagger to carve an opening in the Veil. Nansee holding the portal open with his multiple hands. Stepping through the portal the demigod had made for her had been like voluntarily pushing herself through a sieve. Then arriving in true Cairo with Khefar's lifeless body, power still riding her.

She knew her friends had backed off when she had asked them to, and she was grateful for it. With her extrasense and the dagger's power still clinging to her, and her anger over Khefar's condition still boiling, she'd been in a dangerous place. Not out of control, as she'd been in the cemetery back home, but close to not caring who stood between her and Khefar's safety. Any threat, any attack, would have unleashed the power that had thrummed through her pores. On some level she'd known: his safety was her safety, and getting him back meant she'd be able to come back.

As glad as she was to be relieved of his dagger, to be in control of herself and her power again, the taint of Shadow inside her felt larger, more solid. She'd beaten it back, thanks to Khefar's help, but it was still there, still waiting. The power drain had left her feeling tingly and needy. She wanted to channel that power again. Having both Light and Shadow coursing through her body had been a heady, thrilling experience. She wanted to feel it again. And, she could admit to herself, she *needed* to feel it again.

She returned to her spot leaning against the protective wall overlooking the shorter building to the left of theirs. To the west, she could see the glittering surface of the Nile. It seemed wider than it had yesterday when she'd last stared at it, but even if a river breach had been imminent, they couldn't have moved with Khefar still unconscious. They needed to find out how much time they had to get the Vessel of Nun to its rightful place.

More than that, they needed to know where that rightful place was.

Zoo joined her. "Glad to see you're better."

Kira forced her discomfort away. It wasn't Zoo's fault that she remained uncomfortable around him. "I'm glad to be better."

"We were worried about you," the witch continued. "Our tracer winked out the moment you guys stepped through the portal. Nansee couldn't track Khefar either, and Balm said you cut her connection to you. It was a tense couple of days until you called for Nansee to get you two out."

"I'm sorry you guys worried about us. I had no idea time ran differently over there. It felt like a handful of hours at the most."

"Balm has been trying to reach you," Zoo said.

Kira tensed. "I know. She's been calling to me since we came back through the Veil."

"You're not going to talk to her?"

"No."

"Why not?"

"She knows why." Kira wasn't ready to talk about what had happened to her on the other side, but she knew she'd have to process it somehow. Balm wouldn't leave her alone, and the first moment she settled down to sleep—and now that Khefar was healed, the crash would come soon—Balm would pounce.

"It seems like I've undergone a few changes," Khefar said, snagging her attention. He studied his braids in a mirror Wynne had given him, the plate before him empty. Kira wasn't exactly sure why his wounds had healed but his hair hadn't regenerated while the sun energized him, but the sides of his head were now neatly trimmed, the remaining braids like a faux-hawk in a strip down the middle of his scalp.

"I used a razor to neaten up the edges after the first sunrise," she told him as he looked at himself in the handheld mirror. "I figured I would leave it to you to decide if you wanted to keep the rest."

"I will." His expression darkened. "It took a long time to gain those braids. I'll keep the rest to remind me of that she-devil's face."

"I won't forget it either. She killed a handler without compunction. She tortured you until you died, for fun. This Shadowling is way too dangerous to remain loose. Especially if her master is Set."

The wind seemed to kick up, as if she'd called up the god of wind and desert. Maybe she had. She looked out over the rooftop. It was still early morning, but Cairo never truly slept. Sounds of traffic and life filtered up from the streets below, people going about their daily business all but oblivious to the metaphysical turmoil brewing around them. "Do you think He's emerging?"

Khefar returned the mirror to Wynne. "It would seem so. It certainly explains why Ma'at and Isis elevated us. And it explains why there's been a concerted effort to capture magical Egyptian artifacts."

"That's what I thought." She sighed. "Good thing we didn't think this would get simpler now."

"Whoa." Zoo held up his hands. "When you guys say 'Set,' you're talking about the old Egyptian god?"

"Yep."

"I want to say that's nothing but crazy talk, but I've just had breakfast with a West African demigod." Zoo looked a little ill in the morning light. "I traveled from the middle of London to Cairo in less time than it's taking me to say it, and I've seen enough to make me question my sanity. But I still have a hard time believing that some crusty old Egyptian god is our new big bad."

The breeze grew stiffer, as if indignant with the male witch's flippant tone. "I would caution you against poking at sleeping gods in their own beds, witchling," Nansee advised. "Gods are powerful when we have believers, but the ancient ones, the elemental ones, are powerful even with few worshippers."

"Dude, you just got served by a demigod," Wynne said, elbowing her husband with a grin. "Way to go."

Kira climbed to her feet. "Well, we know Set has at least one follower. At least, we think she follows him. Her name is Marit, and even if she follows no one, she's dangerous. Between the two of us, Khefar and I took out a bunch of her Shadowling followers, but I can't believe we've seen the end of her. She can probably grow back that hand I lopped off, but she wasn't happy with me for taking it. I think we can count on her making an appearance before we put the Vessel of Nun back where it belongs."

"You have a gift," Nansee said, his expression one of wonderment. "A definite gift for making enemies."

"I certainly wasn't going to try to be best buds with her. You know she killed a handler for no reason. You saw what she did to Khefar. For fun. Because she wanted some way to pass the time while waiting for me." Kira shook her head, unable to clear the memories from her mind's eye. "We'll meet again. I can promise you that."

"While I appreciate the sentiment, Kira, I don't need you to take revenge on my behalf," Khefar said then. "Unless this isn't about me, but part of something bigger."

She stared at him, wondering why it sounded like he was against her all of a sudden. "Is there something wrong with that?"

"Revenge, in and of itself, solves nothing." He climbed slowly to his feet. "What happened out there, Kira?"

She folded her arms. "Nothing."

"You told me that Nansee said we were gone two days' worth of time," Khefar said, his voice pitched just above the din of the waking city. "I don't know the time calculation between this side of the Veil and that one, but I do know there was time between you pushing Gunderson through the portal and coming to my aid. What happened?"

"I met someone."

"On the other side of the Veil?" Zoo blurted out. "I thought there were only Shadowlings over there."

"Yeah, kinda surprised me too." Kira kept her eyes on Khefar. "She told me her name is Solis."

"Solis?" Wynne echoed. "I thought we were talking about somebody named Marit."

"We were. Now we're not." Kira noticed that Khefar and Nansee both avoided her gaze. *Figures.* "Why don't one of you explain exactly who Solis is? Funny how you both seem amazingly unsurprised that I met her."

"I wasn't sure we were really Between," Khefar told her. "With the Shadowlings moving about so freely and little else, I was afraid we were someplace worse."

Her shoulders heaved, but she couldn't muster up the mirth to laugh. "There's worse? Considering what I saw them do to you, I can't imagine worse."

"There is always worse." He covered her fingers with his own. She could barely feel his hand. "Maybe you should talk to Balm."

"No." She pulled her hand free. "And don't try to distract me with all the touching. Maybe someone should finally start to tell me the truth around here. This Solis looks like an older version of Balm, except her eyes are green, not brown. She tells me she doesn't answer to Light or Shadow, but to the place of Balance between. And then she presents evidence like a trial lawyer, trying to convince me that neither Khefar nor I are human."

"So that's why you asked me if I was human earlier?" Khefar asked.

She nodded. "Solis implied that there was something that Balm was hiding from me—aside from Solis's existence, that is. I can tell you that Balm was screaming in my head to get out of there after I pushed Gunderson through. But when the sandstorm blew up and Solis appeared, Balm fell strangely silent. She's been trying to contact me since we got back, but I haven't wanted to talk to her."

"Kira, I promised you answers when we got back. That much I remember. I don't remember much else after I told you to get the other Chaser through the portal."

She threw up her hands. "Well, we're back. I'm tired of being kept in the dark about my own damn life. If you know something, if there's anything you know about who or what I am, you need to tell me!"

Regret splashed across Khefar's features. "I don't know anything about your past. I swear that I do not. I'm sorry."

"You are not sorry. You are just one more person determined to keep me in the dark about my own damn life!" She paced away from him, wanting to pummel him, wanting to leave him, but still needing him. "I can't believe you didn't tell me about that place—about her!"

"Kira." He stepped toward her. She glared at him but he ignored it, clamping his hands on her shoulders and lowering his face close to hers. "You're a Shadowchaser. When you use your magic, you call it pushing through the Veil. The Balm of Gilead calls you Daughter. How am I to believe that you did not already know about Solis, or the place between Light and Shadow? You're the Hand of Ma'at—She of the Scales! Your life and purpose is all about Order and Balance. Why by all the heavens would I think you unknowing?"

She stared at him, at his eyes burning with conviction. Here at least was truth. Finally. "I believe you. There's no reason for you to believe that Balm would keep whatever she is, whatever Solis is, from me. But why? Why would she do that?"

"I don't know."

She sank onto the carpet. "And I suppose if those two exist, then there's probably a third version, a Lady of Shadows."

"That's probably a safe assumption," Khefar said. He held his hands up, his fingers and thumbs forming a triangle. "There is Light. There is Shadow. And there is Between, which is supposed to be neutral, the place where the Scales stand. These three aspects are like three sides of a triangle. Balm, Solis, and the Third are like the triangle: three distinct sides that together make one unit, one shape."

His eyes grew as hard as obsidian chips. "Light is Light and Shadow is Shadow. Neutral is both and neither. As you've no doubt experienced with Solis, neutral isn't always so."

"And Light isn't always bright and joyous." She ran a hand through her braids, trying to reconcile her new knowledge with her old life. "Balm is screaming in my head, so I'm going to have to have a showdown with her sooner or later. That's my thing, and I'll deal with it. What we need to do now is find out how long we have to get the Vessel where it belongs. Have we confirmed the Nile is rising?"

"Wynne and I went out yesterday," Zoo said. "All people were talking about was how high and fast the Nile is flowing for this time of year. The government says that they're handling it, so no one's truly worried. Of course, as far as we know, the government doesn't know something supernatural is involved. We do. We looked at the river ourselves, and if it were up to me, I'd be making plans to evacuate. We've got some contacts here, so getting gear should be no problem."

"Okay."

"I have an idea of where the Vessel needs to go, but I want to see if we can get confirmation," Khefar told Kira. "And I'd like to offer a prayer of thanks for making it through. Care to join me?"

"I'd like that." She gathered the portable altar she'd set up while waiting for Khefar to resurrect.

"I'll watch over you while you pray," Nansee offered.

"Isn't that kinda weird?" Kira whispered to Khefar as he sat cross-legged in front of her. "One god watching over you while you pray to another?"

"I think we've already proven that Nansee is not your typical god. He doesn't need people to pray to him as much as he needs people to talk to."

"I'm not the jealous type, Kira," the demigod said, strolling the edge of the roof with his hands behind him as if the ground wasn't several stories below. "I'm okay if you see other gods."

She rubbed her forehead. "You know, it's hard to remember that he actually is a god."

"I'll take that as a compliment." Nansee reached the corner, then executed a graceful leaping spin that would have put Baryshnikov to shame.

Khefar leaned forward. "You're egging him on."

"I know. But ignoring him doesn't make him go away either."

"Hmph." Nansee coughed. "Don't you have some praying to do?"

Kira spread out a square of gold silk, then placed her mirror flat in the center of the square. She laid the replica sistrum within easy reach. Knowing she'd end up in Cairo, she hadn't asked Wynne and Zoo to bring any of her real altar artifacts. With her archaeological credentials—and assuming they would be exiting in a less exotic manner than that in which they had arrived—she'd never make it through Customs and Egypt's Supreme Council of Antiquities would assume she'd acquired undocumented pieces illegally with the intent of smuggling them out of the country. Plus there was the fact that none of them had exactly arrived officially in Egypt to start with; no passport stamp on landing here from Between. Somehow she didn't think the authorities would be too thrilled with the story that she'd entered the country through an otherworldly portal or that Wynne and Zoo had traveled with a demigod bringing an ancient artifact that would prevent the destruction of Egypt and the rest of the world.

She stripped off her gloves, then reached out to link hands with Khefar. "You start, and I'll use my extrasense to charge the mirror."

He nodded, then dropped his gaze to the mirror. "Mother of All, Lady Isis, She of Many Names, hail."

Kira joined in. "My Lady Ma'at, Goddess of Justice, She of the Eternal Truth, bless us with Your presence."

Blue power skated along the edge of the mirror, then poured into it like a rolling fog. The surface brightened to golden white. The feather imprint at her throat burned. She looked up, saw the Isis knot at Khefar's throat burnished with golden light. Their goddesses had heard them.

It was enough for Kira, but she knew there would be more to their audiences with Isis and Ma'at. The surface of the mirror went from a subdued glow to blinding brilliance. Kira squeezed her eyes closed as the outside world slipped away. She rolled with it like bodysurfing a wave, caught between euphoria and intrigue.

Finally, the light subsided. The first thing she noticed was that it didn't feel like a rooftop was beneath her. She cautiously opened her eyes. The sight of lush vegetation hugging the walls of a stone temple greeted her. The sound of rushing water greeted her ears. "Where are we?"

"Abu, now known as Elephantine."

Kira jerked around. Two golden-skinned women stood before them. Fine linen shifts draped their bodies, and both wore elaborate jeweled collars embedded with gold, lapis, and carnelian. One wore a headdress bearing a replica of a throne, the other wore one with a gleaming ostrich feather.

She dropped to the brushed sandstone a split second after Khefar did. "My Lady."

"Welcome, Hand of Ma'at," the goddess said in Her multilayered voice. "It pleases Me that you have endured for My sake, and your own."

"With Your grace and blessing, Lady of Truth," Kira said, tucking her chin in an attempt to resist the temptation to look up at the goddess. The only other time she'd ever actually conversed with Ma'at and heard the goddess's voice had been when she'd died. She wondered if it was possible to talk to Her like this more often, or only when the world was at stake.

"You talk to me often, young one," the personification of Truth and Order said. "I hear you and answer in ways that you need."

She thought about how different Ma'at was from Nansee, which immediately reminded her of something the spider god had mentioned a couple of weeks earlier. "So would you come to breakfast if I invited you?"

"Kira!" Khefar's voice was a low hiss as he clamped a hand around her wrist.

Isis laughed, a musical sound that had Kira shaking in pleasure. "You have spent too much time with Nansee. But then, the Spider of the Western Shore has a proclivity for being where he should not. Don't you, Kweku Ananse?"

Nansee stepped from behind a tree to the left of the temple. This version of the demigod, however, dressed in traditional Ashanti garb, was much younger, virile, and almost sexy.

"Why are you here, old man?" Khefar said, obviously not impressed with Nansee's appearance.

"I could not resist being in the presence of two of the most famous beauties of the Kemetic pantheon," the young Nansee said. "Is that so wrong?"

Ma'at smiled. "These young ones are so brash."

"Especially this one," Isis agreed. She turned back to the demigod. "Thank you for helping Our children in ways that We cannot."

Nansee gave a gracious bow. "My pleasure, ladies."

"We will need to impose upon you for your assistance once again, I fear."

Nansee's smile faded. "You mean the Vessel of Nun."

Ma'at inclined Her head. "The Vessel must be given back to Satet on Abu. She waits in the place that measures the Nile."

"The nilometer on Elephantine Island," Kira murmured. It made sense. The island was located on the First Cataract of the Nile, which had served as the natural barrier between Egypt and Nubia for millennia, and had long been considered by the ancients as the source of the Nile. Egyptian agriculture was completely dependent on the annual inundation of the Nile and the nutrient-rich soil it deposited every year. The nilometers were ancient devices used to measure the level of the Nile, to warn of flooding or drought. There were two nilometers on Elephantine: one a pit-style one dedicated to Khnum, the god of the source of the Nile; and another more like a staircase leading down to the river, dedicated to Satet.

"I will be more than happy to take Kira and Khefar to Elephantine Island," Nansee said gallantly. "We will return the vase to its rightful owner and stop the premature inundation of the Nile."

"You must not use your usual method of travel, Spider," Ma'at cautioned. "Your last journey weakened the Vessel."

Kira's heart jumped in her chest. Khefar had told her Nansee's travels were worse than what they'd felt going through the portal. If that was true, they couldn't subject the vase to further metaphysical travel. If the Vessel suffered further damage, it wouldn't be strong enough to hold back the force of the Nile.

"How much time do we have?" Khefar asked.

"Another day, perhaps less," Isis answered. "You must return Satet's vase as soon as you can."

"Your journey will not be easy, my daughter," Ma'at cautioned. "Other forces are working to stop you."

"You mean Set." Kira gritted her teeth.

"Our brother Set slumbers still," Isis said, "but his rest will soon be at an end. As We have called to you, so does He call for His children."

Kira thought of Marit. Blood pounded between her ears. "Let Marit come and try to stop me. I'll be ready for her."

"Do not let your anger impede your actions, child of Mine," Ma'at chided.

Kira lowered her head. "Yes, my Lady. Forgive me."

"Your fervor is . . . appreciated. Set can be temperamental and unpredictable, and He will gift His children with those qualities. It is more important that you disregard everything but the safe return of the Vessel of Nun to its proper place. You, Daughter, must be the one to restore the vase to Satet's embrace."

"What I am to do?" Khefar wondered.

Isis regarded him. "As you have always done, loyal one. You must prepare to wield the Dagger of Kheferatum."

Kira caught his gaze. It took a long moment for Khefar to nod. She understood his reluctance. If the goddess meant for him to prepare to use the dagger, it meant he'd be faced with a situation in which he'd have no other option but to draw it. She just had to hope that it didn't mean he'd have to draw it against her.

"The time grows short, children," Isis said, her gaze gentle. "Know that Our blessings are with you."

The vision of the island, the temple, and the two goddesses faded. Kira opened her eyes to find herself on the rooftop, her hands still clasped in Khefar's. Nansee still walked the edge of the rooftop as if only moments had passed. Her numb behind told her otherwise.

She glared at Nansee as she pulled her hands away. "Thanks for crashing."

"Your goddesses didn't seem to mind," Nansee said, sounding completely unapologetic.

"You're a demigod," Kira argued. "You can talk to them any time you want to."

"What, do you think there's some sort of Divine Facebook where we keep up with each other?" Nansee hopped off the ledge. "Now you know that you don't have to be so formal when reaching out to Ma'at. Surely that accounts for something."

"We need the ceremony just as much as They do," Kira shot back. "It imparts a specialness. It seems wrong to send a text message to your god."

"We can argue later," Khefar said, rolling to his feet before helping Kira up. "Right now, we need to figure out how to get to Elephantine Island. It's roughly six hundred miles south of here."

"Air is out," Kira said. "It would flag all kinds of security if we chartered a flight on the spur of the moment, especially if we have the Vessel of Nun with us."

"What about one of the feluccas?"

Kira shook her head. "Boat would be too slow, and we'd only get as far as the next cataract."

"That leaves car or camel," Nansee said.

"Car," Kira and Khefar said in unison. "Definitely car."

Chapter 20

They quickly packed their belongings, Nansee working some particular magic to make the bulk of them compress into four lightweight backpacks. The Vessel of Nun hung in front of Kira in a reinforced and padded duffel. She would have preferred something sturdier, but the usual archival containers would have practically screamed "steal me," and she really didn't want to chase down a thief on Cairo's busy streets.

Cairo in November was a completely different beast than London. The largest city in the Arab world was ancient and modern and beautiful and plain, a study in contradictions in its gold and grit, mosques and churches, noise and peace, pollution and pristine desert.

She wanted to be excited over being in the city again. The Central Museum was located in downtown Cairo on Midan Tahrir, a relatively new section compared to other districts that had been drained and developed in the mid-nineteenth century. Kira had only viewed the museum's eye-popping collection twice, when she and Comstock had spent two days browsing antiquities like kids in a toy store at Christmastime. Unfortunately she wouldn't get to visit the hall of mummies or Tutankhamun's burial mask on this trip. If they didn't find a way to return the Vessel of Nun to its rightful place, no one else ever would.

They made their way into the Khan el-Khalili market. The Khan was one of the oldest known continual marketplaces in the world, dating from the fourteenth century. Egyptians and tourists alike shopped its canvas-covered streets. Most of the crowded thoroughfares specialized in certain types of merchandise. Perfumers and spice merchants, for example, occupied the ever-fragrant Muski Street.

The Khan was truly the heart and soul of Cairo, thronged with people, animals, and products of all types. If it wasn't available in the Khan, it couldn't be had anywhere in Egypt, or perhaps the entire Middle East. According to the Marlowes, there were more than a few people in the market who sold what they wanted: information.

They stopped in front of what was ostensibly a stall hawking adventure guides, posters, and handouts offering a variety of tour packages, from camel caravans to luxury outings sailing on the Nile at sunset. A smiling man wearing a beige galabia and a simple turban greeted them. "Welcome, welcome. Are you wonderful couples looking for a romantic cruise?"

Wynne gave Kira a wink, but she studiously ignored her friend, who'd covered her hair with a dark scarf. Zoo stepped forward. "My name's Marlowe. I spoke to Hassam a little while ago."

The man's smile faded as he looked at each of them in turn. He stepped back, lifting a striped curtain that revealed a larger area behind the counter. "Please, come inside."

Kira surreptitiously swept the area with her extrasense. There were a few hits but they weren't close. She nodded, and they moved behind the counter to the inner portion of the shop. The interior boasted a few low stools, more posters and maps, a small cooking stove for warmth and brewing coffee. Another man dressed in jeans and a black Oxford shirt who looked to be in his late thirties sat on a stool, a laptop perched on his lap.

He looked up, surveyed the group. "I don't know if now is a good time for the type of excursion you requested," he said, his voice holding a trace of a British accent. "The government is saying that the Nile has reached unprecedented levels in the last couple of days. There are even rumors that Aswan won't be able to hold it."

"That is precisely why we need to go, Hassam," Zoo said. "You agreed to this."

"So I did, Zeroun," the man said, surprising Kira by using Zoo's given name. "That was before I had all the necessary information."

"What sort of information?" Khefar asked.

"I've been warned to watch for strangers, particularly the couple with braided hair," Hassam said. "Word is that they mean to destroy our way of life, and should be reported to the authorities right away."

Kira tensed. She dialed up her extrasense a little bit more. If anyone came toward the shop with the intent to apprehend, she'd get advance warning. She didn't want to destroy part of the market making their escape, but she would if she had to. Nothing could impede their mission, not even innocents.

"Hassam, you know me," Zoo said. "You call me by

my name as if to remind me that we're friends. Didn't I introduce you to your wife? Didn't you name your second son after me?"

"So I did." Hassam rose. "Yet you appear just when the Nile seems to have forgotten her children, threatening us in winter as we sleep. When dust storms come out of the west and south. Darkness edges out the horizon and now you are here." He regarded them warily. "I am left to wonder, old friend, if your appearance can be trusted in such unusual times."

"We can be trusted," Khefar said then. "We come to right the wrong."

"Who are you?"

"My name is Khefar," the Nubian answered. He then slipped into Arabic. At least Kira thought it was Arabic, but he spoke so fast, she couldn't follow. Hassam answered him, and they proceeded with a rapid-fire exchange that made her head spin. Zoo nodded as he listened, so Kira had to assume the discussion was favorable.

Zoo then asked a question, his Arabic not as fluent as Khefar's. But then, Zoo's family was Hungarian and Khefar had called Egypt home for four millennia. He probably had been in Cairo when it became a Muslim city.

Hassam nodded, walked over to a cabinet, and removed a set of keys. He handed them to Zoo, then nodded to Khefar. "May Allah be with you and the Light shine on you."

They left the shop. Kira fell into step beside Khefar. "Do I even want to know what you guys offered him to make him agree to rent us the truck?"

"I did not offer anything," the Nubian replied. "I merely told him the truth."

"What truth? About Isis and Ma'at and Set? That truth?"

"Of course not. Not really. I merely built upon his friendship with Zoo and my fluency in Arabic to deepen the rapport and convince him we only had good intentions. And that he could make more money if he chose to add a specific sort of clientele to his customer base."

Zoo coughed. "And I promised that Gilead would buy him a brand-new Range Rover whether or not we damaged this one."

"That would certainly do it. Where's this Rover?"

"There." Zoo pointed to a battered white Range Rover, at least five years old, with the travel company's logo stuck to the driver's door.

Wynne stared at the vehicle. "Are we sure this thing is going to get us where we need to go?"

"Only one way to find out." Zoo unlocked the utility vehicle. They piled their gear into the back of the SUV, then climbed in. The charcoal gray interior had also seen better days, but at least the seats were solid. Or not so solid, since Kira could sense weapons hidden beneath the cushions.

"Where are we going?' Zoo asked. "You didn't mention a destination in the shop."

"That was deliberate," Khefar said. "Hassam may be a good man, but he's also a businessman. No doubt he's already sent word that we've come to visit him. We need to be prepared."

"I'll ride shotgun with you then," Kira offered. "I can keep watch."

"You can get rest," the Nubian said, blocking her way to the passenger side. "I know you've been avoiding real sleep since you brought me back through the portal. Nansee can ride shotgun while the Marlowes take the back seat. We've got six hundred miles to travel, and the roads here aren't like the U.S. highway system. It's going to take us a while to get to where we're going."

They arranged themselves in the Rover, Khefar and Nansee in the front, Zoo and Wynne in the second set of seats. Kira climbed in the back with their gear. She needed to rest, she knew. She dreaded the idea though. Balm still called out for her, and the head of Gilead was getting harder and harder to ignore. Her only saving grace was her current mission returning the Vessel of Nun. Balm wouldn't try to interfere with that, but as soon as Kira attempted to get more rest, Balm would probably be knocking on her mental door, demanding to talk.

She needed to talk to Balm. For years she'd been searching for answers, and she'd always believed her surrogate mother held most, if not all, of the answers. That Balm refused to share them even now perplexed and infuriated her.

Wynne turned to lean over the back of her seat. "Are you okay?"

"I don't think I have to worry about getting some shut-eye," she said. "The suspension will keep me awake."

"You should try. You know we'll wake you up at the first sign of trouble."

"I know. But my mind's racing. I doubt if even counting sheep will work."

Wynne grinned. "Then maybe you should dream about that couples' vacation I mentioned a while back."

Kira rolled her eyes. "There you go again with that fairy tale."

"'Denial' isn't just a river in Egypt, *chica*," Wynne said. "Say what you want, but I ain't blind and y'all ain't quiet."

Kira felt her face flame. "You're impossible."

"Yep," Wynne agreed cheerfully. "But you love me anyway."

"I'm going to sleep now," Kira announced, then turned her back on her friend. Wynne just giggled in response.

Kira shook her head but couldn't erase her smile. Wynne had the kind of spirit and temperament that couldn't be repressed for long. Kira needed that, now more than ever. When everything else went to hell around her, she knew she could trust these people to have her back.

Closing her eyes, Kira finally gave in to the urge to sleep.

Khefar drove out of Cairo and took El Maryouteya Road south toward Dashur, alternating his gaze between the windshield and the rearview mirror. If the roads held, they had a good twelve hours' drive ahead of them. Egypt's cross-country roads were notoriously fickle, however, and he didn't hold out much hope for a straight shot from Cairo to Aswan. With the need to be unobtrusive, even taking a boat on the Red Sea would attract too much attention. He wanted the journey to be uneventful, if only so that Kira could get the rest she needed for the final phase of their mission.

The Nile snaked to the east of their location. It had definitely risen, and people had thronged the bridges over the river as they left Cairo, gawking at the unusual sight. In less than a day, the life-giving waters would crest its banks, inundating the verdant strip of land that embraced it, rendering the people subject to its mercy as they'd been in the centuries before the Aswan Dam was installed.

Worry settled heavily on Khefar's shoulders. He worried about whatever and whoever had been brought in to oppose them. He worried about whether they would reach Elephantine Island in time, what they'd be required to do to return the Vessel of Nun to Satet's arms. He worried about the pressure Kira endured, the swath of Shadow that streaked her soul. Most of all, he worried about Isis's warning that he had to be prepared to use the Dagger of Kheferatum.

He was always prepared to wield Atum's blade; he just preferred not to call its true power. Creating and destroying were always last resorts to be used in extreme circumstances. In four millennia, he could only recall three instances in which he'd called upon the dagger to erase existence, instances that were burned into his psyche. Even Marit did not deserve to be unmade, despite what she'd done to him. Who else then could Isis have meant, except for Kira?

He glanced in the rearview mirror again. Kira had curled up in the back of the Rover with their gear, out of his line of vision. He hoped that Balm would leave Kira alone long enough to get some rest. From what she and the others had said, Kira hadn't allowed herself more than catnaps after bringing him back through the portal. She needed serious downtime. Even the Chaser of Chasers needed time to regroup and recover from what she'd witnessed on the other side of the Veil.

How could Balm not have told Kira about Solis and the other "sister"? How could the head of Gilead have kept her surrogate daughter in the dark about something so fundamental to the Commission's existence—to Balm's existence? He couldn't understand Balm's motives, but, then, he never had. He could understand why Kira didn't want to talk to her. She'd never trust that what Balm told her was true.

She hadn't told him much about what had happened with Solis, the Lady of Balance. He just knew that Kira had come back through the Veil questioning her humanity. If Balm had sent her best Shadowchaser into the fray so ill-prepared, no wonder the other Shadowchasers were being picked off or turned.

"Ease, my boy," Nansee said, breaking into his thoughts. "I'm sure the steering wheel means you no harm."

"It's not the wheel I worry about," he retorted, his eyes once again sweeping their surroundings. Nothing but bright blue sky, golden sand, a swath of green, with occasional glimpses of the fast-running Nile.

"There's no need to borrow trouble, Khefar," the demigod said. "I'm sure we'll be neck-deep in it soon enough."

Khefar cut a glance at the spider. "Do you sense anything?"

"At the moment there is nothing save storm clouds gathering on the western horizon."

The western horizon. Khefar touched the Isis knot at the base of his throat. The west, where the dead went, following the sun into the afterlife. The west, where the desert stretched, the ancient domain of Set. Now storm clouds frothed in the far distance, rainclouds that should not be. Foreboding crept over him, settling into his bones. Things were going to get worse before they got better.

"Something else troubles you?"

Khefar forced his shoulders to loosen. "I'm sorry. This land holds several lifetimes of memories and failures for me."

"Well, we're not going to add another failure today," Zoo said from the backseat.

"No, not today," Khefar agreed. "Is Kira finally asleep?"

Wynne glanced over the back. "Yeah, she's crashed. Usually she's out for about five or six hours at least, so as long as we're not attacked and Balm doesn't disturb her, she should be able to recoup."

"Good." He relaxed further. "I don't know how long we'll have peace and quiet. Balm will find us before the Shadowling. At least I hope so. Not that I plan to make it easy for them. This road takes us past Saqqara to Dashur. We'll need to schedule a couple of refueling stops. I'd rather we make those breaks as quick as possible, then we'll keep switching roads as we head farther south. Our opponents probably assumed we took the road closest to the Nile or headed out to the desert. If they don't try to intercept us beforehand, I suspect we'll encounter them somewhere south of Dashur just before or after sunset when the light is bad. If not, then I suppose in twelve or fourteen hours we'll make it to Aswan, hopefully none the worse for wear."

Nansee looked out his window toward the desert. "The Golden Ladies said we couldn't take the Vessel sliding, but they didn't say anything about me working a bit of charm on the road."

"What sort of charm is that?" Wynne asked.

"I have a way with roads. Let's just say that while everyone else is traveling at regular speeds and distances, I'm adjusting the web of the roads, making it faster here, a shorter distance there. I think I can at least cut our journey in half without putting too much undue stress on the Vessel of Nun."

"Awesome!" Wynne enthused. "That's just the kind of break we need!"

"Maybe," Khefar said. "I'm not going to underestimate the other side. Even if we do outmaneuver them, we still have to get the Vessel to Satet. If I remember correctly there's a temple to Satet on Elephantine. The goddesses said that Kira has to be the one to return the Vessel to its rightful place, but I have a feeling it's not going to be easy even if Marit and her Shadowlings stay out of sight."

"Kira can return the Vessel," Zoo said. "But she's not going to be alone. Neither are you. We've got your backs. It's what we do, and we're pretty damn good at it."

Wynne nodded. "Like it or lump it, we're all in this together."

"Hey, I'm army from way back," Khefar said. "I know the power of the team. We just have to make sure our Shadowchaser remembers that."

Chapter 21

Kira sat on a rough-hewn bench with faded tapestry cushions, her back against a gray stone wall. Thick glass windows were set into the corridor every few feet in a vain attempt to brighten the hallway. She didn't know what this place was that her adoptive father had brought her to; she'd stopped caring and paying attention once she realized they were sending her away.

She could hear the deep but muted rumble of waves breaking against a rocky shoreline. Kira knew now that they'd come to an island called Santa Costa, a tiny speck of sun-drenched rock and dirt in the middle of the Aegean. This building was a part of a sprawling sun-bleached complex perched atop a cliff, a structure that couldn't decide if it wanted to be a Hellenic temple or a European castle. For Kira, sitting alone in the hallway as she'd done so many years ago, it still felt more like a prison.

She wondered if this was her memory or Balm's. This was where she'd sat as her family had given her away, had abandoned her to the woman who'd honed Kira's talents, saved her life, then forged her into a weapon. Beyond the thick paneled door lay Balm's office, and the two people deciding her fate.

Her thoughts triggered the scene, taking her for the first time into the office. The room looked as if it belonged to someone who knew what electricity was, but didn't trust it. A fire burned in the stone fireplace. Tapestries and paintings attempted to warm the dark gray walls. Lanterns and candles were used for lighting, strategically scattered about the room.

Balm sat behind a free-form desk that looked as if it had been carved from a single piece of redwood burl, her back straight, her hands folded atop the gleaming surface, still young, still beautiful. Kira's adoptive father slumped in the green high-back guest chair across from the head of Gilead, his face in his hands.

"Are you telling me that you're neglecting your duty, Gavriel?" Balm questioned, her voice as smooth and soothing as her name. "A duty, might I add, that you volunteered for?"

"We've done everything we can do," her father continued, his voice thickening. "But she—she refuses to listen to us, and her—her problem just keeps growing. Bethany's at her wits' end."

Balm's expression didn't change, didn't show an ounce of sympathy. "You knew what you were getting into, Mr. Solomon. So did your wife."

Kira stared, her mind locked with shock. Balm had known her already? Balm had coordinated her adoption with the Solomons?

"We can't help her," her father said then. "We certainly don't dare to touch her anymore. Not after what she did to Gilly!"

"Do not blame Kira for this, Gavriel," Balm said.

"You assured us that you couldn't have children of your own, which was a condition of the adoption."

"Gilly is our miracle child, and now she's in a coma, because of that, that—"

"Mind your tongue!" Balm shot to her feet. "You knew how important this was, for Kira to be raised in a loving, normal household. You knew she needed a safe environment in which to explore all that humanity has to offer."

All that humanity has to offer? Even in this pseudo-dream, Kira felt numb. What did Balm mean? Had Solis told her the truth—was she truly not human?

The Balm of Gilead leaned over the desk, her eyes blazing red-gold in the lantern light. "You neglected to inform us about Gillian, you didn't tell us about the changes Kira has experienced. You did not tell us about how you allowed her to roam the countryside like a wild animal scrounging for roots and vegetables as best she could. You didn't tell us any of that, Gavriel Solomon, yet you continued to accept the stipend sent to you while you duct-taped garden gloves to the child's hands."

"What else was I supposed to do? We did the best we could."

"Your best was not even adequate," Balm told him. "Your only saving grace is that you voluntarily brought the child back to us."

She straightened, then picked up a slip of paper from her desk, held it out to him. "Thank you for your time, Mr. Solomon. The Gilead Commission no longer requires your services."

Gavriel Solomon rose to his feet, his stance

unsteady. He stared at the check in Balm's hand, the only sound in the office that of the fire crackling in the fireplace. After a moment, he reached out a shaky hand, fingers wrapping around the check. He slipped it into his front pocket. "What's going to happen to her?"

"That's no longer your concern, is it?" Balm asked, the soothing tone of her voice completely at odds with the fire burning in her eyes. "If it indeed ever was. Clarence will see to it that you make it back to the mainland. May the Light shine upon you."

Balm made the blessing sound like a curse. She retook her seat and picked up a stack of papers, effectively dismissing Gavriel Solomon as a white-robed acolyte opened a paneled door on the far side of the office. The papers in Balm's hands fluttered, then caught fire.

She dropped them to the desk, then pressed her hands atop them, snuffing out the flames. It was a long moment before she moved again, straightening with a sigh. "I'm sorry, Ana," she whispered. "I thought I'd done right by Kira. I promise, I'll do right by her now."

Balm pushed to her feet again and crossed to the heavy timbered door that led to the hallway. Kira knew what happened after that, her first meeting with the Balm of Gilead, the day her life irrevocably changed as she chose to live with her abilities instead of die in misery.

The vision changed. Balm once again sat behind her desk, Kira in the seat her father had occupied all those years ago. Candles and lanterns still lit most of the room, but a task lamp and laptop sat atop the one-of-a-kind desk. The head of Gilead looked the same as she always did, the epitome of serenity in a body that seemed to have stopped aging in its thirties. Yet they both knew things had changed. Too many things.

Balm broke the heavy silence first. "Do you wish to talk about what you saw on the other side of the Veil?"

Of the verbal minefields Kira could navigate, talking about the in-between place would be far safer than what she really wanted to discuss. "You mean Solis, who'd be a dead ringer for you if you aged another twenty years? She called you Lady of Light."

"That's been one of my names. Just as she's been called the Lady of Balance."

"And is there a third? Equal sides of a triangle like Khefar said?"

"The Nubian talks too much." Balm pushed back from her desk. "Yes, there's a Lady of Shadows as well. Some say we served as inspiration for the Moirae, the three Fates of Greek mythology, though they were far kinder than we can be. The universe is always about Balance and being balanced."

"So I've learned."

"You know there's always been a Balm in Gilead, a Lady of Light. Because there is Light, there is Shadow. And because there is Balance there must be a way to measure that Balance. Light, Shadow, and the in-Between. It's a quirk of the universe, or perhaps just human nature, that called us into being. There have always been these aspects personified in some form or another, just as the ancient Egyptians took the concepts of truth and order and personified them into Ma'at."

Kira rubbed at her forehead. "Are you telling me that you're a goddess, all of you are goddesses?"

"It would depend on the definition of 'goddess,'" Balm told her. "If you believe that a being born into this existence can then ascend to a higher state of being in order to embody a fundamental tenet, then yes, we three could be described as goddesses. I don't need anyone to pray to me, though I suppose you could characterize those who work for Gilead as my followers. I am an earthly construct of a universal concept, granted certain rights and abilities by Universal Law. Before I assumed my current state, I was a normal woman." She smiled. "Well, as normal as a hybrid can be."

Kira's mouth dropped open. "The Balm of Gilead is a hybrid?"

"I was, a long time ago. My family were akin to what you might call dryads, and we lived in the cedar forests of Lebanon. There have been a few human Balms too, but the Gilead Commission decided that hybrids, being part-human and part-Other, were better suited to the role."

More truth, more questions being answered, finally. Except the answers Kira received seem to lead to even more questions. She stared at Balm, understanding why the woman was long-lived. Dryads tended to live as long as the trees they bonded to. The ones in Sequoia National Forest in California had amazing tales to tell, when one could tempt them out into the open. This version of Balm could easily be a thousand years old, if not older.

"You said there were others before you, but you

have a lot of knowledge that I didn't find anywhere in Santa Costa's extensive library."

"That's because that information isn't, and shouldn't be, easily accessible," Balm answered. "Most of that knowledge was imprinted on me when I became Balm. I suppose you can say who I am and how I am is quite like being the Dalai Lama."

"So you're the reincarnated soul of the original Balm?"

Dark curls glistened in candlelight as Balm nodded. "That's close enough. I use the memories of those who've gone before me and the wishes of those who will come after to run the affairs of Gilead. The Commission is charged with finding the candidate to be the next Balm but otherwise takes my direction."

"Okay, if all that is true, how was I going to be able to follow in your footsteps?" Kira asked. "You said you wanted me to take over for you one day."

"That is true, at least until I realized your temperament was better suited to being a Shadowchaser. A soul can become as weary as a body. It needs rest and rejuvenation too. Though it was a long time ago, if I try I can remember living with my clan in a wonderful cedar grove. Sometimes I make it back there, just to touch the trees, but it doesn't happen nearly often enough. I've put some in the gardens here, but it's not the same as being in native soil."

For a moment, Balm did indeed look in need of rest. "Yours is a young soul, Kira, strong and full of fire. I thought that perhaps, if you were agreeable and amenable, that you could be groomed to assume the duties and burdens this soul carries."

"But you said someone has to be a hybrid and has to be able to ascend," Kira pointed out. "I'm pretty sure I'm not cut out for goddess stuff, much less qualified."

"Probably not." A ghost of a smile. "If becoming a Shadowchaser is like jumping into sulfur springs, then the soul training to become Balm is like strolling into Kilauea."

"I'll stick with being a Shadowchaser then, thanks." Kira stared at the woman on the other side of the desk, a woman responsible for sending young men and women up against the worst Shadow had to offer. It would be a heavy burden for any soul to bear, even more so for a soul that had existed for thousands of years.

"I'm surprised at how forthcoming you've been with information this time around," Kira said, also surprised at how calm she felt. "Does this mean that you're finally willing to answer questions now?"

"I was always willing to give you answers, Kira. I just wanted you to come up with the questions on your own."

Twisted, but so like Balm. "All right, then. Tell me who Ana is."

"She was your mother. She died shortly after you were born."

The loss of a woman she didn't know, had never met, cut through Kira like a dagger thrust. The visceral emotion stole her breath. She bent over double in the chair, trying to collect herself.

"Did she die giving birth to me?"

Balm hesitated. "There were complications with your birth, but her death wasn't your fault." The Gilead leader's voice firmed. "I'll not have you thinking such things. You can stop that here and now."

Kira nodded. "Of course." What would be the point of feeling guilty over something she'd had no control over? Of course, that logic hadn't worked concerning the innocents she'd killed in Atlanta, and it didn't work with this newfound knowledge about her mother.

She leaned forward. "Tell me everything you know about her. What was she like? Did you know her personally?"

"I knew Ana," Balm said softly. "I was very close to her family, and Ana and I were good friends. You're like her in many ways. Stubborn, brilliant, protective, fierce, and willing to sacrifice anything for those you love."

"Was she . . . was she human?"

Again Balm hesitated. "For all intents and purposes, yes, Ana was human. Her branch of the family made a conscious decision centuries ago to breed out their paranormal nature and become fully human. All they wanted was to live their lives as normally and humanly as possible, to live in Balance in all things. Aside from a few surprises, just about everyone in your mother's immediate family could pass as human, even medically."

Kira looked down at her hands. So Solis had been right. She wasn't human. She'd merely been masquerading as one. "And by 'a few surprises,' you mean me. So what sort of hybrids am I descended from? Is any of my family still around?"

"Your family were part of a group of beings considered to be the guardians of thunder and lightning by various peoples in Africa, including the Dahomey,"

Balm said. "As for relatives, your mother was an only child. Her extended family took part in a great diaspora long before Julius Caesar set his sights on uniting the world. I wouldn't know how to locate them now."

"What about my father?" Kira wondered. "Did you know him?"

"I'm sorry, Kira. I don't know who your father was. Ana never told me."

"Why?"

Balm looked away. "I am giving you truth, Kira. What is the benefit of having every little detail?"

Kira ground her teeth in frustration. So many answers, so many questions still unanswered. "Because we're talking about my life. The basis of who and what I am. I have a right to know!"

The other woman finally nodded. "Ana wasn't married. She might have been ashamed that it happened. I tried to convince her there was nothing to be ashamed of, that the people who loved her, loved her unconditionally." Balm closed her eyes briefly. "I don't know if she believed me, but I'd like to think so."

"Did she even know if he was human or hybrid?"

"If she did, she never revealed that to me. I can only speculate that, given your peculiar ability and affinity for channeling and throwing power and your extrasense, your father was more than likely a high-level hybrid of some sort."

Kira stared at the other woman, trying to read Balm's indecipherable expression. She remembered her talk with Solis and took a wild guess. "You think he was a Shadowling, don't you? A Shadowling who assaulted Ana."

A slight wrinkle momentarily marred Balm's brow. "It is one of the many options I considered. Again, I never had proof or confirmation, just pure speculation on my part. I can only guess, based on the fact that Ana didn't reveal your father's identity and that she didn't want me to be biased against you. As if I could ever be biased against a child of hers."

Kira dropped her head. What else could her father have been but a hybrid, or a full-on Shadowling? The most that full-blooded humans could be were either psychics or witches. None of them could do what she could. Hybrids were the mutated offspring of humans and the children of Light and Shadow. Werefolk, the fey, vampires—almost all the so-called mythical creatures on the planet came from those types of unions. Now she knew why the taint of Shadow she'd felt would never go away, just as Solis had said. The Shadow-poisoned dagger hadn't infected her—it had awakened a dormant part deep inside her. The answer had been staring at her since puberty; she had just refused to see it.

"Why didn't you tell me any of this before now?"

"Because I promised Ana." Sorrow crossed Balm's features. "She wanted you to have as normal a life as possible, as human a life as possible. Nurture would trump nature, she always told me. It was a core belief of her family and I saw for myself that it was so. So I interviewed dozens of couples in order to find one good enough to raise Ana's daughter. I thought I'd found that with the Solomons."

Balm fiddled with the wireless mouse beside her laptop. "Ana was sure that nothing would happen when you reached puberty, that the care her people had taken to embrace their humanity would subjugate any hybrid instinct you might have developed. To be honest, I wasn't so sure. Not based on anything concrete, mind you. The Solomons were supposed to report any physiological changes to me at once."

Red sparks lit the depths of Balm's eyes. "As you saw, Gavriel and Bethany hid your changes from me. I am used to making hard choices and living with the ramifications of those choices without dwelling on regrets or what might have been. But it . . . grieved me to know that you were mistreated, that you suffered and that my promise to your mother was in jeopardy."

Kira didn't doubt Balm's words. Here, at last, was truth in all its plain, brutal coldness. "I spent so many months being angry, hating myself, feeling guilty for what I did to my sister, for causing my parents pain to the point that they chose to throw me away." She curled her hands. "I felt all of that because I thought they loved me. I thought they picked me out of all the other children because they wanted me. It took me years to believe that they weren't going to send me back, that they really wanted to keep me, that it was okay to call them Mom and Dad and believe we were a real family. But it was a lie!"

"Kira—"

"Don't try to tell me different, Balm!" Kira shot to her feet, angry tears blurring her vision. "They only wanted me because you paid them to want me. You paid them to pretend to love me just so I wouldn't become a bad seed! And it worked too, until they had a real human daughter. Until they saw what life could be like if they didn't have to raise the freak!"

"Enough!" Balm's hands slapped the desk, the sound thunderous. Power thrummed through the room as she rose, her eyes sparking fire as she glared at Kira. "I will not have you describing yourself in such a way! I put the Solomons through a rigorous vetting process. If you felt any affection from them, it was true, not manufactured. They did have your best interests at heart, at least at the beginning. But people can change."

"They changed when they had Gilly."

"That was probably the start of it, yes." Balm continued to stare at her. "Are you going to blame Gillian for that? Are you going to stand there and tell me that you believe your sister's affection for you was also purchased?"

Kira's heart tightened as she thought of her sister. She'd spent years trying to find Gilly after leaving Santa Costa, wanting to apologize, wanting to make sure Gilly had recovered, wanting her forgiveness. It had never happened, and she could only assume that the Solomons wanted to make sure she never found them or Gilly again, or that they were all dead.

"No. The only thing I am sure of is that Gilly loved her big sister." She sighed, trying to push the emotion away. "So you bought Gavriel Solomon off and decided to raise me yourself here on Santa Costa."

Balm nodded as she retook her seat. "My goal was always to protect you, Kira. To fulfill your mother's wish and see that you had a happy and normal life. But your power had already manifested and you had endured several months of suffering without any guidance or training. I couldn't place you with another family. I had no choice but to break my vow to Ana to see that you were happy. I thought it better to see that you survived, that you managed your abilities and could willfully manipulate that power instead of letting it manipulate you."

The head of Gilead ran her hands repeatedly over the smooth wood surface of her desk, a gesture that spoke volumes about her emotional state. "I thought once I'd taught you to control your abilities, you would turn to a life of quiet study and contemplation that would enable you to one day replace me as head of Gilead. I thought it would be the best way of fulfilling my promise to your mother and letting you have the best of both the human and paranormal worlds. Your natural curiosity paled in the face of your bottomless rage, however. I reluctantly agreed to send you to Shadowchaser training, and you took to it like a fish to water, despite how difficult we made it for you."

"My training was more intense than everybody else's," Kira said. It wasn't what she wanted to say, what she wanted to talk about, but Balm had deluged her with truth and information and it was hard for the analytical part of her mind to process everything. "I just assumed my training was harder because you didn't want to be seen as playing favorites."

"I didn't." Balm managed a smile then. "More than that, I wanted you to be able to handle anything and everything that the universe chose to gift you with. I didn't tell you anything about your background because I thought that knowledge would be detrimental to what you really needed to learn, which was how to be comfortable in your own skin. You are a good

Shadowchaser, the best the Commission has seen in centuries. We could not squander your abilities by forcing you to remain here. I also felt it important for you to experience the world and what it has to offer. If you decided you wanted to return to Santa Costa, to Gilead, it would be of your own free will after making an informed decision."

"Comfortable in my own skin." Kira laughed, wiping at her eyes with a shaky hand. "You think I was comfortable in my skin before I learned all this? Knowing that I'm not human, that I was *never* human—is that supposed to make me more comfortable now?"

"Daughter—"

Kira recoiled. "Don't call me that."

"Very well." Balm's expression went utterly, completely blank. "I don't want to keep you in this dream state for much longer. I'd prefer that you come to Santa Costa so that we can finish this talk face-to-face, but I don't suppose you'll do that."

Kira knew she'd hurt the other woman. She regretted it, but couldn't help it. Balm had raised her after the Solomons had failed. Balm had raised her because of a promise to Kira's mother, nothing more. That duty was done. All that remained was Kira's duty as a Shadowchaser. Besides, how could she finish the talk when she didn't know what else there was to say?

"I still have a mission to complete here in Egypt," she said, trying to swallow the emotion. She switched to the subject that had always been her safe haven: work. "Wynne and Zoo tell me that Gunderson has been taken back to Gilead."

Balm rose, her composure becoming more brisk, businesslike. "Yes. He'll be given a chance to recover, but his time in the field is over."

"Don't be too harsh with him. Marshall was more than his handler, and losing him hit Gunderson hard. He should never have been a Chaser, Balm."

Balm crossed to the high window that overlooked the Aegean. "I understand. I had my reservations, despite the fact that he survived the Crucible. However, the Commission thought London would be an easy enough section for him. Once he is able, I'll place him with the research division."

Kira nodded. "Not that my opinion means much, but I think that will be a good fit for him."

"Your opinion matters a great deal," Balm told her. She looked out the window. "One final thing, Kira. I held your mother in the highest regard. She spent her pregnancy and the last days of her life here, and I like to think that I enabled her to have that time in peace and love. Fulfilling a promise to her was never a duty, and you were never a burden. Whether you choose to believe me or not, there hasn't been a day that has gone by without me wondering if I've done right by Ana, if I've risen to the level of faith she placed in me. What keeps me awake at night is wondering not about the fate of this world, but about whether Ana would be disappointed in me." She turned away from the window. "I have a few mementoes of Ana's. If you like, I can send them to you."

Kira had to swallow several times before she could speak. "Yes, thank you. I'll let you know when I get back home."

Balm clasped her hands together. "All right. I'll see to it. You should probably wake up now. I think your friends have need of you."

She turned her ageless face back to the window. There was something vulnerable about the sight, the yearning expression of Balm's smooth features, that haunted Kira even after she left the dreamwalk, and Santa Costa, far behind.

Chapter 22

"Kira?" Wynne's voice, insistent, worried. "Kira, are you okay?"

Kira opened her eyes, trying to get her bearings. She stared up into Wynne's anxious face. "No, but I will be."

Khefar sat beside Wynne with his usual frowning expression, which meant Zoo and Nansee had the front seat. Zoo was a terrible driver, so Nansee was probably behind the wheel. Egypt's desert roads were bad enough without turning Zoo loose on them.

Khefar reached over, fingers brushing at her cheeks. "You were crying in your sleep. What's going on?"

"It's nothing." And everything.

"You were talking to Balm, weren't you?"

"Yeah." She sat up, not liking the feeling of vulnerability with them staring down at her. "Are we there yet?"

Wynne traded a glance with the Nubian. He shrugged as if to say, no big deal. It irritated Kira to the point of speaking up, but Wynne spoke before she could. "Almost. But Nansee says we've got company."

"What?" Kira sat up, running her fingers through her braids. "You could have led with that, you know."

"Finding out what's wrong with my friend is more important than telling you a Jeep's been following us for the last couple of miles."

"Couple of miles?" She looked out the rear window. The setting sun had burnished the winter sky a brilliant golden orange that stained the columns of rocks and sand to their west. Several yards back she could make out the headlights of another vehicle. "Are you sure it's them, and not innocents?"

"We've switched roads a couple of times and they've kept pace with us," Khefar said. "No idea why they haven't attacked yet, but the farther we go, the closer we get to our goal."

"Unless they've set a trap for us." Nothing like a little conflict to make her forget her personal problems. "Where are we exactly?"

"Just outside of Thebes," Nansee said, sounding entirely too cheerful. "Desert to the west, farmland to the south and east. Valley of the Kings, Hatshepsut's Temple, the Ramesseum."

"Stop here, Mr. Tour Guide," Kira ordered.

"Are you sure this is a good place?" Khefar wondered.

"No, but we ain't got a lot of choice," Kira answered. "We don't want to endanger any of the monuments. South of here are too many hotels. We certainly can't cross the river into Luxor proper."

"Right. Into the desert we go." Khefar tapped Nansee's shoulder, but the demigod had already turned west off the main road. The Rover bounced its way along, scrabbling for purchase on the sand and sandstone. If there had been any doubt that the Jeep was following them, it was obliterated as the vehicle swerved off the road behind them.

Wynne clapped her hands. "Okay, so it looks like

we're going on the offensive. Zoo, I hope your guy packed quality."

"Only the best for you, babe," her husband answered, checking the sight on a handgun. "Check the footlocker Kira's sitting on."

Kira slid off the metal box, then flipped it open. Wynne whistled as she peered over the backseat. "Merry Christmas to me!" She pulled out a rifle and scope. "Russian, but nice. It might take me a couple of shots to get the feel of it. I sure wish I could have brought Junior with me."

"Junior?" Khefar asked.

"Her favorite rifle," Kira explained, Wynne's actions going miles toward making her feel better. "Their weapons are their kids."

Kira stripped off her right glove, then called her extrasense. She really didn't want to touch the rifle, but having Light-enhanced bullets would help in taking out their opponents quickly.

"Hey, *chica,* just touch the bullets, not the rifle," Wynne exclaimed. She picked up a small box. "The bullets are new. Not nearly as much feedback."

"Oh yeah. Right." Kira wrapped her fingers around the box, dialing up her power. "Do you think you can shoot out the tires? That would be the quickest way to end this."

Wynne sniffed. "Give me something hard to do. Front or back tires?"

Kira smiled. "Shooter's choice."

"Nansee, can you open the back hatch window?"

"Of course." The window hummed as it slid down. Night had all but fallen; just a sliver of reddish-gold tinged the western sky above the cliffs and desert rocks and a scattering of diamond stars about them. Kira crouched down as Wynne sighted along the scope.

"Four in the Jeep, and they don't look happy—or all that human," she murmured. "Right front tire in three . . . two . . . gotcha!"

The rifle spat out a bullet, then another. The Jeep swerved, then pitched violently, rolling over in the sand twice before coming to rest on its passenger side.

"Awesomeness!" Elation sang in Kira's veins for a split second. Then she felt a skittering sensation across her extrasense. "Khefar."

"What is it?"

"Seeker demon."

She stripped off her jacket, then reached down, wrapping her hands around the duffel containing the Vessel of Nun. "Wynne, you and Zoo keep shooting until there's nothing moving out there, then you shoot some more. Nansee, make sure you keep from being a target as much as possible."

"What are you going to do?" Wynne asked, loading a clip into an automatic handgun and passing it to her husband before taking the duffel from Kira.

Kira pulled off her second glove, flexed her fingers. "We're going to take down another seeker demon."

"Nansee," Khefar called, "slow down but don't stop. We're jumping out."

Nansee slowed the Rover. Kira vaulted over the rear door, tumbling in the sand. Khefar landed a couple of feet from her. They rolled to their feet, both drawing their blades as a familiar horrible shape, a cross between a Doberman and a Komodo dragon, scrabbled out of the Jeep's wreckage.

"How do you feel, really?" Khefar asked, as if a demon dervish of death wasn't bearing down on them.

"I'm feeling like kicking a bit of Shadow ass. How about you?"

"Feel like you're avoiding the issue, but all right."

She shifted her stance, keeping her eyes on the seeker demon, the Jeep behind it. "Surely this isn't the time or place?"

"I always like to know the mental state of the people I fight with," the Nubian said. "But no worries. Let's take care of this, then we can take care of the rest."

"Try not to get injured this time around," she called to Khefar, not really wanting to focus on "the rest" or why he thought it needed intervention. "Make sure nothing else is coming out of the Jeep."

Khefar pulled free the Dagger of Kheferatum, the blade gleaming in the near dark. "Get injured and let you have the glory of returning the Vessel of Nun by yourself? I think not."

Kira slid her Lightblade free, calling her power. For a moment the world shifted crazily; it almost seemed as if she'd gone through the Veil again. She could feel Light and Shadow swirling inside her, power arcing in shades of blue-green and the thinnest whispers of yellow. The difference was that this time, she controlled it. The power did not control her. She'd make sure it never controlled her again.

The Rover sped away, kicking up plumes of dust. Dimly she noted a couple of other shapes crawling from the Jeep's wreckage. She hoped one of them was

Marit, and she hoped the female Shadowling was pissed.

With her heightened senses, Kira could hear the spit of gunfire. She knew Wynne and Zoo didn't like silencers since they tended to skew long-range shots, but they didn't need to alert the local authorities to the supernatural battle. If her friends had to resort to normal firepower, she had to hope the fight would be over quickly and they'd be on their way long before local police arrived.

"I'm going to try to draw it away from the Rover and farther up the hills," she said to Khefar.

He cursed. "It's not heading for the truck. It's making a beeline for you."

"All the better. Take care of the other Shadowlings, then come help me as soon as you can."

Kira didn't give him a chance to argue with her, just broke into a run for the cliffs. Time elongated as she climbed the steep slope, became almost a fluid, living thing. The desert of Deir el-Bahri was eerily quiet in the deepening dusk.

Some Shadowchasers didn't like fighting at twilight, believing the old wives' tale of Shadowlings being strongest when shadows were longest. It was probably why Marit had decided to press them. Kira didn't believe old superstitions, though. If she believed that, she'd have to accept that those who served the Light were completely vulnerable when the sun went down. One thing she refused to be, ever again, was vulnerable.

In a slight open area with plenty of rock at her back, she called more power. The desert shimmered with ancient memory, the lives of hundreds of thousands of people. Against the darkness the living stood out in sharp relief: Wynne and Zoo with their rainbow-colored auras, methodically reducing the Jeep and its lone Shadowling occupant to scraps; Nansee in deific white making the aged truck move like a sports-car on a straightaway; a yellow-tinged Shadowling fighting a muddy-colored silhouette that Kira belatedly recognized as Khefar.

Of course. Solis had said the Nubian was no longer human. She'd called him god-struck too. That explained the streak of gold-white in his metaphysical form. The muddy color, a mix of every color, seemed to flow either from or into the dagger that shone with the deep primordial red of fire, lava, blood: creation and destruction.

She scanned the desert. Where was the seeker demon? Thinking it was after the Vessel had been a miscalculation on her part. Marit obviously had it out for her if she wanted Kira dead more than she wanted the Vessel destroyed. Where was the female Shadow-ling anyway?

"Marit!" she called into the night. "Siccing a seeker demon on me just because I lobbed your hand off? A bit of overkill, don't you think?"

As if in answer, the wind picked up. *Gods, no.* The last thing they needed on top of nightfall was a sand-storm. She had to put her faith in Nansee to keep her friends and the Vessel safe, and in Khefar to take care of the other Shadowling. Handling Marit—if she was the one controlling the seeker—would take both their skills combined. If Marit controlled the seeker, that made her an Adept at the minimum, someone who had spent years practicing and manipulating Shadow-magic. Their time on the other side of the Veil would have been much worse if Marit hadn't underestimated them as grossly as she had. Something told Kira the Shadowling wouldn't make the same mistake twice.

"Come on, Marit, I thought we were friends. We got along so well behind the Veil."

The clattering of claws on hard-packed dirt and rock was the only warning she had as the seeker demon scaled the hill faster than she'd thought possible. She threw her Lightblade up as the demon sprang, jaws slobbering, claws extended. She swiped at it, slicing across its forearms as its hind claws raked across her back. She bit down hard on her lip to keep from crying out as searing pain blossomed along her spine, dropping her to one knee. A seeker's claws were poison; its saliva and blood contained acid, which was exactly why the only way to kill a seeker demon was quickly.

"Is that the best you've got, bee-yotch?" She regained her feet, scanning for the demon. "I'm beginning to think you're not worth the trouble."

Sand kicked up around her. Kira dialed up her extrasense, her body glowing turquoise. The wound on her back sizzled as her natural defenses worked to eject toxins from her system. Hybrid defenses. If she were human, she'd be dead already.

Her Lightblade lengthened to a shortsword as she poured more power into it. Her braids fanned out about her shoulders, the entire valley sparking blue-green. But it wasn't so bright that she couldn't see the gleaming phosphorescent yellow of the seeker demon racing back for a killing strike.

"Ma'at, be with me," she breathed. Screaming, she dove forward as the seeker demon launched itself in the air. They hit each other with a meaty thud, the force spinning them around before they hit the sand. The seeker slashed at her with its foreclaws. She jabbed at it with her Lightblade, her magic protecting her against the acid dripping from its jaws. It bounded away from her, disappearing into the dark.

She crouched, blade at the ready, her body singing with tension. Fighting in the dark was never good. The fight was reduced to sound and shadows and the light thrown by her blade. The only sense she could trust was her sixth one.

Her senses, both mundane and magical, stretched out, searching for any advance warning, no matter how minute, as to which direction the seeker demon would come from. She heard snarling and a couple of thuds. Khefar had engaged either the seeker or one of the Shadowlings. She really hoped he was getting his revenge on Marit instead.

Her heartbeat and her breathing sounded abnormally loud in the darkness. She couldn't give in to panic or fear, but both crowded in her chest. The longer it took to take down a seeker demon, the more the fight would go in the demon's favor. She couldn't afford more than one or two more clashes with the beast.

Thudding in the sand. She spun just as the demon crashed into her. Pain blossomed in her chest, and she swung at the creature again, slicing it across its rib cage. It shrieked, the sound deafening at close range. Then its jaws clamped down on her left wrist with the force of a hyena's bite, grinding the bones. She screamed as pain lanced through her arm, burning into her brain. Twisting, using her mangled arm as leverage, she pinned the seeker to the desert floor. Her Lightblade swung high into the air above her head, throwing off blue-green sparks of light. She brought the blade down, putting every bit of force and will that she could muster into the blow.

The Lightblade pierced the seeker demon's skull. The creature scrabbled and clawed as her power flowed into it, burning it from the inside out. Despite the pain emanating from her wrist, she felt a detached sort of joy as the creature disintegrated beneath her hands.

With her back screaming in agony, she managed to pull her blade free of the sandstone. The force of it knocked her off balance, sending her sliding and tumbling down the rocky incline. After an eternity of rolling and bouncing, she found herself face-up on the desert floor, staring up at the sky. *The stars are so beautiful,* she thought. *What is it like to be so removed from the pain you witness every day?*

"Kira? Kira!" She heard Khefar running toward her, saw headlights bouncing off the canyon walls.

"I'm here. Nauseous, but here." She managed to straighten to a sitting position as Khefar skidded to a stop, his dagger still free in his hand. Her Lightblade had retracted to its normal length. "What about the others?"

"Nansee and the Marlowes seem to be unhurt. Don't know about the truck. They're on their way back here, if the dizzying path of the headlamps is any indication." He knelt beside her. "Are you hurt?"

"Yeah." She winced. "The seeker got my back and

turned my left wrist into a chew toy before I managed to send it back to Shadow." She cradled her left wrist close to her chest. Gods, it hurt like a bitch.

"Dammit, Kira, why didn't you say something?" His fingers ran over her back, causing her to shiver. "Your shirt's shredded. How badly did the seeker demon get you? Why aren't you keeled over now?"

"It's no big deal. Since I'm not human, it'll take more than a scratch from a seeker demon to kill me."

His hands paused. "I suppose that's why I only feel welts, not bloody furrows."

"I could feel my extrasense fighting the poison, pushing it out. It's still going, and I can't pull back my extrasense yet."

She couldn't see his expression but his silence spoke volumes. So did the fact that he drew his hands away from her. "This not a human thing. Is this something that Balm told you during the dreamwalk, or is this still from your conversation with Solis?"

"Solis told me, and Balm confirmed it." She pushed to her feet. Her wrist began to throb in concert with her heartbeat, the pain dizzying. "My mother's family were hybrids, but her branch spun off in order to become completely human. Tried to, anyway. Didn't quite succeed since they had some surprises pop up now and then in the family tree, according to Balm. No idea on who fathered me, but Balm believes a high-level hybrid assaulted my mother. That might be a good indication of which side he was on."

Khefar swore. "Gods, Kira. I'm sorry."

"Yeah, the hits just keep coming, don't they?" She sheathed her Lightblade. Her extrasense leveled off, but dialing back her power only intensified the pain in her back and wrist. "I'd rather you didn't tell Wynne and Zoo. I don't need everyone shunning me, and if word gets out, it might make my job a lot harder to do."

"You can trust me to keep your confidence, Kira," he said, his tone full of reproach. "Have I given you reason to doubt me?"

Other than stepping away from her as soon as he found out about her heritage? "Nah, I don't doubt you. Did you see or hear Marit anywhere in that melee?"

He slipped a hand beneath her right arm to help her to her feet. "Unfortunately, only a couple of Shadowlings and a hybrid were in the Jeep. If Marit was somewhere nearby, and she was the one controlling the seeker—"

"Don't say it." It took a lot of talent to control a seeker demon. If Marit truly controlled the creature, it meant she was more than just a Shadowling, hybrid, or even an Adept. It meant she had power enough and talent enough to be an Avatar.

The truck sped up to them and slid to a stop with a flourish of rocks and dirt. Wynne hopped out, weapons at the ready. Nansee leaned out the driver's window. "Children, I know you're having fun out here, but you must hurry. The Nile is still rising and the dam at Aswan is in danger."

"No problem," Kira said, heading for the back of the truck. "Let's get moving."

"Big problem," Khefar corrected. "Unless there's a supernatural first aid kit in this SUV."

"Someone hurt?" Zoo called. "We've got a first aid kit, and I am a witch, remember?"

"See?" Kira said. "There's no problem."

Khefar squinted at her through the glow of the headlights. Or maybe he glared. "The seeker demon ripped her back and mangled her wrist. She's doing good to be upright at this point."

It was her turn to glare. "So much for keeping my confidence, huh, Medjay?"

"You think our friends have suddenly been struck blind?" He reached into the Rover, pulled out his jacket. He zipped up completely before he approached her. She guessed he was going to make sure she didn't touch his skin, even accidentally.

It hurt, dammit, and she didn't like the knowledge that he could hurt her.

"Kira, let me take a look," Zoo suggested, a pair of surgical-grade gloves already on his hands.

"Take a look while we're on the way, okay?" she said, using her right hand to pull her gloves out of her pocket. "Let the Nubian keep watch in the back while Wynne takes shotgun with her shotgun."

Despite her protests, Khefar helped her into the rear passenger seat beside the male witch. "Be angry with me all you must," he whispered to her, "but I am first, last, and always concerned with your welfare. Deal with it."

He slammed her door shut, leaving her open-mouthed with surprise as he stalked around to the back compartment, then climbed inside.

"I think you've met your match," Zoo said with a smile. He gently manipulated her left arm, trying to examine her wrist in the light cast by the overhead. It looked just as messed up as it felt. Her left hand had swollen in response to the poison infecting it. "If you don't keep him, we will."

"I thought you were on my side," she complained, grateful for the distraction.

"I am," he answered, his voice pitched so that only she could hear. "Which is why I'm doing my best not to freak my wife out over how badly your wrist and back are mangled or how much power you're pulling to keep the pain at bay."

She lowered her head. "Thanks, Zoo. You're a good friend."

"No prob," he whispered back, then raised his voice. "Your back isn't as bad as I thought it would be, so I'll clean it up in a jiff and let you find another shirt. We've got a couple of more hours' drive ahead of us. I think you and Khefar need to rest up. I'll wrap your wrist and you'll be all set to play hero when we get to Elephantine."

"Yes, sir," she said, saluting with her right hand. She could already feel Zoo's innate healing energy wrapping around her wrist, gently blending with her extrasense to speed her recovery. The seeker demon had broken at least one bone in her wrist when it bit down; its acidic saliva would have created nerve damage for any other Shadowchaser. As it was, Zoo's efforts were like putting a bandage on a knife wound: better than nothing but not what was needed.

What she needed, what she wanted, was the one thing she didn't have. Time. She needed time to reconcile herself to everything that Balm had told her. Time to digest her heritage and what, if anything, it meant. Time to grieve for a mother she never knew, and a mentor who'd also been her handler. Time to figure out what to do with a near-immortal warrior who'd become her lover and her fail-safe, and a Shadowling with a grudge. Above all, she needed time to figure out what she was going to do next.

Kira didn't have time for any of that, she realized, as the Range Rover crested the hill and turned back toward the Nile. Even in the dark of night, she could see that the ancient river had risen even further, threatening Luxor and Karnak and the small towns surrounding them.

Time had just run out.

Chapter 23

Night had a firm grip on the land by the time Nansee got them to Aswan, but they didn't need sunlight to see what they faced.

People were evacuating, heading for high ground. The Nile had already reached flood stage, lapping against the retaining wall and natural rock boundary. Another hour and farmland would be in danger.

Khefar peered out the back window. "With this much traffic, I don't know how we'll be able to get to the island undetected. And every available boat is being used to get people to higher ground."

Kira ground her teeth in frustration. Her extra-sense had done a good job of ridding her of most of the pain, but fighting the seeker demon's toxins had left her weak, hungry, and very irritated. On top of that, she couldn't believe that the encounter in the desert was the last of the opposition they'd face before returning the Vessel of Nun to Satet's embrace. Marit was out there somewhere waiting for them, probably with more Cult of Set members at her beck and call. Of course, with panicked Egyptians fleeing the rising Nile in droves, Shadow wouldn't need to do much more than stand back and watch them fail.

"Can I ask a stupid question?" Wynne piped up from the front seat.

Kira slouched, then winced, belatedly remembering her wounded back. "Why not? It's not like we're going anywhere."

Wynne turned around to face them. "Y'all wanna tell me why we're trying to get to Elephantine Island when the border and the Aswan High Dam are south of here? Shouldn't we be taking the Vessel of Nun there?"

"Because this was the ancient border of Egypt, back when the breaks in the Nile—the cataracts—determined the boundaries," Khefar explained. He pointed southwest. "That's where the First Cataract is, one of six main rapids along the Nile. On Elephantine—it used to be called Abu back in the day—there are a couple of temples to Khnum and to Satet."

"We need to go to Satet's nilometer," Kira said. "There's a statue of Satet there, in a cavern below the water line. I need to place the amphora in her arms."

"So how are we going to get there?" Zoo asked.

Kira stared out over the rushing water of the Nile, the lights glowing on the largest of a scattering of islands across from Aswan. She could feel time slipping away from them. Somehow they had to get to the island, sooner rather than later.

"Nansee, can you transport us over there?" she asked.

Khefar answered before the demigod. "No. Isis said the Vessel couldn't take another slide like that. We'll have to find some other way."

"It's the only way we've got," Kira told him. "I'll do my best to protect the Vessel on the slide. Or we can spend precious hours trying to find and steal a boat and cross a flooding river to the nilometer. In the dark. With Shadowlings wanting to stop us."

Khefar said something that would have been pretty if it hadn't been a curse. "And if the Vessel of Nun cracks under the strain? What happens then?"

She looked toward his dark form. "Then you do as Isis commanded. You wield the Dagger of Kheferatum. But instead of destroying, you use it to create—or in this case, to re-create a fully restored Vessel of Nun."

"Can you do that?" Zoo asked. "Sweet."

"I don't know if I can do that or not," Khefar told them, his tone much like that of two rocks grinding against each other.

"Are you saying you've never tried to re-create something in the four thousand years you've carried Atum's dagger?" Kira couldn't believe that. Khefar had been human, after all. He had to have been tempted at some point to bring something into being. Like his family.

Khefar remained silent for a long, telling moment. "It's not an easy thing, nor should it be," he finally said. "Trying to re-create something on the level of a god's artifact . . . I can't imagine it."

"Khefar." She reached out with her right hand, wrapping her fingers around his wrist. "The dagger has been used for centuries to destroy. I think it's long past time for it to try to create something."

He drew his hand away as if bothered by her touch. She didn't want to take it as a rejection, but she couldn't stop the twinge of emotional pain his gesture caused. *Dammit.* Her genetics weren't her fault.

"Besides," she added, forcing the words past a suddenly tight throat. "You may not have to do it at all. Maybe we'll slide the short distance across the water and the amphora will be fine. We won't know until we try. And the bottom line is, we have to try."

"But Nansee can't interfere."

Why was he being so stubborn about this all of a sudden? Was he just wanting to contradict her? Or didn't he trust her, now that he knew she wasn't fully human? "They pulled out a seeker demon on us, Medjay," she reminded him. "I'm not going to be able to take down another one. The longer we sit here and twiddle our freakin' thumbs with debate, the more opportunity they have to release another one on these people. I don't want to take the chance of more innocents being hurt."

Nansee spoke. "The Golden Lady did say that I could lend assistance. I travel pathways as I wish. What is wrong with you tagging along?"

"Doing something is better than doing nothing," Wynne said.

"Agreed," Zoo piped up.

"It seems I've been outvoted." Khefar's voice filled with exasperation. "Fine. Let's all slide over to Elephantine. And if the Vessel of Nun breaks, we'll just have to hope the Dagger of Kheferatum will be strong enough to mend it."

Wynne and Zoo loaded up on weapons as Kira settled the duffel containing the amphora across her shoulder. Tension pulled at her. She didn't know what was going on in Khefar's mind, but she didn't have time to deal with it. Still, she'd need his help getting the Vessel of Nun back to Satet's statue. With the Nile rising all around them, she was willing to bet that the water filling the cavern beneath the nilometer would be cold and fast-moving. She wouldn't be able to safely carry the Vessel and swim.

"I gotta know something," she said to Khefar as they waited for Nansee to conceal the Range Rover.

"What is it?"

"Are you pissed at me about something in particular, or is this just a general reaction to a crappy day?"

"I'm not mad at you."

"Uh-huh." She adjusted the duffel's strap. "You couldn't wait to cover up, and you've pulled away each time there's even a possibility I might touch you. Is it because I told you about my conversation with Balm?"

"Your conversation with . . ." He sucked in a breath. "Gods no, Kira. I don't care about that!"

She wanted to believe him. Stupidly, she needed to believe him. "So if it's not that . . . Are you gonna cover up every time we disagree, like you're punishing me? It's important for me to know that going forward, because I don't want to get used to being able to touch you and then have you take that away from me because I don't blindly agree with you."

His hands clamped down on her shoulders, startling her. "It's stupid that you have to point that out to me, and stupid that you're right. It's stupid of me to do that, whether I intend to or not. I'm sorry. We'll talk about everything after this is done, I promise you. Okay?"

She nodded, then realized he couldn't see her clearly in the dark. "Okay. I'll hold you to that."

"I know you will."

"Is everyone ready?" Nansee called.

They gathered together in front of the magically concealed truck. "It shouldn't be as bad as the last one," the demigod announced. "That was a fair distance from London to Cairo."

Kira watched as the demigod began to glow. He lifted his hands, three pairs of them, to literally pry open the air before him. "Okay, kiddies. Last one through is a rotten egg."

Zoo stepped through first, guns ready. Khefar followed him, then Wynne. Kira cradled the amphora to her chest, then stepped through the portal.

Nansee was right, it was better than the last trip through a portal. This time the sensation of being turned inside out lasted mere moments instead of minutes. She considered it a bonus to emerge on the other side on her feet.

She sucked in a cool, stabilizing breath. Finally she was on Elephantine Island. Her mission was nearly over.

There were few lights still on at this end of the island, though Aswan on the eastern side of the river was still well-lit. Wynne and Zoo had fanned out, sweeping the place to scope out any potential danger. While Kira had never had the chance to visit Aswan in her studies, she knew that several excavations had uncovered and restored temples to Satet and Khnum. If she were lucky, she'd get to visit the sites after restoring Satet's Vessel to her arms.

Carefully, she lowered the duffel to the ground, then removed the amphora. "How is it?" Khefar asked. "Is it still intact?"

"It is." Kira cradled the amphora tucked in the crook of her left arm like a newborn, then rose to her feet. "Let's get this done and get out of here."

Their flashlights cut through the darkness, highlighting their way. Pale granite steps cut into the rock, leading down toward the river and into the cavern beneath. Vertical columns flanked the stairs, marking the depths the river would reach during the Season of Inundation. At this time of year, the nilometer should have been mostly dry, the waters of the Nile receding by October. Unfortunately for them, it wasn't.

"It's flooded," Khefar said, arcing his flashlight over the water cresting the top of the nilometer. "And we don't have air tanks. How are we supposed to replace the amphora now?"

"Just as we planned, as Isis and Ma'at charged us. I'll take the amphora in, and restore it to Satet."

"But you'll drown!"

"Like you won't?"

"Kira." He grabbed her shoulders. "I'm expendable, you're not. I've lived hundreds of lifetimes to your one. We don't know what's down there, or if the flooding will cause a collapse. I'm better suited to go in, you know that."

It didn't matter that he was right, or that she knew better. The thought of him drowning, or being trapped, filled Kira with cold dread. "It has nothing to do with who's better suited. I've got my extrasense to protect me. You can drown just as easily as I could."

"Probably." He gave her a jaunty smile, and she could almost hear the adrenaline rushing through his veins. He lived for this hero stuff. "If I'm successful, the waters will recede. Come get me and lay me out in sunlight. I'll be all right once I dry out."

"I'm the one who's supposed to go in," Kira reminded him. "Did you forget what Isis said?"

She saw him grit his teeth. She knew he was worried about her, and it warmed the cold place growing inside her.

"If it reassures you any, I grew up on an island. I used to free-dive and body surf during my down time on Santa Costa. I can do this."

"Oh for Pete's sake," Wynne exclaimed. "You both go in. Khefar can provide cover and light while Kira puts the vase thingy wherever it's supposed to go."

They stared at each other. "She makes a lot of sense," Khefar said wryly.

Zoo laughed. "That's my woman."

"Okay, Wynne's voice of reason wins out," Kira said, the passage of time and the open location making her nervous. "Nansee, can you spin webs on both of us, in case the cave is bigger than we think? Then you'll be able to pull us out if there's a need."

The demigod inclined his head. "Of course."

He carefully wrapped etheric thread around Kira's waist, then Khefar's, fashioning a secure harness for each. "I'll be able to monitor you through this. Take care of yourselves."

Khefar drew his dagger, balancing it securely in his left hand, a large waterproof flashlight in his right. He stepped down the stairs leading to the ancient well, the river loud around them. "Are you ready for this?"

"As ready as I'll ever be," she replied, entering the water. On Santa Costa, swimming in the ocean had been escape as much as exercise and training. Only far below the surface could she escape the roiling waves that constantly pounded the shore. Swimming in those still sapphire depths had given her comfort during her tumultuous teen years, making her feel as if all of Light cocooned her.

Light flared now, Ma'at's feather glowing at the base of her throat. Khefar's Isis knot also emitted a golden-white light, shimmering in the water as they entered it up to their necks.

"I think you can use the light of Ma'at's feather to guide you to Satet," Khefar told her. "I'll cover you."

Kira nodded. Concentrated hyperventilating pushed carbon dioxide out of her lungs and bloodstream and gave her something else to focus on besides the number of seconds Khefar would be underwater. The longest she'd ever floated beneath the surface was just under fifteen minutes, and that had pushed her limits. The longest she'd held her breath while actively swimming had been somewhere around the seven-minute mark, swimming through caverns beneath Santa Costa during her trial to claim her Lightblade.

But that had been with two good hands, not with one wrist mangled by a seeker demon.

"I'm ready." She called her extrasense, allowing her power to completely suffuse her body as Khefar slipped beneath the water. She had to trust that her power would provide a measure of protection against the metaphysical might of Nun's primordial waters on this side and the rushing rage of the floodwaters on the Normal side of reality, just as she had to hope that the Dagger of Kheferatum would protect Khefar.

Sucking in a deep breath, she slipped into the river. She knew the water, or the water knew her. Ma'at's feather sparked at her throat, adding its pearly glow to the violet her magic kicked out. The river carried her, the feather guiding her to the back of the cavern.

Flickering golden light snagged her attention. The current carried them deeper into the underwater cavern, to uncarved rock beneath Elephantine. The light resolved itself into the shape of the Isis knot at Khefar's throat, his braids fanning out around his face as he floated before her in the water. Then relief turned to dread as she realized that he held the Dagger of Kheferatum defensively and that the shape beyond him wasn't the statue of Satet, but the largest Nile crocodile she'd ever seen. It was easily twenty feet long and more than a thousand pounds, and swimming straight for Khefar.

She fumbled to draw her Lightblade as she kicked toward him. For a crocodile to be here, in this place— that was no accident. The croc had to be ancient to be so huge, and an old crocodile probably meant old magic. She didn't know if her magic would be enough to take it on.

They were in trouble.

Khefar saw her. He crossed his arms in a clearly negative gesture, pointed at the Vessel of Nun, then beyond her to the right. "*Go!*" he mouthed at her.

The mission, the mission was all. She held the amphora close, knowing she had to trust the Nubian's ability and skill to fight, to win, to come back from the dead. But they hadn't counted on a twenty-foot crocodile wanting to reenact scenes from Tarzan movies.

The cave wall loomed in front of her. She could barely make out the sweeping headdress of the goddess, the upraised hands. Kira's lungs burned already, adrenaline crowding out oxygen, her muscles twitching with the need to help Khefar. Her shoulder blades itched with the need to look behind her, but she resolutely ignored it. Either Khefar had done what he needed to do or she'd be looking into the yawning maw of ancient death. Neither was a scene she wanted to see.

Instead she lifted the Vessel of Nun, settled it onto Satet's outstretched hands. An invisible pulse of power rippled through the water, then the goddess smiled. The Vessel of Nun was back where it belonged.

Kira flipped around in the water. A dark slick of blood spread through the water before her. The Dagger of Kheferatum burned a bright, fiery red as it sliced through the blood, burned through the water. Khefar raised it high, plunging the dagger into the ancient reptile's belly. It writhed and roared, then began to collapse in on itself. In less than a heartbeat, the gargantuan beast became a speck, then nothing, completely unmade by the power of the Dagger of Kheferatum. The reverb from the metaphysical and literal implosion rippled through the water, knocking them both back.

Khefar's body floated gracefully. He made no motion to return to the nilometer entrance. He had finished the crocodile and had used up all his air doing it.

Kira's heart beat triple-time as she kicked her way to the unconscious Nubian, catching him before the river could sweep him away. Her extrasense extended to wrap around him as she fought against the biological imperative to breathe, knowing she needed every bit of oxygen for her brain, her muscles.

Anansi! She reached out with her extrasense, the chamber glowing with violet-blue light. *Nansee, get us out of here!*

Black spots danced before her eyes, her lungs protesting every second without oxygen, blood pounding in her ears. *Just a little more, please Ma'at, please Isis, a little more . . .*

She gasped, water sweeping down her throat. The darkness spread from her vision through her body. It was all she could do to hold on to Khefar as the current took them away.

A jerking sensation, a change of direction. She hit the sand hard, the impact forcing her to suck in a breath. Air—sweet, blessed air!

Breathing begat coughing as she rolled to her hands and knees, vomiting up a stream's worth of the Nile. Sand caked her soaked clothes, her braids. She had never been so happy to see dry land in her life.

Nansee squatted beside her. "How do you fare?"

"Thank you," she gasped out, still struggling to catch her breath. "Thank you for saving us."

"I can say the same thing to you, Hand of Ma'at," the demigod replied. "What happened?"

"Croc," she gasped. "Huge, magic. Khefar made me go on with the Vessel instead of helping him. After I gave Satet the amphora, I saw him use the dagger to unmake the crocodile. But it knocked the air out of him."

Khefar. He lay a little apart from her, still, so still. She scrambled over to him. It didn't matter that he would resurrect with the dawn. Dawn was still hours away. He'd saved her life, saved everyone's lives. She'd damn well try to return the favor.

She rolled him over, pushing water out of his body. "Come on, Khefar. You took on a Nile crocodile. You can't let a little water get the best of you."

Nansee dropped beside her as she began CPR. "Kira . . ."

"I know." She continued the chest compressions. "I know he'll come back. But I don't like seeing him this way. I don't want to ever take that for granted, to ever not try to save him."

"Khefar!" She shoved at him, pushing more water out. "Damn you, Medjay—don't you die on me!"

He coughed, spluttered, then blessedly ejected the rest of the Nile from his lungs. "There's my girl." He smiled up at her, his hand coming up to cup her cheek. "Told you I'd be fine after you wrung me out."

"Just have to play the hero, don't you?" she asked, a stupid grin stretching her lips.

"You're saying that to *him*?" Zoo asked, laughter ringing his words. "That's funny as hell."

Kira sat back, light-headed and giddy. According to the levels carved into the nilometer's steps, the Nile was already beginning to recede.

"We did it." She looked at each of them, her eyes resting lastly on Khefar. "We did it together."

"That's what teams do," Khefar said, wrapping his hand around hers. "Better together than you could ever be alone."

"Go Team Kira!" Wynne crowed.

A collective groan filled the air. "Speaking of

going," Kira cut in, "I think we need to go back to Cairo, go get our stuff, and especially go get patched up, filled up, and rested up. I know no one really wants to do another slide, but I don't really want to spend six hundred miles on mostly desert roads in a Range Rover again."

"I think I can handle one more slide, especially if it gets us back to the Khan market," Wynne said. "Crisis averted, it's time for shopping!"

Zoo laughed. "On second thought, maybe the drive will be better. By the time we get back, Wynne will be too numb to get her shop on."

"Hey!" Wynne exclaimed.

"I vote for sliding," Khefar said. "If Wynne's unhappy, we're all unhappy."

Wynne pouted. "You know, I may have to start shooting first and ask questions later."

Kira smiled, then laughed. She was all right. Her friends were all right. The world was all right. At the moment, she had everything she needed. "Okay, back to the Rover, then on to Cairo by slide. Nansee, will you do the honors?"

"I would be delighted."

Chapter 24

The night sky spread like black velvet above them, stars twinkling like rhinestones in dark fabric. The lights from Cairo glimmered on the horizon, providing a sparkling backdrop for the small group gathered around the Rover. They'd been back in town for two days, recovering in a suite of rooms in the Mena House Oberoi. The luxury hotel just beyond the Great Pyramid complex was exactly what Kira had needed to recharge her batteries.

Kira looked affectionately at her small group. Dear friends as teammates, a demigod as a companion, and an immortal as a lover. Life had definitely taken an interesting turn.

Just before sunset, they had made their way to the Giza Plateau, joining her at one of Bernie Comstock's favorite places. Now, with his urn in her hands, his watch tucked in her pocket, his loss hit her keenly.

"There should be words," she said, leaning against the hood of the truck. "At times like this, you're supposed to have words to say."

"Your heart is full of words," said Khefar, a tall dark statue standing at attention in the night. "He knows that."

"He's right, my dear," Comstock added. He stood

in front of them, the desert visible through his suit. "I know the words you hold in your heart. That's enough for me."

Kira gripped the urn's lid, sniffling back tears. "This isn't the end, is it?" she wondered. "I don't want it to be the end. I've lost too much already."

Comstock smiled. "You should know better than that. With all that you've seen, all that you've learned, how can you think that this is an ending?"

"Death is just the beginning," Khefar said softly. "He'll be with you whenever you need him."

"You're right. You're both right." She clutched the urn close. "It's just that—I don't want to let you go!"

"Kira." Comstock reached out, his palm hovering near her cheek. "Sometimes you have to let go. It's the only way that your arms can open enough to embrace what's next." He looked at Khefar. "You'll stand with her and hold her?"

The Nubian nodded. "For as long as I am able."

Comstock turned back to Kira. "And will you stand with him and hold him?"

She wiped at her tears. "For as long as I am able."

The old man beamed. "Good, good. That's all I can ask." He looked out at the landscape, the massive temple complex. "This is a good place to be, but don't worry. I'm sure I'll be around when you need me. After all, there are several mementoes you have yet to examine."

Kira handed the lid to Khefar, then pushed off from the truck, taking a few steps away. "Have a good afterlife, Bernie."

She poured out the ashes. A breeze brushed past

her, catching the particles and carrying them away on the breeze. Comstock's ashes joined the shifting sands of Egypt, just as he'd wanted.

Khefar stood beside her. "What's next?" he asked, draping his arm about her shoulders.

"Gilead's arranging transport for us back to London. I'll have to stay there for a few days longer. There's still a lot to do with Bernie's possessions, and I haven't even been in the antiques shop yet. His former colleagues still need to be told about his passing."

"And the rest?"

"I can save that for home, whenever I get there. I have to reconcile who I am with what I am, and I'd much rather do that on my home turf."

Her gaze traveled over the group again. "I just wanted to thank you, all of you, for your help on this," she told them. "I honestly could not have done any of this without you. Tracking down Gunderson, recovering the Vessel of Nun, returning it to Elephantine, saving Egypt and the world from a flood. One person couldn't have completed this mission. You guys are an awesome team. You've proved that multiple times."

She smiled. "Of course, the real test will be to see how we work when the fate of the world doesn't hang in the balance. For now, Wynne and Zoo, I need you two to go back to the States and handle patrols in Atlanta while I finish up in London. Think you guys are ready for boring, run-of-the-mill Shadowchasing when you get back?"

Nansee snorted. "My dear Chaser, I don't think you

know the meaning of the word. Nothing about you is run-of-the-mill."

"The demigod's got a point," Zoo added.

"Yeah, he sorta does," Wynne agreed.

"Somehow you and 'boring' don't go in the same sentence," Khefar said. "But if you want to try it, I think we'll try it with you."

"Not to be Debbie Downer," Wynne said, "but you do still have a Shadowling with a grudge out there somewhere. We'll have to report all the stuff about the seeker demon and Marit to Gilead."

"I know." For a moment Kira felt really tired. "Writing a full report is the first thing I'll do when we get back to London. You guys will need to do a mountain of paperwork yourselves in Atlanta. Section Chief Sanchez is completely by-the-book. Oh, and I need you guys to stop by the DMZ and make sure Demoz hasn't sold the city out from under me."

The Marlowes nodded.

Nansee spoke up. "If we are done here, Kira, I know of a charming café nearby where we might enjoy a late dinner. . . ."

"Everything revolves around food for you," Kira said, amazed. "I didn't know gods were so fixated on stuff like that."

"You'd be surprised what we can fixate on," Nansee said, wriggling his eyebrows. "The stories I could tell."

"I'm sure. I think I'd like to hear a couple of those. We've got some time before Gilead gets us out of Cairo."

Kira stared at the Great Pyramids. Her whole life she'd been searching for answers. Now that she'd finally gotten them, they'd only produced more questions. Somehow she had to find a way to process everything she'd learned and experienced, in order to be ready for the next thing on the horizon. She knew, without a doubt, that her duties as a Shadowchaser and the Hand of Ma'at were far from over.